KISS YESTERDAY GOODBYE

A Serenity Bay Novel

Book 1

By

DANNI ROSE

Thank you to my friends and family for your help and support in making my dream a reality. I couldn't have done this without your love and encouragement.

CHAPTER ONE

"What's so important we need to have a city council meeting tonight?" *My one free night this week*. Beth Kingsley sat in the chair closest to the secretary and rubbed her forehead to ease the headache from hell. "Are we here to discuss which brand of toilet paper to buy—again?"

Abbey, the manager at Beth's coffee shop and fill-in for the council's sick secretary, leaned down to study her computer, "Don't know. The mayor—" She disappeared under the desk.

Beth smiled. "What are you doing?"

From below came a mumble. Beth shrugged, kicked off her shoes, and stifled a yawn.

The owner of a successful business, she'd wanted to give back to the community. That was why she sat at the conference table waiting for the meeting to start instead of at home relaxing. She looked around. The other council members chatted with the audience.

Today had been plagued with one crisis after another. At her coffee shop and bakery, Delectable Delights, Beth had to fill in for two employees who'd been out sick. All day she'd looked forward to a night at home with a glass of wine and a long, hot soak in the tub. She took a deep breath and could almost smell the sweet scent of her lavender and vanilla bath salts.

"Aha." Abbey popped up wearing a silly grin. She held a cord and plugged it into the computer. When the machine started, she pumped her fist.

Just then, the chamber doors swung open. Mayor Bill Derr entered the room, a bounce in his short-legged stride. Behind him walked a man Beth never thought she'd see again.

"Why is he here?" Her eyes narrowed.

Abbey looked around. "Who?"

"Look at him. He struts like Alexander the Great entering Babylon." Beth grimaced. *This can't be happening.* Her stomach twisted. *Why is he here?*

She studied him. Gone was the boy who'd rescued a young girl. In his place was a man with sleek sophistication and a sexy-as-sin body with the sensual appeal of a Greek god. But she wasn't fooled by his looks, because she knew the truth. Like the harsh, jagged scar on his right temple, he was pure danger.

"He looks familiar, but I don't remember meeting him. No

woman would ever forget that face." Abbey licked her lips the way she did when she looked at the double chocolate cake with fudge frosting. "That man is six feet of sexy. Yummy."

He'd been a handsome boy, but now Jason Fischer's sultry French Canadian good looks took Beth's breath away. He wore a tailored suit that displayed the raw power of a man who had the world at his feet.

Beth squirmed in her chair.

Abbey said, "His picture should be on the cover of *GQ*."

"It was." Beth clamped her fingers around the edge of the table and held tight. If she let go, she'd run from the room. *Can this day get any worse?*

Jason followed Mayor Derr to the podium. The mayor, a brilliant smile on his face, waited until everyone sat. Then he called the meeting to order. "Today we have with us a man renowned for his keen mind, revolutionary ideas, and financial wizardry—Mr. J.D. Richards."

The only things missing from his introduction were the blaring trumpets and waving banners.

"J.D. Richards?" Abbey blew a soft whistle. "The man with the golden touch and more money than the Federal Reserve?"

Mayor Derr continued. "Mr. Richards is CEO of Ziron Corporation, a Fortune 500 company, and the reason for this meeting."

Without shifting her gaze, Beth told Abbey, "When he lived in Serenity Bay, he was Jason Fischer. People called him that worthless Fischer boy."

"Are you sure? Maybe you're confusing him with someone else?"

"I'd never forget a lying bastard."

Abbey gaped at her. "You knew him well?"

"I thought so." Beth would never admit she still struggled to live with his betrayal. Her anger flared as she remembered the honey sweetness of his kisses, and how her body tingled when he brushed his fingers over her skin. Yeah, she'd known him but not as well as she'd thought she did.

The mayor announced, "Four months ago, Mr. Richards contacted me with an idea for a project he wanted to undertake. When we began our discussions, he asked that I hold off bringing the proposition to the council until he worked out the financial arrangements. After he had explained his concerns about profiteering, I agreed." The mayor rocked on his feet. "Last week, Mr. Richards called to say all the pieces were in place, and it was time to meet with the council. Tonight he's come to present his generous proposal and ask for your approval."

She frowned. A project in Serenity Bay?

Mayor Derr spoke through his grin. "Please welcome J.D. Richards."

A few people in the audience and the council members applauded. She pressed her lips into a tight line. This is my nightmare come to life.

Jason stood and looked at each member of the council. Every muscle in Beth's body tensed when he looked at her longer than he did the others. The dark anger in his eyes made her stomach sour.

Abbey asked, "What do you think—?"

"Shh." Beth had built a life in this town. It wasn't the one she dreamed of, but it was more than she'd thought possible. If someone threatened the contentment she'd worked so hard to find, she wanted to know why.

"Thank you, Mayor Derr." Jason smiled. "Some of you may remember when I lived in Serenity Bay. Since leaving, I've achieved success in my business and financial dealings. I want to share my success with this community that did so much for me."

The deep, smooth tone of his voice flowed over her, sweet and hot. Nine years hadn't changed his ability to make her body heat with desire. Beth muttered, "What is he plotting?"

"That's why I contacted Mayor Derr and presented my proposal to build a community center in Serenity Bay. He agreed the town needed a place where friends and families could gather. A center to offer recreational and educational activities. We had discussed different options and possibilities before we agreed on a plan."

Beth's eyes narrowed at the triumphant smile on his lips.

"Today I am here to ask for your approval to build a recreation and activities complex in Serenity Bay."

What? The muscles in Beth's shoulders tightened. This can't be happening.

"The complex will have an indoor swimming pool and gym. It will have rooms for classes, meetings, and parties. There will be tennis and bocce ball courts along with a large picnic area. The complex will be built on land converted into a city park and overlooking the bay."

There were dropped jaws, raised eyebrows, and gasps of surprise throughout the room.

"The center will be named in honor of my parents, Matt and Helen Richards, and I will donate the complex to the town." He placed an architect's blueprints on the display easel. "I present the Richards Recreation & Family Complex."

Beth rolled her shoulders to ease the tension. Who were Matt and Helen Richards? Jason had changed his name, had he reinvented his family too?

Her stomach roiled. No one who knew Jason would believe he wanted to share his good fortune with Serenity Bay. He'd hated this town. She hid behind a stiff smile but worried it might melt from the heat of her anger.

"I want the center to be a welcome addition to the community. To make sure the complex gets built with few problems or complications, I plan to stay in town during the construction to oversee each stage of development."

Applause filled the room as the council members and audience got to their feet—except Beth. Her legs, limp as day-old cooked spaghetti, could never support her.

Her anger exploded. Seeing Jason reminded her of all she'd lost. She still struggled to cope with her nightmares. How was she supposed to deal with Jason's return?

"I don't understand. How did you know him?" Abbey gaped at her. "Wait. Is he—?"

"Yes." Beth hissed as she cut off Abbey's question. She looked around the table. No one heard their conversation, they were too busy beaming at Jason.

She wanted him to hurt and watch as his soul bled the way hers did—every day. Then, with strength earned one tear at a time, she straightened her shoulders and lifted her chin.

The council would support the project. For years, they'd wanted to build a recreation center, but hadn't been able to put the funding together. The complex Jason offered was more than they hoped to have and at a price they couldn't afford to turn down. If she voted against the proposal, she'd have to explain her reason. But a vote in favor of the project would keep Jason in town.

She didn't think it was possible, but the mayor's smile got wider. Sure, it was easy for him, he'd assured his re-election while she drowned in a dark pool of painful memories.

The board discussed the proposal and invited the audience to participate. After the last question, the mayor asked, "Do I have a motion to approve Mr. Richards' generous proposal?"

One of the board members lifted his hand.

"Do I have a second?"

Another hand went up.

"All those in favor of approving this proposal, please raise your hands."

Beth stopped breathing as each council member voted for the proposal. With grim determination, she released her death grip on the table and raised her hand.

The thunder of clapping hands filled the council chambers, and proud smiles lit the faces of the members of the council. The motion had passed with a unanimous vote.

She shuddered and glared at Jason. He'd abandoned this town, its people, and her. Why come back now? Did he know?

Abbey's eyebrows dipped. "What will you do?"

"I'll avoid the louse and count the days until he leaves." Beth gazed out the windows at the lush beauty of northern Minnesota. She loved to see the full moon's reflection rippling over the water. During the day she'd watch the sun's rays gleam and bounce off the water in the bay or walk on a path through the lush, green forest. Her walks reminded her there was more to life than work, and the cool calm of the nights soothed her soul. But tonight she found no peace.

Her shoulders slumped. J.D. Richards, or Jason Fischer, or whatever he called himself, had returned to Serenity Bay.

When the meeting adjourned, Beth grabbed Abbey's arm and pulled her to the refreshments table. "I need caffeine."

Before they reached the coffee, an employee rushed to Abbey and, with arms waving, whispered in her ear. This evening, Abbey supervised the employees who were in charge of the refreshments provided by Beth's shop.

"There's a crisis in the kitchen," Abbey whispered.

"I can handle it." Beth cringed at the desperation in her voice.

"No. You stay and play councilwoman. Remember, keep smiling. It will confuse the enemy." Abbey rushed away.

Smile. Right. Beth rolled her eyes. I survived his betrayal; I'll live through this.

Desperate to fortify her fractured nerves, Beth poured a cup of coffee. Then behind her, she heard the rumble of a deep voice. She turned to find Stephen Howard, her friend and attorney, standing next to Harmony Owen, owner of the New Age shop. She fought to hide her smile and wondered when Stephen would give in to the sparks flying between them.

Harmony wore her long, tie-dyed skirt and peasant blouse along with several silver bracelets. When she talked, she waved her hands, and her bracelets made a soft, tinkling sound. As usual, she wore a bright smile and happily greeted everyone nearby.

Stephen wore a pinstripe suit and a frown. "Jason's gift is generous, although surprising."

Harmony glared at Stephen. "I think it's wonderful that someone who's accomplished so much remembers the town where he lived."

Stephen said, "I can't imagine why Jason Fischer would want to give a gift to this town."

"You think everyone has a sinister motive." Harmony rolled her eyes. "Not everyone lies."

"Maybe not, but everyone has secrets." Stephen raised an eyebrow. "Even you."

Harmony shook her head and turned to join another group.

More of Jason's fans joined Beth and Stephen. One person after another applauded Jason's generosity. With each word of praise, her hands tightened around the coffee cup.

While Beth chatted, she tracked Jason's movements as the mayor introduced him to the council members. The mayor's smile was open and sincere, while Jason's looked like a shark in search of prey. *Am I his next meal?*

A woman clutched Jason's arm and leaned close. Whether he wore a custom-made silk suit or jeans, he was the most virile man in any room. Beth's smile tightened into a grimace. Nothing had changed. He still drew women the way a bright flower attracted bees.

She took a deep breath when Jason and the mayor walked towards Stephen and her. With a clink, she set her cup on the table and clamped her hands together behind her back. She pasted a smile on her face and wondered if it fooled anyone. Her stomach knotted as she prepared to greet the man who taught her love existed only in fairy tales.

"J.D. Richards, this is Stephen Howard."

"Richards?" Stephen questioned as they shared a brief handshake. "It used to be Fischer."

"The Richardses took me in when I moved to Chicago, made me part of their family."

"Oh. Well, welcome back." Stephen had nodded before he walked away.

Beth took a deep breath and cleared her throat. Was Harmony right? Could Jason be more generous and forgiving than she knew? She huffed. No. He'd proven he cared about no one but himself. Whatever his reason for returning, he would never get close enough to hurt her again.

"Beth, meet J.D. Richards."

"J.D. say hello to Elizabeth Kingsley, Beth to her friends. She owns Delectable Delights, the best coffee shop, bakery, and caterer in the state."

She tried to thank Mayor Derr for the compliment, but her tongue stuck to the roof of her mouth.

"In fact, Delectable Delights provided this evening's refreshments." The mayor's voice rang with good cheer. Why shouldn't it? His world was bright and sunny, while a nightmare of epic proportions threatened to destroy hers.

No longer able to put it off, she looked into eyes the color of dark chocolate and seething with emotion. Breathe in—breathe out. She flinched when Jason extended his hand. If she didn't accept his welcome, the news of her snub would be the main topic of gossip in every home at breakfast tomorrow.

Beth fought the urge to rub her damp palms on her skirt. She shook his hand but jerked at the touch of his skin. She'd locked away the memory of how she loved having his arms wrapped around her, but it returned in a rush. Need heated her blood and pulsed between her legs.

He smiled, but his eyes held no joy. She shuddered. When they were young, his eyes had been bright with happiness and love. Now they were cold and swirled with deadly intent.

She dug her nails into the palms of her hands. "We've wanted to build a recreation center for a long time. Your gift is very generous."

He crossed his arms. "I want to thank everyone for all they did for me when I lived here."

Mayor Derr looked across the room. "Excuse me. I need to speak with someone." He rushed off.

Beth crossed her arms. "Why did you come back?"

"I owe a debt to the people of Serenity Bay."

"You despised this town and everyone who made your life miserable." She frowned. "Why give a gift to people you hate?"

"Hate is a strong word." He shrugged his left shoulder. "I want to repay a debt."

"You want to thank people who treated you like dirt?" Beth stared at him.

"When I got your letter, how could I turn down such a gracious invitation to return?"

"What—?"

"J.D.?" Mayor Derr scurried to Jason's side.

"Please, call me Jason."

A bright smile lit the mayor's face. "There's someone I want you to meet. Will you excuse us, Beth?"

A frown had flashed across Jason's face before a polite smile replaced it.

She nodded and watched as he walked away. Her emotions raced like an out-of-control rollercoaster. He still made her ache for his touch. She frowned. Why did he think she wrote to him?

Someone grabbed her arm, and Beth yelped.

"Sorry." Abbey's eyebrows drew together. "Are you okay?"

"I need to get out of here."

"What's wrong?"

"I'm exhausted." She looked over Abbey's shoulder and met Jason's glare. "You have everything under control. I'm going home."

Abbey's lips parted, but Beth turned away and waved over her shoulder. "I'll see you at the shop tomorrow."

Beth parked her SUV in the garage she'd added onto her house. She loved the Queen Anne style home her great-grandfather built over a century earlier, but a garage was a necessity if a person wanted to survive winters in northern Minnesota.

Beth pressed her head against the steering wheel. She dealt with the challenges of owning a business and being a council member, but when Jason walked into the council room, she'd once again been that fifteen-year-old girl in need of rescue.

She climbed out of the car. Then she grabbed the tote bag with her computer and the month's receipts. The last bag she pulled out had the ingredients she needed to try a recipe for a banana cake with cream cheese frosting.

While she struggled to open the door, her cell phone rang. She'd forgotten it when she left for work this morning. She rushed into the kitchen to answer the call but stumbled and dropped the bags. Her things skated across the floor.

With a frown on her face, she grabbed the phone. "Hello."

A harsh voice killed her hope for a peaceful evening. "Elizabeth, this is Archer Kingsley."

Damn. She should have checked the caller identification. "You don't need to introduce yourself."

"I wasn't certain you remembered me."

"What do you want, Father?" She grinned. He hated when she called him father. It reminded him he was old enough to have a grown daughter, one he no longer controlled.

"There is no need for sarcasm." He scolded. "Your mother told me you called to say you aren't able to attend her birthday celebration. That is not acceptable."

"In case you've forgotten, I decide what's *acceptable* in my life." Although she no longer lived in his home or under his thumb, her father expected her to rush to follow his orders. "The party is an excuse to show off for your business associates. Or have you arranged another marriage for me? Whatever your scheme, I won't be part of it."

Archer ignored her words the way he ignored anything he didn't want to hear. "If you don't come, you will embarrass your mother. Regardless of how you feel about me, I know you're fond of Deidre."

There it was. The emotional blackmail he used with surgical precision to force her obedience. Beth's hand curled until her nails cut into her palms.

"Will you disappoint your mother?"

When Beth had been young, her father scolded her for being too soft. *If you let others see what you're feeling, it gives them the power to control you.* Archer should know, he was an expert at controlling others.

A frustrated sigh slipped through her lips. "If I attend, will you promise not to lecture about my duty to the family name or you?"

"This is a celebration of your mother's life. It would not be a proper time to discuss how you've failed your family."

"I'll reconsider my decision, but I'm not making any promises."

"It will be good to see you perform your family duty on this occasion at least." The line went dead.

Beth's shoulders slumped. She'd prefer to have a root canal without anesthesia than spend time with Archer.

On his personal plane, Jason worked during the flight to

Chicago. He called Andrew, one of his senior vice presidents. "I want the loose ends on the Hawkins deal tied up before I leave Chicago next week."

"That deal is at a critical point. You should be here. How long will you be away?"

"I'll fly in from time to time, but otherwise I'll work from home until the construction is complete. In the meantime, Matt will manage the daily operations."

"You don't oversee small projects. What's different about this one?"

"I want it done right." He trusted Andrew but didn't share personal information with anyone except those closest to him—his family.

"If you want the Hawkins contracts signed before you leave town, we need to close the deal at tomorrow's meeting," Andrew said.

"I want that company and don't want more delays. Let's meet in the morning to discuss the negotiations and the best way to handle their board of directors." He loved a battle of wits, and the challenge to close this deal made his blood race. "I'll talk to you tomorrow."

He scrubbed a hand over his face. The pain of his past had returned, but it wouldn't stop him. He wanted revenge and planned to get it no matter the cost, but only after he had his answers.

Jason made another call, and one ring later he was bombarded with questions. "How was the meeting? Were they surprised? What was their reaction to the complex? Was it all you wanted? Did they ask about the change in your name?" A frustrated huff sounded across the connection. "Well, say something."

"I'm waiting for you to take a breath."

Callie's laughter made him smile. His best friend, she was the best adopted-sister a man could have.

"Oh, all right. Did you recognize anyone?"

"Several people who knew Jason Fischer attended." He chuckled. "And before you ask, surprise doesn't begin to describe the stunned looks on their faces."

"Did anyone ask about your name?"

"One person did. Stephen Howard a guy I knew in school, asked."

"Did anyone comment on your past or make any snide comments?"

"None that I heard."

"I wish I could have been there. With all you've accomplished, none of those people would dare talk down to you now. If they try, you let me know, and I will take great pleasure in kicking their butts."

"Calm down, slugger. I appreciate the support, but I can handle this battle. If I need help, you'll be the first person I call."

"Growing up in Serenity Bay wasn't easy. Are you sure about this?"

He'd told Callie more about his life in Serenity Bay than anyone. When she heard the story of how Beth dumped him, her outrage soothed his pride. The memory of her rant brought a smile to his face. But Callie didn't know the whole truth. His pride kept him from telling her the depth of Beth's betrayal and his need for retribution. "It's time to put my ghosts to rest."

"Then you make them eat every insult they ever uttered."

CHAPTER TWO

You were never more than a fling I used you to amuse myself. I would never marry the son of the town drunk. Don't come back. It would embarrass me to be seen with you. Elizabeth Marie Kingsley.

That letter shattered Jason's dreams. He hadn't wanted to believe what he read and went to confront her. She repeated every word in the letter as though she'd memorized them. Each word drew blood until he'd been drained dry.

To escape the pain, he left Minnesota, but the ache of Beth's betrayal followed him. He got a job that forced him to get out of bed each day, but at night he struggled with his despair until he met Matt. With Matt, Helen, and Callie's help, he made a new life for himself. Jason locked his feelings in the darkest closet of his heart and became J.D. Richards.

Then he received another letter postmarked Serenity Bay, MN.

Mr. Fischer, If you want to learn the truth, you should return to Serenity Bay and talk to Elizabeth Kingsley.

The letter wasn't signed.

He swept a hand through his hair. Had Beth sent the letter or was someone else trying to manipulate him? Why did he need to return to Serenity Bay? What *truth* was he supposed to discover?

For years he dreamed of going back to town in triumph. To show people who'd called him worthless how wrong they'd been. No longer was he a hoodlum they could grind under their shoes. He rubbed his hands together. The time for vindication had arrived.

He intended to uncover Beth's secrets and to teach her what those who betrayed him learned—if you cross J.D. Richards, expect retribution. Jason Richards didn't walk away from a fight, and even if he was late to this one, he planned to win.

When he walked into the council chambers, he'd fought the desire to stare at Beth. She was more beautiful now than she'd been at eighteen. Her hair was still the color of wheat in the summer sun, and her lips had that slight pout that made a man hungry for a taste.

When they'd been together, what had touched his soul had been her caring, loving heart. But her love had been a lie, and nothing could ease the pain of betrayal. This time, lust wouldn't blind him to her character. She was a viper who waited for her prey's most vulnerable moment to destroy him.

His shoulders drooped. He could negotiate a merger with a

hostile opponent but was lousy at choosing women to trust. All his life he'd wanted a wife and children, but failed. So he buried his disappointment and bitterness in his work. Now there were few women he trusted other than his mother and sister.

With a bright smile, the flight attendant set a cup on the table. "Would you like anything else, Mr. Richards?"

"No. Thank you." He inhaled, and the honeysuckle in her perfume reminded him of the cologne Beth wore when she was eighteen.

Her lips were hot like the blood flowing through his veins and weakened his resolve. "We have to stop."

"Take me with you, please. Don't leave without me."

"It's just two months. Then you can come with me. In the meantime, I'll find a job and an apartment. I know it's hard to be apart, but I want to have a place for us to live when you get to the city."

"Then, before you go, make love to me."

"We agreed to wait until we got married. I don't want you to regret what we do."

"Please, Jason. I need to believe you'll come back for me."

"Mr. Richards."

"Beth, I want you—"

"Mr. Richards?"

Jason's eyes blinked open. The flight attendant's eyes were wide with surprise. No doubt shocked he'd fallen asleep. He never slept on these flights.

"We'll be landing in twenty minutes, sir."

"Thank you." He straightened his shoulders. I'm nobody's fling.

A week later, Jason returned to Serenity Bay. He stayed in a house owned by friends who lived in Chicago and vacationed in northern Minnesota. It was a renovated nineteenth century Victorian. The builder in him loved the workmanship of the home. Ornate and elegant, the house had been restored with attention to the details.

The *worthless Fischer boy* had never gone into the homes of Serenity Bay's elite. He'd lived on the poor side of town, and people called him a hoodlum. Archer even tried to have him arrested for a crime he didn't commit.

Now, J.D. Richards received an invitation to the homes of the wealthy and influential. Presidents asked his opinion and courted his friendship. Although only thirty-one, he had earned the admiration of those he called friends and the respect of those who challenged him. Now no one was foolish enough to call J.D. Richards worthless.

Jason spent his first morning back in town working in the study, or at least he tried. His jaw tightened as he tossed aside the contract he'd read for the third time. Instead, he made phone calls.

"Jackson here."

His no-nonsense-let's-get-down-to-business investigator's greeting always made him smile. "Have you learned any new information about the months Beth traveled?"

"Everyone I've talked to said she traveled in Europe with her mother. I checked with my contacts. She's never had a passport."

Jason rubbed the back of his neck. "What are you going to do now?"

"I've talked to several of Kingsley's household staff. He fired a maid a short time before Elizabeth left for Europe. I want to find her."

"You think she knows something?"

"Well, the timing seems coincidental."

"—and you don't believe in coincidences." Jason chuckled. "All right. I'll call again in a couple of days."

After Jason had ended his call to Jackson, he dialed again. He never had a chance to say hello.

"I'm so glad you called." The greeting was warm with an underlying hint of concern.

"I left Chicago yesterday, Mom. Don't tell me you miss me already?"

Helen Richards' laughter rang through the connection. "Don't tease me. How are you?"

"I'm fine. You don't have to worry about me. I'm not the scared boy who left town nine years ago. I'm older now and tougher. No one pushes me around anymore," he sighed, "except you."

"I don't understand why you went back. That town holds so many bad memories. You don't have to prove yourself to those people."

"In my mind, I know you're right, but a part of me needs the closure."

"All right, but be careful. We love you and want you back where you belong."

"Try not to let it upset you." Even though she supported his decision to return to Serenity Bay, Helen would worry.

"I love you."

Jason said, "I love you, too."

When he laid the phone down, he grinned. Time to take the next step in his plan. He'd visit her in the middle of the day. She'd be less likely to expect him, and she wouldn't have time to practice her lies.

Beth's shop was on Main Street in the heart of the business district. There wasn't an open space in the lot, so he parked around the corner.

His heart pounded hard and fast as he walked into Delectable Delights. He took a deep breath and inhaled the rich, earthy scent of fresh-brewed coffee mixed with the aroma of sweet baked pastries. The atmosphere vibrated with the buzz of conversation and laughter.

The shop invited people to stop in to visit with friends and family. There were areas of easy chairs filled with customers who chatted and enjoyed their coffee. Along the walls were several overflowing tables. The atmosphere of the shop would encourage customers to linger over coffee and to feast on a tempting treat.

There was one problem; Beth wasn't here. Jason assumed, in the middle of a workday, she'd be in the restaurant. He knew trying to predict another's actions could undermine a plan no matter how well designed. When he decided on a course of action, he considered roadblocks and hurdles, but never made assumptions. Until today. *Where is she?*

Behind him, a door whooshed open. He turned. Beth walked out of the kitchen. This woman was self-assured and confident. She was no longer the child of his memories. Her hair fell in a braided waterfall to her waist, and her eyes were the translucent blue of the oceans around exotic islands. But it was her body that made men dream of tangled sheets and long, mind-blowing nights of sex.

Beth picked up a pot of coffee and walked to the tables. She talked with the customers while refilling their cups. At last, she stepped away from a table and turned. The bright smile on her face faded to a frown, and her eyes narrowed.

This is how it felt when time stopped.

Beth embodied grace, elegance, and radiated a seductiveness that captivated others. Jason clenched his teeth. She'd crushed his heart once; he'd be a fool to give her a chance to hurt him again. It would be easier to do if the sight of her didn't make it so hard to breathe.

He couldn't judge her reaction. She appeared cool, indifferent until she pushed a strand of hair behind her ear. Her hand trembled.

Her gaze drifted to the kitchen door. If she ran away, Jason intended to follow her. They would talk. He went to her with a smile pasted on his face. "Hello, Beth."

She huffed. "Mr. Richards, or is it J.D.?"

"My friends call me Jason."

"We aren't friends." Her words were colder than winters in Minnesota.

He nodded at the coffee pot she held. "That smells good."

"It's the best in town. Do you want a cup?"

"I would love one—strong and black."

"You used to drink your coffee with cream." She pressed a hand to her lips.

He bit off a laugh before it could escape. Beth remembered.

She waved to the one empty table in the shop. "Have a seat, and I'll get you a cup."

"Great. Will you join me?"

"What?"

"I came to talk to you. We didn't have time to visit at the council meeting."

Beth looked away and frowned. What was she thinking? The silence in the shop caught his attention. All conversations had died. He looked around. The customers and employees watched and listened to every word they exchanged.

She lifted her chin. "My office is this way."

He'd won this skirmish, or had he? Beth never gave up without a fight. He'd bet she didn't want witnesses when she told him to get lost.

She walked behind the counter. "Abbey, I'll be in the office. Call if you need help."

Abbey shifted from foot to foot while she stared at Jason. "Okay."

Beth walked through the door, and Jason followed. Not until her desk stood between them did she look at him. They watched each other like two combatants searching for weaknesses. She waved at the chairs behind him, and he sat in the one opposite hers.

"I didn't know you wanted your own business."

"People change." She shrugged. "Dreams change."

"Yes. Sometimes by choice." Every muscle in his body tightened, but he leaned back and crossed his legs at the ankle. Never let the prey see you sweat. "Sometimes it's forced on us."

"Why are you here?"

"I like your shop."

Her eyes narrowed. "You didn't answer my question."

"I wanted to visit old friends." He smiled.

"You couldn't wait to leave town or your friends. What's the real reason for your return?"

He held onto his smile. "To build the recreation complex."

"Why would you give a gift to people you hated?"

He exhaled. His infamous reputation for ice water running through his veins was a lie. Hot, burning anger ran through him now. He needed an excuse to stay longer. "Can I have a cup of coffee?"

Beth stared at him.

Would she ignore his request?

After several moments had passed, she picked up the telephone. While she waited, she ran her tongue across her lips.

He watched the seductive movement, and the heat of his anger turned to lust. When Beth snapped her mouth shut, his gaze returned to her eyes.

He covered his mouth and coughed to hide his laughter.

"Could you set up two cups of coffee? One a double espresso, and the other my usual."

Silence.

"I'll come out." Beth set the telephone on her desk. "They'll be ready soon."

"Excellent." He tilted his head. "What have you been doing for the last nine years?"

"I don't know what you're up to, but we aren't friends and have nothing to talk about. Whatever your reason for returning to town, it has nothing to do with me."

He crossed his arms over his chest. "Are you sure?"

"Why are you here?"

"It's time people in this town learn the consequences of judging others."

Her eyes flashed. Was it a reflection of the light or intense emotion?

"Is that why you're here?" she taunted. "J.D. Richards has returned to teach us a lesson?"

"I want people to admit they were wrong about me." He stood and leaned across her desk. "It doesn't matter where someone lives or who their parents are. No one should be called worthless because he lives in a trailer park instead of on River Road."

Beth jumped to her feet, and her chair slammed against the wall. "I'll get the coffee."

Jason sat with his back straight as the edge of a ruler. He shouldn't have let her see his anger, but she'd pushed too hard. Now wasn't the time to ask questions or confront her, but it would happen soon. If there was any hope he could make peace with the past, he needed answers and vindication.

Besides, the letter hinted Beth hid something. Jason didn't know what secrets she had, but he refused to leave town until the truth was revealed.

He inhaled a deep breath and slowly released it. Calmer now, he flexed his fingers and looked around Beth's office.

Neat. No clutter, no papers, not even a paperclip on her desk. Three-ring binders stood on the shelves, lined up in a straight line like soldiers for inspection. On the cabinet next to her desk were several photos. Pictures of women, children, christenings, weddings, but not a single picture of her or her parents.

The sound of a throat clearing caught his attention. He turned and looked at Beth standing in the doorway holding two cups. He stood as she shoved a cup of coffee at him. She went to her side of the desk, picked up her fallen chair and sat. He settled back into his chair.

"You own a home out on River Drive." He watched her while he took a drink of espresso. "This is good."

"How—how do you know where I live?"

"People talk." He would never let her know he had reports from an investigator. "I'm surprised your father let you leave the family home. He was rather protective of you."

"My father doesn't tell me how to live. I wanted a home of my own, and now I have it."

"Are you married or involved with someone?" He wanted to know if she'd answer his question.

"That's none of your business."

He flashed his most charming smile. "True, but tell me anyway."

There was a sadness in her eyes when she said, "My husband died."

"I'm sorry." Jason's eye narrowed. "Why didn't you come to Minneapolis?"

Beth's heart skipped a beat. "What?"

"The day I left, you begged to go with me. But after I left, you changed your mind. Why?"

"I liked my life and didn't want to leave."

"You hated your life here. What changed after I left?"

"It's ancient history. Besides, it didn't matter to you."

"What do you mean it didn't matter? We made plans for a future together, but instead, you dumped me and said I was a fling. It mattered."

Then why didn't you come back when I begged for your help? She folded her hands together. "It took nine years, but I've learned you can't change the past and to try is a waste of hope. I got on with my life. You should do the same."

He uncrossed his legs and leaned forward. "Will you have breakfast with me? We can catch up with each other."

"My life is boring."

"I don't believe anything about you could bore me. We can meet before the shop opens."

Beth pressed her lips together. Jason never gave up. He'd wheedle and push to get what he wanted. "When do you want to meet?"

"I'll pick you up tomorrow at six-thirty.

She stood. "Fine. I'll see you in the morning."

He walked out with a swagger in his steps.

She mumbled, "I can't wait."

By the time she got home, Beth's head ached from clenching her teeth. She skipped dinner, went to her bedroom, and paced. *I can't go to breakfast.* She crossed the room. *Why did he return?* She walked back. *I needed his help, and he ignored me. Now he wants to be friends? Never going to happen.*

If she left the house early, she'd be at work before he came for her. He might be so angry he'd give up on his demand to see her. She grabbed her pillow and screamed into it. When they'd been young and in love, she'd admired his determination. Now that she was the prey, his persistence wasn't as admirable.

Beth took two aspirins and crawled into bed. If only there was a pill to make Jason go away. She closed her eyes determined to put him out of her mind and lose herself in sleep.

The sinister light of the moon passed over Jason. His face looked hard, angry, and dangerous. Then clouds gathered to hide the moon's glow, and he vanished into the darkness.

Alone and frightened, her scream echoed through the bleakness. "Jason."

"You didn't want me. You threw me away."

"That's not true. I had to protect you."

"You're lying."

"It's the truth. I would do anything for you. I love you." Murky shadows surrounded her and strangled her with their icy claws. She couldn't breathe.

Beth sat up to find her sheets tangled around her. She fought to get free then crawled out of bed. Beth stumbled to the bathroom and barely made it to the toilet before heaving. With deep, long draws of air, she tried to slow her breathing and ease the nausea. It didn't help. She choked on the desolation that always tortured her after her nightmares. She sat on the floor and did nothing to stop the fall of sweat and tears down her cheeks.

The gagging stopped, but her stomach ached. Beth held onto the counter and struggled to her feet. Her sweat-dampened nightgown clung to her skin. She wrestled to get the gown off and ignored the sound of fabric tearing. When the cool air touched her skin, she shivered.

She ran a washcloth over her damp skin. By the time she put on a fresh gown, her heart had returned to a normal rhythm although her stomach still churned. She returned to the bedroom and turned on every lamp in the room. The light hid the terror and skeletons that came out in the dark, but nothing stopped the memories or guilt.

CHAPTER THREE

The next morning, as he walked to Beth's front door, Jason congratulated himself for the success of his plan to gain her trust. Soon Beth would answer his questions and share her secrets. Then he'd walk away and wipe this town from his life—and his heart.

His friends and family joked that he had the determination of a bulldog with a fresh piece of meat. They were right. His blood raced when he went into a battle, whether the fight took place in the boardroom or in a coffee shop with a difficult opponent like Beth.

He wore a cocky smile as he rang the bell.

The door opened, but instead of Beth, an older woman welcomed him. "Hello."

"Hello. I'm here to see Elizabeth Kingsley."

"Miss Beth already went to work."

"Oh." He clenched his hands. "I must have misunderstood where we planned to meet. I'll go to the shop."

He stalked to his car, dropped onto his seat, and slammed the door. *Damn her!* He slammed his hands on the steering wheel then gripped it so tight his hands ached. The tires screeched when he pulled out of the driveway. Beth could scratch and hiss if she wanted, but he wouldn't leave Serenity Bay until she answered every question and paid for her sins.

Jason broke the speed limit as he drove to Delectable Delights' and pulled into the parking lot. He stomped to the door and knocked. No one answered. He pounded on the door. A man in a white baker's uniform came from the kitchen and shouted, "We open at seven."

"I'm here to meet with Beth," he yelled through the door.

"Come back later."

"We planned to meet at six-thirty."

"You're late." The baker opened the door. "Weren't you here yesterday?"

"Yeah. Beth and I are old friends." *Well, we were friends—nine years ago.*

"She's in her office." He locked the door and turned back. "This way."

Jason followed the man but waited outside Beth's office. The heat of anger flowed through his veins.

"Hey, Erik. Did you need something?"

"Someone is here to see you. He said his appointment was for six-thirty."

Before she could answer Erik, Jason strolled into her office.

Beth smiled at him, but her eyes were shards of ice. "Thanks, Erik."

"I misunderstood where we were meeting." Jason sat in a chair. "I went to your home before I came here."

"Sorry. I'd planned to get together with the staff today and forgot about breakfast." Beth shrugged. "Not that we have anything to discuss."

"Yeah, I figured it was something like that." He leaned forward. "Tell me why you said I was a fling. Did you mean it? Was that why you changed your mind about leaving town? If you didn't want me to come back, why did you write to me?"

"At the council meeting, you mentioned a letter. Why do you believe I wrote to you?"

"Who else would contact *Jason Fischer*?" Frustrated, he huffed. "If you answer my questions, I'll leave." *After I teach you it's not wise to tease a shark.* "But first I want to know what happened nine years ago."

"I told you, I've let go of the past and don't wish to discuss it." Beth stood. "Besides, I have no secrets I want to share with you. So go away and leave me alone."

Jason pounded a fist on the desk. "You are the one person who can answer my questions. I won't walk away until you tell me what I want to know."

Beth tightened her hands around the arms of her chair. "There's nothing to tell. I would never have sent you a letter because I never wanted you to come back. We have nothing to discuss, so go away and leave me alone."

She looked cool and calm until he looked into her eyes. Fear. *What is she hiding?*

Erik came to the door with a butcher knife in his hands. "Is there a problem?"

She pointed a finger at Jason. "Would you show Mr. Richards out?"

"This isn't finished, Beth. You can get angry and make a scene, but I won't leave town until you tell me what happened nine years ago." He shoved past Erik and stalked out.

Later that afternoon, Abbey walked into the office. "How are you?"

"Miserable." No matter how busy Beth got, her thoughts returned to Jason, his anger, his threats. "Why can't he leave me alone? I told him I don't want to discuss the past, but he won't let it go."

"Are you sure he hasn't changed—"

She rubbed her hands over her arms. "If he'd cared, he'd have come back when I begged him. Now he thinks he has a right to make demands. Well, he's nine years too late."

"Why did he decide to ask questions now?"

"He received a letter and claims I sent it." Beth put her hands on her hips. "I would never have written him."

"Have you seen the letter?" Abbey frowned.

Beth shook her head. "He hasn't shown it to me."

"Why would someone want him to come back to Serenity Bay?"

"I don't know, and I don't care." Beth briefly closed her eyes. "Now he's building the complex and won't leave town until it's done. That will give him time to harass me. When he left this morning, he was furious. Maybe he's so angry he'll leave me alone."

"That's not going to happen."

Beth glared at Abbey. "What? How do you know?"

Abbey held up a finger and scurried away. She returned with Jason. He carried a large florist's box. He walked to her and held the box out to her.

As though he carried a snake, Beth took a step back and wrapped her arms around her waist. "What's that?"

With a cocky grin, he said, "Flowers."

Beth waved her hand. "Yes, but why?"

"To apologize. I don't lose my temper often, but talking about the past is difficult for me." He glanced at the box. "Anyway, I'm sorry."

He'll stand there holding that darn box until doomsday if I don't take it. Beth took the box and mumbled, "Thank you."

"I'll see you tomorrow." With a satisfied smile on his face, he walked out.

Abbey bounced on her feet. "Is there a card?"

Beth shrugged.

"It won't open itself."

"I don't want them."

Abbey pointed at the box. "If you don't open it, I will."

Beth sighed but untied the ribbon. She was careful not to tear it. The ribbon was her favorite color—peach. That was why she wanted to save it, not because he gave it to her.

In the box were long-stemmed, peach-colored roses mixed with baby's breath. They were her favorite flower. Nestled on top of the bouquet was an envelope with her name on it. She recognized Jason's handwriting. She reached for the envelope, but stopped and curled her fingers.

It had taken years to gain her self-confidence, and she refused to act like a coward. She grabbed the envelope and took out the card.

Please accept these flowers, along with my apology, for my outburst this morning. I hope you'll give me a chance to make it up to you. Jason

"What a sweet apology. I'll get you a vase." Abbey rushed from the office with a huge smile on her face.

"Yeah, isn't it sweet?" *Why won't he leave me alone?*

The next day Beth reorganized the shop's storage room. If she kept busy, there wouldn't be time to obsess over Jason's accusations or her traitor heart. It didn't work. She thought about why it was so important for him to return to town and ask questions now. By the time she finished in the storeroom, all she had were more questions and another headache.

Not only had she obsessed about Jason's return, this evening she'd see him at the press conference. The mayor and city council were to announce the construction of the recreation complex followed by a reception at the mayor's home. Jason was the guest of honor.

When it was time to get ready for the conference, Beth went to her office to change into the dress she'd brought to work. This morning she'd tried on every cocktail dress in her closet until she chose her favorite. She changed into a curve-hugging black dress and a pair of killer high-heels that made her feel sexy and confident. Tonight she would need all the self-confidence she could muster.

By the time she finished dressing, her hands shook so badly she had to put on her lipstick twice before she got it right. She looked in the mirror. "You survived the worst days of your life and can live through this evening."

She walked out of her office and found herself surrounded by employees. With a laugh, she turned in a circle. "Well, how do I look?"

Erik wagged his eyebrows, "Every man at this shindig will lust for your body."

Beth laughed so hard her side ached. If she could have a brother, Erik was the man she'd choose. She kissed him on the cheek and hugged him. A bright red blush ran up his neck and covered his face.

He clapped his hands. "Customers wait, and pastries burn. Jamie, you relieve Abbey. If she doesn't get back here soon, she'll burst."

Their laughter rang out before everyone returned to their stations. Seconds later, Abbey charged into the kitchen. She walked around Beth and let out a wolf whistle. "Wow."

"Should I have worn the blue dress?"

Abbey grinned and wagged her eyebrows "You are gorgeous. Jason will kick himself for letting you get away."

"I didn't dress to impress him."

"No, of course not. But he'll still kick himself." Abbey snickered. "Now go show him the woman you've become."

"I didn't dress for Jason."

Abbey handed Beth her purse, "Absolutely not."

Beth walked the two blocks to the council's offices hoping the fresh air would calm her nerves. She entered the chambers but stopped when she saw a crowd gathered around Jason. He hadn't seen her, so she went to the side of the hall to study him.

His good looks and self-confidence had drawn others to him even when he'd worn jeans and a leather jacket. Today in his tailored silk suit he radiated power no one could ignore. Regardless of what he wore, he had a body made for hot, sweaty sex. *Abbey's right. He's a hunk.*

Her gaze swept over his body and up to his face. She stopped breathing. Jason watched her. A smug smile on his face, he walked to her. He held out a single peach-colored rose with a lace ribbon tied around the stem. Her mouth opened, but no sound came out.

"I want to apologize again for losing my temper." He gave her a sweet smile. "Will you forgive me, and let me prove you can trust me?"

Several of the guests watched them, no doubt in search of a juicy bit of gossip. Whether she took his peace offering or not, there was plenty to discuss over the back fence.

When Beth took the rose, a thorn bit into her finger. "Ouch."

"Be careful." He grinned. "Beautiful flowers often have

thorns."

"So do people."

"I'll be meeting a lot of people tonight and hoped you'd help me with introductions."

"The mayor will be glued to your side and introduce you to everyone."

"True, but I prefer you at my side."

"I won't hang on your arm like an ornament."

"I don't think so little of you." Jason's gaze never wavered. "You are an intelligent, successful woman, and it would be an honor to have you next to me."

What game is he playing? "As a council member, I'll help in any way I can."

Jason gave Beth his I-closed-a-multi-million-dollar-deal smile. With a touch, he led her to the stage.

Mayor Derr rushed to them. "Before we start, would you like a drink, water or soda?"

Jason asked her, "Do you want a drink?"

A pink blush covered her face. "No. Thank you."

"We're fine. Perhaps later."

The mayor slapped his hands together. "If you'll come with me, we can start the press conference."

She stepped away. "I want to wash my hands. I'll return in a minute and join the other council members at the podium."

"We'll start when Beth returns." Jason gave her a bright smile and wondered if that sound he heard was her teeth grinding.

To his credit, Mayor didn't ask questions, but his eyes were wide with curiosity. While they waited, the mayor filled the time with polite chatter. Jason did his best to listen to him, but watched and wondered whether Beth would return. When she walked back, the tightness in his chest eased. He took her hand and followed Mayor Derr to the stage.

"The reporters agreed not to ask questions until after the announcement." The mayor said, "The photographers will take pictures while you talk, but I'm sure you're accustomed to that."

Beth's back stiffened.

Jason wrapped an arm around her waist and whispered, "The mayor will direct this circus. He'll do most of the talking and handle the press. We're here for the show."

Mayor Derr clapped his hands. "Let's begin, shall we?"

Beth lined up with the council members behind the mayor and smiled, and Jason stepped to the side. She smiled, but there was no happiness in it. Was she worried that he'd learn her secrets?

"Ladies and gentlemen, I'm glad you could join us this evening. Tonight we are here to announce the construction of an addition we've wanted in this community for years." The mayor spoke through the wide grin on his face. "I'm certain you've heard of business magnate and philanthropist, J.D. Richards, CEO of Ziron Corporation. What you may not know is he got his start in Serenity Bay."

Adrenaline pumped through Jason's veins. He'd looked forward to this day. He wanted to show these people how wrong they'd been about him. The *worthless Fischer boy* had become a man others admired and respected. With Beth here to witness his triumphant return, his victory was complete.

"Several months ago, Mr. Richards contacted me about a project he wanted to undertake. After we worked out the details of his proposal, we took the plan to the town council. The vote was unanimous in approval of Mr. Richards' venture."

Jason watched, entertained, while the mayor played the room with the skill of a veteran politician. Reporters recorded his words while the photographers took picture after picture.

"Please welcome J.D. Richards who will tell you about the project he wishes to undertake in Serenity Bay." The mayor beamed and applauded louder than anyone in the room.

Jason walked to the podium, and the fire of victory raced through his veins. "Thank you for your warm welcome. As Mayor Derr said, Serenity Bay was my home for many years. Since leaving town, I have been fortunate in my business and financial endeavors. I want to share my good fortune with those who contributed so much to my life."

He'd dreamed of vindication, and now he had it. He intended to savor every moment and let it wash away the years of humiliation he'd endured. Out of the corner of his eye, he saw Beth frown before she replaced it with a smile. He'd love to know what she was thinking.

"After several discussions with the mayor, we agreed Serenity Bay could use a recreation center. A place where parents can spend time with their children or friends, and they can take part in a variety of activities."

There were gasps when Jason set a drawing for the proposed complex on the easel. "The Council approved my proposal for a recreation complex that will serve this community for years to come. There will be a large community room for social gatherings and classrooms for educational use. The complex will have an indoor swimming pool and gym for athletic events. Outside we've planned courts for bocce ball and tennis. We plan to build the complex on a ten-acre park that will overlook the bay at the north end of town."

He looked at the people who knew him when he lived in Serenity Bay. The shock and surprise on their faces soothed the wounded ego of the boy who'd been told again and again he wasn't good enough.

"To make sure the planning and construction move along smoothly, I will stay in town to oversee the project." He paused. "After the construction is completed, I will sign the papers giving the Richards Recreation & Family Complex to Serenity Bay."

Satisfaction coursed through his veins when the council members and the audience joined in applause that echoed through the chamber. He took a deep breath and inhaled the sweet scent of vindication.

The mayor asked, "Are there questions?"

Several hands were raised. It took Jason and the mayor twenty minutes to answer the questions plus another twenty for pictures. During a lull, Jason left the mayor to wrap up the press conference.

He wore a smile when he went to Beth and held out his hand. Those closest watched with interest when she laced her fingers with his.

The flashes of cameras lit their way from the stage. A few reporters followed and shouted questions. Jason stopped to talk with them, but his patience was wearing thin. He wanted to get Beth alone.

One journalist commented, "The two of you seem close."

Jason smiled at Beth. "We're old friends."

The reporter smirked, "You seem like more than friends."

Jason fisted his hands. Would it be worth a few hours in jail to punch the jerk? Instead, he turned to answer another question.

Behind them, Mayor Derr thanked everyone for attending the press conference. When he reached Jason, he said, "That couldn't have gone better." The mayor wore a proud new-father smile. "I understand the guests have begun to arrive at the reception. We should be on our way. Do you need a ride?"

Jason shook his head. "Thank you, but my car and driver are here. We'll meet you at your house." He slid his arm around Beth's waist. Her muscles tensed, but she didn't pull away. Careful to hide the smug smile he knew was on his lips, he steered her to the door.

Marco stood at the curb with the door open.

She tried to step away, but Jason held tight and led her to his car.

"I need to get my car. It's at the shop."

"A beautiful woman shouldn't wander through town alone at night."

"This is Serenity Bay, one of the safest towns in Minnesota."

"I'd like you to go with me to the reception. Then you can tell me the gossip about the other guests."

She looked at him with narrowed eyes. "What are you trying to do?"

He shrugged. "I want to prove I can be your friend and am worthy of your trust."

"Why?" Beth glared at him.

"Once we were best friends. We knew everything about each other. It's good to have friends who know your past."

She stared at him. Would she insist on getting her car? If she left on her own, he doubted she'd go to the reception. She turned to the limousine. He held her arm as she got in.

Marco drove to the mayor's home which was a beautiful example of Victorian architecture. Jason looked over the three-story house with a builder's eye. Whoever restored it had preserved the original structure, and the workmanship was first-rate. Wherever Jason traveled, he looked for local contractors to work on his projects. He'd ask the mayor for the builder's name.

The mayor and guests clapped when Jason and Beth entered the house. Long past being flustered at such attention, he squeezed her hand. "Keep smiling, and we'll get through this."

Mayor Derr rushed to them. "If you'll come with me, I'll introduce you to everyone."

Jason knew the people who attended the reception had been invited based on their importance to the mayor's reelection, but he liked Bill, so he smiled and shook hands. The whole time, he kept Beth at his side. She didn't complain, but the look she gave him promised retribution. He looked forward to the challenge.

Like the mayor, several guests had moved to Serenity Bay after Jason left town and didn't know his history. However, there were people who had known him, and he thoroughly enjoyed the surprise and shock on their faces. When Mayor Derr made his introductions, most said they were glad to meet him and acted as though they hadn't known him. A few welcomed him back, and everyone thanked him for his generosity.

One woman, bolder than the others, asked, "Did you return to show everyone what you've made of yourself?"

Jason stared at the woman with his iciest smile. Her face flushed a deep red when he said, "Our focus should be the recreation complex, and how it will benefit the community."

The woman mumbled a few words and hurried away.

After that, the mayor deflected personal questions. Jason decided Mayor Derr didn't want anyone to insult the man who was building their sports complex and getting him reelected.

While Jason and Beth talked to him, her parents walked into the house. Jason wanted to rub his hands together. He knew Archer's reputation for cutting corners and fleecing investors to line his pockets. He had to consider J.D. Richards a prime target, but it was Archer's reaction to his introduction to the *worthless Fischer boy* that held Jason's interest.

When Beth saw her parents, her muscles stiffened. Jason wondered about her negative reaction. It was true Archer had never treated her like a beloved daughter but could their relationship be more strained than he knew? He looked into her eyes and was surprised to see them filled with anguish. Without understanding why, Jason gave into the need to protect her and pulled her close.

Archer looked around the mayor's home. It was nice, but his home was more impressive. He'd brought in a designer from New York to stage his home and make it a showcase for his wealth and power. Archer grinned. He was the biggest shark in this pond, and he made sure everyone in town knew it.

It had taken years to sharpen his teeth, but after he had finished college, Archer shed his past the way a snake sheds his skin. He'd buried the poverty-stricken details that had been his life until he escaped to college. Then he clawed his way into the world of business and married the boss's daughter. The day he took control of the company and changed the name to A.K. Industries was his reward for the bowing and scraping he'd done. It had taken time to arrange, but soon he'd have full ownership of the company.

Archer looked around the room. Was anyone here worthy of

his attention? Mayor Derr chatted with a man and woman. That must be Richards. Archer steered his wife to them. He didn't care if he talked to the mayor, but he intended to meet the great J.D. Richards. Archer's sole reason for attending this reception was to talk him into an investment in his latest deal. Richards' name would draw other investors and put more money in his pockets.

The woman at Richards' side triggered a faint recollection, but he couldn't see her face. Archer huffed. He wasn't interested in any decoration on Richards' arm.

Mayor Derr said, "Beth, I believe you know these people."

Archer clamped his lips together. Elizabeth?

The mayor said, "Jason, have you met Archer and Deidre Kingsley, Beth's parents?"

"Never formally."

With a grin on his face, the mayor said, "Archer is the owner and president of A.K. Industries. Deidre sits on the board of several of our charities. Archer and Deidre this is J.D. Richards."

Archer stared at the worthless Fischer boy. Was this a joke? He narrowed his eyes and glared at his daughter. Fischer was a hoodlum and calling himself J.D. Richards didn't change that. Why was she with him? "Elizabeth—"

"Hello, dear." Deidre smiled and kissed Beth's cheek. She shook Jason's hand. "I'm pleased to meet you, Mr. Richards. I've read about you and your company."

Archer stared at Deidre. She'd read something other than the society page?

Richards smiled. "I've looked forward to meeting you. Please, call me Jason."

Jason? They should call him what he was—trash.

Archer had tried to have him sent to prison ten years ago. Someone had broken into his car. He'd insisted Fischer was the thief and had convinced the sheriff to question him. The police couldn't find any evidence to tie the punk to the crime, so they released him.

When she'd been young, no matter how often he'd told Elizabeth to stay away from the boy, she'd found a way to spend time with him. Finally, Archer had come up with a plan to keep the worthless punk away from his daughter.

He sneered at Richards. "You've come up in the world, and now you plan to share your good fortune with the people of Serenity Bay."

"I want to repay everyone for all they did for me when I lived in town."

Mayor Derr jumped into the conversation. "We're thrilled you've returned and can't thank you enough for your gift."

Archer pressed his lips together. What was Richards planning? The mayor didn't know predators the way he did. Archer knew a shark's only interest was their next meal not giving gifts to towns that knew he was nothing but trash.

Archer smirked. "Serenity Bay must look different from this side of the tracks." The glares he got from the mayor and Deidre didn't bother him. Only one opinion mattered—his own.

"It's true, there have been a lot of changes. I've heard it said you can't go home again, but it can be interesting to visit. Don't you agree? Besides, staying in town while the recreation complex is constructed will give me an opportunity to reacquaint myself with—" Jason smiled at Beth, "Serenity Bay."

Archer's eyebrows lifted. Was Richards still interested in Elizabeth? Maybe he could use her to get Richards to fund his Chicago project. When it went bankrupt, he would make millions. If J.D. Richards invested in the project, it would make his success that much sweeter.

Archer handed Richards his business card. "Let's have lunch. I have an investment opportunity that could make you a great deal of money."

CHAPTER FOUR

After three hours of smiling, Beth's cheeks ached. If she had to be pleasant to one more fawning admirer of Jason's, she'd sputter gibberish.

They stood with another council member and his wife and chatted about the recreation complex. He leaned over and whispered, "We've stayed long enough. Are you ready to leave?"

"I'm so ready. My lips have frozen in a permanent smile and might need medical attention."

His lusty laughter ignited a fire in Beth's blood and heat pooled at her center.

They found the mayor, and Jason shook his hand. "Thank you for arranging today's events. Everyone seemed pleased with the plans for the complex. But if anyone raises objections, let me deal with them."

"I will. Once again, on behalf of the town, thank you for your generous gift. The complex is a welcome addition to this community." The mayor pumped his hand. "You remember that we are scheduled to meet next Friday?"

"I have it on my calendar. I'm eager to see the updated drawings."

Cameras flashed while Jason and Beth walked away. Once again, he wrapped his arm around her waist and pulled her close. She tried to step away to put space between them, but he didn't loosen his hold. "The photographers are taking pictures—of us—together."

"They've been taking pictures all night." He shrugged. "Don't let it worry you."

"People will talk. Like that reporter, they'll think we're more than friends."

"People will gossip about anything, even if it's not true, until they find the next juicy morsel. In a few days, we'll be old news."

Beth clenched her teeth. Since she'd escaped Archer's control, Beth didn't worry about gossip. They'd always find someone to talk about. No, she was more concerned about the need she had for Jason's touch. A longing she'd thought dead and that once again burned hot in her.

Jason had shattered her dreams and almost destroyed her, but the past didn't change her body's reaction. She'd be a fool to put her heart at risk again. Somehow, she had to stop wanting his lips on hers.

Once again, Marco waited for them at the limousine. After Beth settled on the seat, Jason sat with his thigh pressed against hers. She moved over a few inches, but he followed her. Why hadn't she driven her own car instead of riding with him?

He pounced. "I am starved. Are you hungry?"

"I'm not—" Beth's stomach rumbled.

"That's a yes." He laughed. "What's your favorite restaurant?"

She wasn't getting out of this. "Chez Belle Ami. It's on River Road. They have a good menu, and the food is excellent."

He asked Marco, "Would you take us to Chez Belle Ami?"

"Wait. I need my car." Beth grabbed Jason's hand. "If you'll go to the shop, I'll get my car and meet you at the restaurant."

"We'll drive you to your car after dinner."

"It's inconvenient to have to drive to town."

"It's not a problem. Besides, you need to make sure we don't get lost."

She looked out the car window. They weren't far from the restaurant, and Marco hadn't needed directions. Maybe Jason thought she'd stand him up? That's exactly what she'd do.

When they walked into Chez Belle Ami, she inhaled the fragrant aroma of rosemary, lavender, thyme, and the other spices used to season the food. The food was excellent, but Beth also loved the old world elegance. White linen cloths covered the tables, the place settings included lead crystal goblets and fine bone china. The atmosphere in the restaurant was intimate and quiet.

Adam Wainwright, the owner and chef, grew up in Serenity Bay, but he'd left to study at the best culinary schools in the United States and Europe. After Adam returned to town, he opened the restaurant. It had gained a reputation for its French cuisine that one critic called *a sensual adventure into the divine.*

While they ordered, Beth racked her mind for a safe topic of conversation. There was always the weather. Instead, she asked, "How did you get a job in construction? You never did that kind of work in Serenity Bay."

He chuckled. "When I moved to Chicago, it was the only job I could get. I've always enjoyed working with my hands, so it was a good fit. But more than that, I was fascinated by the intricacies of running a company. I read books about economics, management, and finance. I enjoyed learning and discovered a talent for business."

"You always liked a challenge."

He chuckled. "That's true. I like to test myself, and I like to win."

"Tell me more about your construction work."

"I enjoy the people. They are honest and down-to-earth."

She tilted her head. "You talk about your employees as though you know them."

"I know a lot of them. My first job was working with the crews. They taught me about the construction business and life." He smiled. "I still go to job sites to talk to them. They often see problems before management and have ideas on how to deal with them."

"Most CEO's don't take the time to talk to their employees."

"Those people are more than employees. They're my friends."

Beth brushed her fingers over her mouth then said, "You said people need to learn not to judge others. Is that why you came back? To teach us a lesson?"

He shrugged. "I left town with unfinished business. It's time to finish it."

"What unfinished business?"

He sat back. "I told you, I want to show these people it's wrong to call others *worthless* because of where they live or who their parents are. Even you didn't believe in me."

"That's not true." Beth shook her head. "I always knew you could conquer any goal you set for yourself."

"If that's true, why did you change your mind? You said I was a fling. Did you mean it?"

The question hung between them. Beth sighed. "Please, let it go. We both made mistakes and rehashing it won't change the past."

He rubbed his chin. "I need answers first. The past and present are tied together. But I can be patient. I won't push—yet."

She knew he'd keep prodding until he got what he wanted. When he was sixteen, he'd wanted a job. He applied at every business in town. No matter how many rejections he got, he kept applying until he got the job at Santos Auto Repair.

She asked, "Did you enjoy the reception?"

"Enjoy isn't the word I'd use. I found the people interesting."

"What do you mean?"

"Two groups of people attended the reception. Those who remember the worthless Fischer boy's past, his father the town drunk, and whose mother ran away with another man. The rest of them wanted to meet famous J.D. Richards."

"You sound cynical."

"I guess I am."

"You had a lot of friends in town. They must be proud of everything you've achieved."

"True, but they weren't at the press conference or reception."

Beth wanted to disagree, but couldn't. The elite of Serenity Bay's society attended, not people who'd been Jason's friends. She laid her napkin on the table. "I need to get home. Will you take me to the shop to get my car?"

Jason lifted his coffee to his lips and drank. He set his cup down and said, "It would be easier to take you home. I'll pick you up in the morning and take you to work."

"That would be inconvenient for you. I have to open the shop tomorrow, so I need to be in early."

"Earlier than five o'clock?"

"Good grief. No."

"Great. I wake early and have nothing scheduled until after lunch. We can have the breakfast we missed."

Excitement sent her stomach into a somersault. She wanted to see Jason again. Then reminded herself, he would push until he got what he wanted. "All right."

When he helped her out of her chair, his fingers brushed over her back. She gasped and inhaled a woodsy scent mixed with a hint of citrus. Perhaps there was more danger in spending time with him than she'd anticipated.

Jason looked into her eyes, and his lips parted. Beth watched him. More than she wanted her next breath, Beth wanted his mouth pressed to hers. Behind her, someone laughed, and she remembered they were in the middle of the restaurant. Beth cleared her throat. "We should go."

They walked out to the limousine. "Marco spends a lot of time waiting for you. Doesn't he get bored?"

"He uses the time to study." Jason laughed. "This week he's learning Swedish."

"Swedish? Is he planning a trip?"

"No, but when I travel, Marco goes with me and likes to talk with the people we meet in their native tongue. He has an ear for languages and is fluent in six. He grew up in Mexico, so listening to him speak German or Japanese can be quite entertaining."

She laughed as Jason helped her into the car. Needing to make conversation to settle her nerves, Beth asked, "What countries have you visited?"

Jason said, "The same ones you have."

"But there must be others, more exotic places?"

"Yes, we've been to, Japan, New Zealand, the Netherlands, Austria. I don't know that they are exotic, but they're not on everyone's travel itinerary."

The car pulled up to her house. Jason held her hand as she stepped from the car and held it as he walked her to the door. *Will he kiss me?* Her stomach fluttered. "I enjoyed our evening."

With a finger under her chin, he lifted her face and kissed her cheek. "Good night."

The touch of his lips had her heart racing. She mumbled, "Good night." Then, as he drove away, she stroked her cheek.

The next morning, Beth sang and danced to the rock tune that blared from her radio. She would see Jason. While Beth braided her hair, her heart pounded in time to the music. When she was dressed, she winked at her reflection and left the bedroom.

Jason said he'd pick her up at six-thirty. At five-forty-five, she went to sit in the parlor to wait. Her right foot swung back and forth. Once again, she checked the time. Five-fifty-four. Nine minutes since the last time she looked. She jumped to her feet and paced.

Beth took a deep breath and inhaled the lemon scented polish on the mahogany furniture. She loved the charm of this parlor with its Victorian furniture and Tiffany lamps. When her grandmother was alive, they had tea and finger sandwiches in this room every Sunday. For dessert, the cook always made a special treat. That was the start of her love affair with white chocolate.

During one of their teas, eight-year-old Beth told her grandmother she planned to be an acrobat in the circus. Nana smiled and hugged her. "You will look beautiful swinging on a trapeze."

The next summer, Beth told Nana she wanted to take care of sick kittens and puppies. Nana had again hugged her and said, "You will be a wonderful veterinarian." She missed Nana and the way she'd given her unconditional love.

The roar of a motor pulled Beth from her memories. She peeked out the window and watched Jason climbed out of a sleek, silver car. Was it his or leased? She'd bet he owned it. He loved cars. When he'd gotten the job at Santos' garage, it had let him do what he loved—play with cars.

She didn't want him to catch her gawking and let the curtain fall into place. When the doorbell rang, she jumped even though she expected it. She controlled the urge to run to the door, but she couldn't hide her grin.

Beth pulled the door open and stared. He wore the smile that had stolen her heart twelve years ago. She felt the flush of anticipation on her cheeks. "Good morning."

"I'm early, but there's no rush. I'll wait until you're ready to leave."

"I'm ready." She cringed at the eagerness in her voice.

His smile grew wider. "Great."

She ignored his cheeky grin. "Are you this cheerful every morning?"

"It's a magnificent day, and I'm escorting a beautiful woman to breakfast. What could be better?"

"Oh. Thanks." Beth bent to pick up her bag, but he took it and grabbed the handle of her grocery trolley before she protested. He took them to the car while she locked the house. At the car, he waited for her with the door open.

When they pulled onto the road, the car jerked forward and raced by the trees. Riding with him made her feel like she was flying. She laughed.

Jason glanced at her and asked, "What's the joke?"

She grinned. "You still like to drive fast."

He gave her a sheepish smile, and the car slowed—a little.

Jason parked behind Delectable Delights, and they went in the back door. As they walked to her office, Beth flipped the switches on the coffeemakers and ovens. They set her bags behind the desk, and he followed her back to the kitchen.

While she prepared breakfast, he sat on a stool and watched. "I don't recall you learning to cook."

"No, it wasn't a skill I was forced to master."

"What changed?"

"I opened the shop and had one pastry chef. He needed help, and I became his gofer. Erik said he'd never be able to show his face in public if the owner of the bakery couldn't even bake a muffin. That was the day he began my education. Now I love to bake and cook, but managing the business takes all my time." She laughed. "I miss being a gofer."

When breakfast was ready, he carried the tray with their food and coffee to her office. He held Beth's chair until she was seated and then sat across the table.

Jason took a bite. "The omelet tastes as good as it smells."

"Thank you. It's truffle and parmesan, one of my favorites."

"What are your plans for the day?"

"Oh, exciting stuff. Update the accounts and do an inventory. Thank goodness I got that college degree, or I wouldn't have any idea why it's important to do an inventory."

"So, you went to college?"

"Yes. I got a degree in business administration and management."

"I'm surprised Archer wanted you to study business."

"He didn't." Beth chuckled. "Father doesn't believe women belong in the business world. Do you remember my grandmother?"

"The two of you were close."

"Nana encouraged me to study business, and Archer didn't dare disagree. He didn't want to risk angering Nana. He was waiting for her to die so he could take control of her estate."

"Why study business?" Jason frowned.

"Like you, I enjoy a challenge, and I wanted to show my father I was more than the Kingsley princess."

"Did you already have plans to open the shop once you had your degree?"

"No." She shrugged. "I was twenty-three, a college graduate, and a widow with no idea what to do with my life."

"Shouldn't you have finished college when you were twenty-one or twenty-two?"

"I didn't go to college right after high school."

"Why not?"

Beth stared at her plate. "Mother took me to Europe."

"Where did you go?"

She repeated the lie she'd practiced since she'd return to town eight years ago. "The usual places—London, Paris, Madrid."

"Did you enjoy traveling with your mother?"

Why is he asking about the year I traveled? "I had more fun turning my idea for a coffee shop into reality. I wanted to get away from Archer's temper and obsessive control of my life. Opening Delectable Delights was my way of celebrating my freedom, my independence."

"You've done well. You have every right to be proud."

"Getting a degree in business management was one of the best decisions I ever made. It also helps that I have a great team working with me. Erik is so talented, and no one manages better than Abbey."

"If you own a bakery, a talented baker is key to your success. The scones we ate were delicious. Did Erik make them?"

She nodded. "We call him the Picasso of Pastry."

He laughed then said, "I'll help clear the dishes."

"I can do this."

"All right. Well, thank you for breakfast. You're an exceptional cook." He stood. "Will you have lunch with me tomorrow?"

She'd enjoyed breakfast, and he hadn't tried to interrogate her. If he would let go of the past, maybe they could be friends. "I'd like that."

They walked to the back door, and Jason said, "Great. I'll pick you up at two o'clock."

"I am off work tomorrow. Would you pick me up at home?" She opened the door.

"Okay. You will be there, right?" He leaned in and kissed her cheek.

"Yes." She closed her eyes and delighted in the touch of his lips. "I'll be there."

After she'd shut the door, Beth slid her fingers over the spot he'd kissed. She turned to go to her office only to find sappy smiles on the faces of the kitchen staff. She laughed. "Show's done. Back to work."

What started as a great day, turned into a disaster. The large coffeemaker blew a rubber gasket. The manufacturer express shipped a replacement, but it wouldn't arrive until the next day. A coil in an oven wouldn't heat. They continued to serve the customers, but when a tour bus pulled in, Abbey said, "Maybe we should close the shop and hide."

By the time her day ended, Beth had agreed.

That evening, when Beth got home, she dropped her bags in the kitchen and dragged herself to the bedroom. She kicked off her shoes and flopped onto the bed to rest for a minute.

When Beth woke the next morning, she looked at her wrinkled blouse and laughed. Even though she'd slept in her work clothes, she felt great. She would see Jason again. After she had taken a shower, she had another clothes crisis trying to decide what to wear. Her room looked like a tornado roared through her closet by the time she settled on a white, strapless sundress with a flared skirt.

Five minutes after she dressed, Jason arrived. The heat in his eyes made the struggle to decide what to wear worthwhile.

After he helped her into the limousine, she watched his shirt stretch over the muscles of his arms and shoulders when he closed the door. He had a body most men would envy, and women would do anything to possess. She curled her fingers to keep from running her hand over his chest.

When the car pulled out, she asked, "Isn't the limousine a bit formal for lunch?"

"I'm waiting for a call from my office. Lupita, my housekeeper, has errands to run, and Marco agreed to answer the calls. With the limo, Marco can practice his Swedish and take messages." He held her hand, "How is your day off?"

She huffed. "I needed this time to recuperate from yesterday."

"Rough day?"

"The worst." She told him about the craziness that had plagued her day. "They say adversity builds character. Well, I don't need more character."

They were still laughing when the car pulled into the drive of the River Inn. The owner of the Inn, Mason Reed, was a friend of Beth's. The huge Victorian home had been owned by his family for over a century. He'd converted it into an elegant bed-and-breakfast and restaurant.

There were only ten tables in the dining room, and they offered one seating at lunch and one at dinner. The menu was whatever Mason prepared that day. Food critics wrote that no one who appreciated fine cuisine could claim to have eaten in the best restaurants in the country until they'd dined at Raison D'etre.

The hostess seated them in front of a picture window. The view would have made a beautiful postcard. The house sat on a cliff which overlooked a slow flowing river surrounded by a forest of pine, spruce, and cedar. It was a romantic's dream come true.

After the waiter had described the day's lunch, Jason ordered wine. "I'm impressed with the restaurants in town."

"We get vacationers in summer for swimming and hiking, and in the winter for skiing and snowmobiling so there's plenty of business to support them." Beth sat back and crossed her arms. "In fact, I know anyone who wants to eat at Raison D'etre has to make reservations a year in advance. How much was the bribe for this reservation?"

He shrugged and grinned.

She tilted her head. "How did you become the CEO of Ziron Corporation?"

His face turned a light pink. "The construction job I got was with Stone Building. Down the street from the job site was a diner where I ate lunch. One day, a guy asked to share my table. We talked about everything and, after that, we ate lunch together every day." He scratched the back of his neck. "It was a couple of months before I found out he owned the company."

The waiter brought a bottle of wine that Jason tasted. After he had filled their glasses, Jason said, "Matt took me home to meet his wife, Helen, and his daughter, Callie. I spent so much time at their house, it seemed natural to move into the apartment over the garage. They treated me like a member of their family." Jason stared into his wine glass for a moment. "Matt and Helen weren't blood, but they became the family I always wanted. They made me part of their family and wanted what was best for me. Unlike my birth parents who made my life hell."

The waiter returned with their salad, and Beth waited for Jason to continue his story.

Jason said, "I was forever asking questions about the business. One day Matt announced he was sending me to college. As much as I wanted to go to school, I couldn't accept his gift. But the family pushed and prodded until I agreed. During the day I worked construction and in the evenings attended college. The day I received my master's degree, Matt promoted me to vice president of operations for the parent company, Richards Construction."

"What about Callie? Did she resent you?"

"Callie has never been interested in running the business, but she wanted someone they trusted to work with Matt. Her interest is marketing. She's a vice president in charge of the Marketing Department." He grimaced. "Three years after my promotion, Matt had a second heart attack. The doctors warned him to slow down or risk an attack he might not survive. The family asked me to accept the presidency."

"They must trust you."

Jason said, "I would never hurt them."

"So you learned to swim with the sharks and changed your name to J.D. Richards?"

One side of his mouth curled into a soft smile. "Richards

Construction was a family-owned business, and the family wanted to keep it that way. Over dinner one night, Matt asked if I'd consider becoming a Richards. I was stunned. I worried that Helen and Callie would resent Matt's suggestion, but they thought it was a great idea. Callie said it would take the pressure off her if her parents had someone else to harass."

Is he in love with Callie? Beth took a drink of her water and then said, "They sound like good people. I'm glad you had them."

"Yeah, me too. It wasn't easy to move to Chicago, but their love and support made it easier to keep putting one foot in front of the other."

Beth took a shaky breath. "So, you became president and revamped the company's operations? I read that Ziron is one of the top corporations in the country and the success is due to your management and the innovations you've implemented."

"With the boom or bust cycle in the construction business, I wanted to lessen the risk of having all our assets tied up in one industry. I diversified the company and streamlined operations. When we took the construction company public and sold stock, the results were better than expected."

"You can be proud of your accomplishments, and now you have the family you wanted."

"Not really."

"But the Richardses love you."

"I wanted a wife and children of my own." He frowned. "When I was twenty-eight, I married Eleanor. She's intelligent, has a great sense of humor, and can navigate the shark-infested waters of my world. I thought she'd be a great wife and mother."

Jason's eyes swirled with contempt. "But what I knew about her was nothing but lies. The real Eleanor was self-indulgent and self-centered. She claimed to be eager to have children, but what she wanted was a life of privilege without responsibilities, especially a family. I found out she'd taken steps to make sure we never had children. The following week, I filed for a divorce."

A deep sadness cut into Beth's heart. He would have been a good father. "I'm sorry."

With a slight shake of his head, he said, "Let's talk about something pleasant."

She nodded. "How did you get a construction job without experience?"

"I asked Matt why they hired me. He said Pat, my supervisor, felt sorry for me." Jason laughed. "My first day on the job, a roofer asked me to get him a turban. I spent thirty minutes searching for a hat before one of the guys took pity on me and told me a turban was a vent."

After a burst of laughter, Beth said, "Before I hired Erik, I tried to make the desserts myself. My first try was an angel food cake. It looked like a pink Frisbee with a hole in the middle. I wanted to try a simpler recipe and made an apple pie. An hour after putting it in the oven, I took it out. It was raw. I forgot to turn on the oven. My last effort was a carrot cake with cream cheese frosting. It took all morning to make, but it looked beautiful. While the staff sampled it, I looked on with pride. When they bit into the cake, carrot shreds the size of earthworms hung from their mouths."

Jason laughed so hard he gasped for breath.

"I hired Erik the next week."

They took turns telling stories of the blunders they'd made getting their start in business. As they talked and laughed, the walls Beth used to protect her heart cracked. But she couldn't put aside the question in the back of her mind. Why had Jason really returned to town?

Back in the limo, Jason apologized before returning a phone call. Beth watched as he talked. His face lit with excitement while the smooth tone of his voice sent chills skating over her skin. She wanted to crawl onto his lap and nibble on his lips. Instead, she clamped her hands together.

Would it be a mistake to invite him in for coffee? As they got closer to her home, her fingers squeezed tighter. There was no danger in sharing one espresso, was there? The muscles in her shoulders ached by the time they'd pulled into the driveway.

He disconnected his call. "Sorry, that took longer than I expected."

Staring at her hands, she asked, "Wouldyoulikeacupofcoffee?"

Jason frowned. "What?"

Heat crept over her face. She tried again. "Would you like a cup of coffee?"

"I would follow you anywhere for a good cup of coffee."

"It's the best in town." She laughed. "By the way, I enjoyed your commentary about the coffee at the reception. There was, 'This has all the flavor of water.' Then later, 'Are they holding down the cost by using one scoop of coffee per pot?'" She got out of the car. "Although, my favorite was—"

"I didn't think you heard me."

"You didn't mean what you said?"

"Oh, I meant every word, but you weren't supposed to hear me."

She giggled. "You'll be glad to know, I have an espresso maker that would have any barista drooling with envy."

"The woman of my dreams." He threw his arms around her.

Heat washed over Beth's face. "Why don't you wait in the parlor?"

"I'd rather go with you. A person can't be too careful with their coffee."

"Oh. Okay."

Jason turned with Beth and kept his arm around her as they walked. "Do you know how to make espresso?"

She stopped and stared at him. "When you own a coffee shop, making coffee is a required skill."

"Others have claimed to have the ability, but in my experience, it's no guarantee the person who makes the coffee knows what they're doing."

"That sounds like a challenge."

"You were always competitive."

She laughed and pointed to the stools at the counter. "Have a seat." Beth walked around the counter and took what she needed from the cupboards. She inhaled the sharp, smoky aroma of the coffee beans she ground.

When she gave Jason his espresso, she held her breath while he took a taste. Then she cleared her throat. "Well, can I make coffee?"

"You definitely know how to make espresso." His eyebrows dipped.

"What's wrong?"

"The espresso at the shop isn't this good, and by good I mean strong."

"I want my customers to come back, not die of caffeine overload." She laughed. "Most of them don't like their drink so strong it would knock an elephant to its knees. When I'm home, I use a special, darker roasted bean for my coffee."

"How do you make it stronger without it becoming too bitter?"

Beth wiggled her eyebrows. "I have a secret ingredient."

"I won't ask you to divulge any secrets." Jason looked around the kitchen. "Was this your grandmother's home?"

"Yes. It was part of my inheritance."

"Is that when you moved out of your parent's home?"

She nodded. "I wanted my independence. When I inherited Nana's estate, it gave me the freedom I'd always wanted."

"It must have been a big leap for you?"

"Nana used to tell me I had her lust for life, but I knew she was being kind. Her life had been interesting and filled with adventures. I lived my life controlled by Archer."

"Your life might not have been adventurous like your grandmother's, but you fought to be your own person. Instead of going to boarding school, you stayed here and became friends with a boy others said was worthless."

"You were never worthless. Besides, you always treated me like a person. Something my father never did. To him, I'm a pawn he used to put his business deals over. I have no real value."

"You always had value." He tipped his head. "What did Archer say when he learned you inherited your grandmother's estate?"

"After Grandmother died, Stephen Howard, her attorney, met with us to read her will. I thought she left me a piece of jewelry or another keepsake. When Stephen told us Nana left me her entire estate, I was speechless."

"And your father?"

"Archer was furious. I told you, he'd been waiting for Nana to die. He was sure Mother would inherit everything, and he planned to take control." She sighed. "His face turned deep red like he was having a stroke. Then he grabbed my arm."

Jason frowned. "What happened?"

"Mother and Stephen stopped him." She shrugged. "Anyway, he accused me of lying to Grandmother to get her to cut him and Mother out of the will. I told him Nana never told me her plans, but he didn't believe me."

"Archer doesn't trust many people."

"No." Beth gave a slight shake of her head. "His attorneys tried to break the will, but Nana and Stephen had written a will so tight it was impossible to challenge."

"Your grandmother sounds like a smart woman with a good attorney."

She nodded. "Archer realized there was no way to break the

will, and he ordered me to give control of Grandmother's estate to him. I refused."

Jason asked, "Did he think you'd do whatever he demanded?"

"I always did." Beth grinned. "When I told him I planned to manage Nana's estate myself, he made all kinds of threats, but I didn't buckle. Until the day I moved out, he never believed I'd go through with it. My one regret is that I didn't stand up to him sooner."

She pressed her fingers to her lips. "I have so many happy memories of my time with Nana, and she knew I loved this house. Father would have sold the house, and I couldn't let him do that."

Jason pushed a strand of hair behind her ear. "I think your grandmother would be proud of you."

"I miss her. She gave me her unconditional love and support." She picked up her cup and walked to the espresso machine. "Would you like another cup?"

He nodded and handed her his cup. When she took it, his hand brushed over hers. Beth shivered the way she did the night they'd made love. She'd never forgotten the feel of his hands on her body and the exquisite pleasure of having him fill her.

CHAPTER FIVE

Jason turned to Beth when she returned with his coffee. The tip of her tongue slid across her lips and lust gripped him. She blushed a bright pink, and he smiled.

He wasn't happy that she still fired his blood. She'd used and betrayed him, but his need burned too hot to be silenced by the past. He couldn't fight the heat coursing through his veins. Maybe he didn't want to.

Wanting to give her a chance to turn away, he moved slow and easy as he leaned forward to press his lips to hers. Then her sweet, soft lips met his, and she sighed. He wanted more than a taste and swept his tongue over her mouth and teased until she opened for him. He slipped his tongue in and tasted the earthy flavor of espresso mingled with the delicate sweetness of Beth.

She slid off her stool to step between his legs then wound her arms around his neck as she returned his kiss. Gone was the young girl who had been frightened by his caresses. In her place stood a desirable woman who met his passion with her own. He wanted her, wanted to touch and kiss every inch of her delectable body.

Jason skimmed his fingers up her arms. He grinned against her lips when she trembled then pulled her close and pressed their bodies together. Jason sank into their kiss. Beth whimpered.

He rubbed his thumb over her lips. "I want to make love to you."

She turned her head and kissed the palm of his hand. "I want that too."

"I have no birth control." Jason pressed his forehead to hers.

"I am taking the pill to regulate my monthly."

"Thank God." He lifted her into his arms and walked towards the front of the house.

"Stop."

He froze, and his jaw dropped.

She giggled and waved her hand to the rear of the kitchen. "That way is faster."

He grinned and rushed to the back stairs. When he reached the top, they kissed until Jason pulled away to gasp for air.

"Which room?"

Her hand shook as she pointed to the bedroom across the hall.

Jason went to her room and stopped next to the bed. He

lowered her legs, and she slid down his body and over his already stiff cock. Need threatened to consume him. He wanted to bury himself in her, again and again, until they fell into an exhausted sleep in each other's arms.

Beth reached around to the back of her dress and struggled with the zipper. With a huff, her arms fell to her side.

He grinned, "I'll do that."

She kissed his chin and turned.

Jason brushed his fingers across her bare shoulders until he reached the dress's zipper. He slid it down but stopped every few inches to tease her skin with a kiss or a lick or a suck. Then he lowered the zipper another inch until he reached the bottom.

Jason turned Beth. He tugged on the bodice and sucked in air when it fell to her waist. He stroked her satin smooth skin. She arched her back, and his hands slid down to fondle her breasts.

He took a step back, and she opened her eyes. With a smile, he slipped her dress past her waist and hips until it pooled at her feet. She stood in a white silk thong and nothing else. While he memorized every delectable inch of her body, his pants stretched tight over his cock.

Beth whispered, "Jason," and her lips nipped at his. She teased his mouth until he took control of their kiss. He drank in her passion the way a connoisseur sips a sixty-two-year-old Scotch whiskey.

Her nails dug into his arms, and her eyes closed as the passion built. He ran his hands over her skin, and she responded with eagerness. He wanted to lay her down and bury his cock deep, but he didn't want to rush. First, he intended to savor the sweetness he'd missed for nine long years.

Jason pulled off his shirt then wrapped his arms around Beth and lifted her until she cradled his cock in the vee of her thighs. When her breasts pressed to his chest, he shifted from side to side rasping her skin against his. He enjoyed the sensual torture but wanted more. He set her on the bed.

Beth lay back with one leg bent and opened herself to his gaze. His breath caught in his throat. She looked more luscious than Aphrodite in the painting he'd seen of the goddess waiting for her lover. Except this was Beth, and she waited for him.

With more enthusiasm than finesse, he pulled off the rest of his clothes. She watched him the way she had their first time together. He pushed his slacks down and released his cock. When she licked her lips, his shaft jerked as more blood flowed to it.

As Jason's control weakened, he fisted his hands while need ran through him like hot lava. He climbed onto the bed and sprinkled light kisses on her eyes, nose, and cheeks.

Beth drew circles around his nipples.

He jerked back.

Her eyes widened. "Am I doing it wrong?"

"No." He swallowed to remove the gruffness from his voice. "I don't want you to call me the five-minute-man."

Beth's breasts bounced as she laughed.

He teased her lips until she moaned. Then he sucked on her bottom lip, pulled it between his teeth, and nipped at the plump tidbit. With a sweep of his tongue, he soothed the spot. When she moaned, his lips slid over her cheek to her ear. He circled the delicate flesh with his tongue and blew on the damp lobe. She whimpered, so he did it again.

Jason kissed his way down her neck until he reached the place where her pulse beat. He nibbled on the spot then glided his lips across her shoulders. Jason let his hands drift over her skin until he could cup her breasts. He suckled each breast and whirled his tongue across the nipples until the buds were tight.

With the tips of his fingers, he brushed his hand along her ribs. Then he tickled and teased her navel before he slid his tongue in circles around the delicate dimple. Beth writhed and clutched the sheet. He gave her only a moment to catch her breath and dropped a hand to stroke through the curls around her slit.

The glow on Beth's face when he swirled his fingers in her cream captivated him. With a slight twist, he dipped a finger into her sheath. She moaned. When he was certain she was ready, he slipped a second finger into her. She ground her softness against his hand. He used his thumb to circle her clit and heard the mewling sounds she made.

Jason's good intentions disappeared. He wanted her wrapped around him. Kneeing over her, he teased her with the tip of his cock. She arched her back, and he pressed on her hips to keep her still. "Let me do this."

After covering his shaft in her cream, he pushed into her one breath-stealing inch at a time. He rolled her nipples between his fingers and took her mouth in a deep, possessive kiss.

Beth turned her head and in a breathy moan begged, "Please...."

"Patience. You're tight. I don't want to hurt you."

She inhaled and exhaled to relax her muscles. He buried his cock deep in her. Jason wanted to linger in the velvet softness wrapped around him, but the muscles of her vagina fluttered around his shaft. His control shattered.

His hips jerked as he stroked in and out until his body vibrated with anticipation. One thought consumed him. He needed the satisfaction his body demanded. Jason plunged and retreated. His hips moved fast and hard.

Beth dug her nails into his arms and lifted her hips to meet his thrusts. Her erratic gasps for breath and frantic moans let him know her orgasm was close.

Unsure how much longer he could hold out, he slid a hand to her clit and caressed it. Could such violent, intense loving kill a man?

Her pussy clenched. The walls of her vagina rippled over his cock and her cream flowed as she screamed, "Jason!"

His back bowed as he thrust—once, twice. The tension in his body built, and his orgasm erupted. Unaware of anything but his release, he shouted while pleasure rolled over him. He remained deep in her heat until he was empty.

Jason's arms trembled. If he didn't lie down, he'd fall. With a push, he rolled to Beth's side. He struggled to breathe, his heart pounded against his ribs, and his body shook. They lay together, arms and legs entwined. Beth ran her fingers over his chest. Now he knew why cats purred.

He fought to tame his thoughts and the emotions that threatened to overwhelm his heart. This had been more than sex; this had been making love. Her gentle touch, the warmth of her body, and the heat of her kisses would live in his heart long after he left Serenity Bay.

Beth tightened her arms around him and sighed.

He propped his head on his hand. "You appear to be thinking serious thoughts when you should be basking in the afterglow."

"My thoughts aren't that serious, and I am basking."

"Good. I would hate to think I was unappreciated."

"Good grief!" Beth's hand flew to cover her mouth, and a dark red blush swept over her cheeks.

"What's wrong?"

"Marco is outside in the limousine. By now he's figured out what we're doing." She tucked her face into his chest. "He'll think I hop into bed with every man I meet like Casanova."

Jason chuckled. "Casanova was a man."

"You know what I mean." She slapped at his chest, and his chuckles became full-blown laughter.

Beth's eyes narrowed. "This isn't funny."

"I sent Marco home."

"You planned to seduce me?" She shook her finger at him. "Do you bed every woman you feed? Is Marco accustomed to your trysts? How does he know when to return?"

"I call him."

"Well, isn't that convenient?" She spit each word. "Am I another *notch* on your bedpost?"

"This is your bed."

She waved her hand. "Don't confuse me with facts. You can't charm your way out of this."

"Angel, calm yourself. I told Marco we wanted to talk. If you threw me out, I planned to walk or call him. The house I'm living in is a few miles down the road."

"Oh."

"Although it would be unkind of you to toss me out in the freezing cold."

"It's June."

Jason brushed his lips over her eyelids, nose, and ears. He nipped at her neck and shoulders. "I hope you found my amorous attention to your liking?"

"It was adequate." She grinned. "Although the memory has begun to fade."

"Adequate? Fading?" His voice rose in indignation, and he laid a hand over his heart. "You wound me."

She slipped her fingers across his chest. "I doubt that."

He leaned over her. "I will have to work harder to satisfy your desires. Unless I've worn you out?"

"Don't worry about me. I'm not even winded." She grinned. "My concern is for you. You're older now and don't have the stamina you possessed when you were younger."

Jason gave her his sexy grin, the one he'd practiced when he was seventeen. "Like a fine, aged cognac, now I am smoother and more potent."

Then he proved how good a lover he'd become. After the third time they'd made love, their bodies collapsed into a tangle of sweat covered arms and legs. She snuggled into his side, and they fell asleep wrapped in each other's arms.

The next morning, Jason hummed as Beth's fingers played over his skin. He rolled to his side and pulled her close. When she whimpered, he frowned. "Did I hurt you?"

"No." She blushed a sweet shade of pink. "It's...I ache."

He leaned over her. "It's been a while since you've made love?"

She lifted a shoulder. "I guess."

He lifted her face. "How long?"

Beth stared at his chin. "The night you left Serenity Bay."

"What? That's not possible." He frowned. "You were married. I don't understand."

She glanced at the clock. Six o'clock.

"I don't have time to explain now, or I'll be late for work."

"But you'll tell me the next time we talk?"

She nodded.

"Promise?"

Beth said, "I promise."

Jason ran his fingers over her cheek. "I'm sorry you're sore."

"I enjoyed everything we did. But now I have to dress. If we hurry, I'll have time to take you home and get to the shop a few minutes early."

"You get ready for work. I'll call Marco. He's an early riser which means he's been up for hours and will annoy me with his cheerfulness. The drive home will be the perfect time for him to give me a lecture and warn me about leading the 'nice senora' astray."

Her brows drew together in a frown. "Do you regret what happened?"

"Never. Last night was perfect. My only regret is that I fell asleep."

Beth smiled, leaned over, and kissed him. It started as a light kiss, but soon it turned hot and needy. She pulled away. "I have to get ready for work."

"I know. Will you have dinner with me?"

"I work until six tonight. Abbey has appointments and has to start later than usual. Let's have dinner at six-thirty at the University Club."

"Shall I pick you up at work?"

"No, I'll drive my car."

"I'll call to reserve a table. You will show up, won't you?"

She gave him a guilty smile. "I'll be there."

"Good. Now get moving. I don't want to start something you can't finish."

"You are breathtaking." At the Club, Jason held her chair. She wore a silk dress in a midnight blue that hugged the curves of her body. But it was her smile that made him hard and want to spend another night, or several, with her wrapped in his arms.

"Sorry I'm late, but the rain made the road slippery." Beth waved her hand. "So, the Wizard of Wall Street was able to reserve the private dining room?"

"It was available."

"Hmm." She asked, "Is Marco outside practicing his Swedish?"

"No, I drove myself."

Her face turned a light pink. "Um—did he say anything about—last night?"

Jason laughed. "He did. I got an earful about being a bad influence. He said you are a delicate rose, and I should take better care of you."

"That's sweet."

"Sweet for you. It was me he accused of leading you astray."

They laughed until a throat cleared. The sommelier said, "Good evening, Miss Kingsley. Mr. Richards, the wine you requested is ready. May I serve it?"

Jason asked, "Would you like a glass of wine?"

"Yes. Please."

"We'll both have a glass," he told the sommelier.

He waited, tapping a finger on the table, while the man poured their wine. Beth appeared more relaxed than she'd been since the first day he saw her in the council chambers. Maybe tonight she'd trust him enough to answer his questions.

"To old friends." He lifted his glass and clinked it with hers. A minute later, the waiter arrived to take their dinner order. After he left, Jason said, "Tell me about Delectable Delights. What made you open a coffee shop?"

"I graduated from college not knowing what to do with my life. I wanted to do more than spend my time running from one charity to another. Serenity Bay is a tourist town. In the summer our population triples and in the winter it doubles. I thought a restaurant sounded like a good business idea, but there were two problems. I had no experience in business, and my ability to cook was non-existent."

"What did you do?"

"After I inherited Nana's estate, her attorney agreed to work with me. I invited Stephen to dinner, and we talked about my idea. We discussed the steps I'd have to take to open and run a business. It boggled my mind. He suggested that I start with a smaller business. The restaurant became a coffee shop with desserts."

"You're fortunate to have had a good attorney to advise you."

She nodded. "Stephen helped me put together a business plan. He suggested I buy a building rather than lease a shop. Then I found an empty space in a great location and hired a contractor who made the changes I wanted. While the contractor worked on the renovations, I interviewed and hired a team of employees. Three months later, Delectable Delights opened."

"It's not easy to start a business. Although, the Beth I knew would have been excited about the challenge."

"You're right. It was fun converting an empty warehouse into a thriving business." She shrugged. "I like to win too."

After they had their salads, Jason asked, "When did you expand your menu and add catering?"

Beth chuckled. "Erik said he wanted to make food to 'nurture the souls of the masses.' That's when we added sandwiches and salads. A few months after we opened, customers were calling in special orders. Erik suggested the change, I ran the numbers, and we were catering."

"What about a personal life? It takes a lot of time and effort to run a business."

She stared at her folded her hands. "I love the shop and the people who work with me are my family. We get together for dinner at least once a week. I'm on the city council and volunteer at the shelter. I'm content."

Content. She was too young, too full of life, to settle for contentment. She'd fought her father to experience life not hide in an ivory tower, and she deserved more. A life filled with love and happiness had been her dream, so why had she settled for less?

He took a drink of his wine then carefully set the glass on the table. "Why did you change your mind about leaving town with me?"

Beth stared at her plate. "I made a life for myself in Serenity Bay. I love my shop, my home."

"You didn't have the shop or your home when you were eighteen. What happened after I left town? Your letter said I was a fling. Was I a fool the princess used to entertain herself?" His pride demanded the truth.

"I never considered you a fling or a fool." She looked at him. "Jason, we can't change what happened. You wanted to be friends; can't we do that without rehashing the past?"

His voice rose. "I deserve to know the truth. I thought you loved me. You made me believe we had a future together until the day I got your letter. I want to let the past go, but first I deserve answers."

She held her hand out in supplication. "Please, let it go. Remembering only makes the pain and anger worse."

"What pain? Anger over what?" He rubbed his forehead. "You hated playing the society debutant and wanted to escape the future your father planned for you. But when you could leave, you changed your mind. Why?"

She pleaded, "Please..."

His eyes narrowed. "Your letters and calls stopped. Then I got that last letter. I didn't want to believe I was a fling. But when I went to see you, you repeated every word."

"What do you mean the last letter? I sent several, but they came back stamped *Moved*."

"You know which letter. The one that told me my life was a lie. Your message was short but memorable." He stared at her, but she didn't look away. Then he spoke the words that destroyed his dreams. *"You were never more than a fling I used to amuse myself."*

She pressed her hand to her heart. "I never said that."

Jason stared at her with eyes as cold as ice. *"I could never be serious about a hoodlum and the son of the town drunk. Don't come back. It would embarrass me to be seen with you. Elizabeth Marie Kingsley."*

The color drained from Beth's face. Her fork fell and clanged on the plate. Her mouth opened and closed before opening again. "I would never have written such awful lies."

The anguish in her voice almost convinced him. "You did. That's what you said when I went to your house. You told me never to bother you again." He took a deep breath to control his anger. It didn't work. His body shook as he exhaled. "I did what you asked. I stayed away. Until I got your letter a few months ago."

"I didn't write to you." Her back straightened like the sharp edge of a butcher's knife. "What did that letter say?"

"It came to my office, addressed to Jason Fischer. It was short and succinct. *Mr. Fischer: Serenity Bay has many secrets. If you want to uncover the truth, you should talk to Elizabeth Kingsley.* It was unsigned."

"With no signature, why do you think I sent it?"

"The postmark was Serenity Bay. Who else knew Jason Fischer?" He rubbed his hand over his chin. "Why did you want me to return? What secret have you kept from me?"

Beth's fingers folded together, and her knuckles were white. "I have no secrets."

"We have been given another chance, but first we need to make peace with the past. I need to know why you changed your mind. Tell me what secrets you're hiding."

Beth pulled her napkin off her lap and twisted it. Tension snaked through him, and his muscles stretched taut. He didn't want to ruin the relationship they were building, but he'd never bury his ghosts if she didn't tell him the truth. "Beth, make me understand."

"If you wanted to know what happened, why didn't you read my letters? When I needed your help, you abandoned me. Now I'm supposed to beg for forgiveness for something I didn't do."

What is she talking about? He ran a hand through his hair. "What letters? Your letters stopped coming until I got your kiss-off."

"You won't believe anything I tell you." Beth couldn't take much more. "You don't trust me. I told you, I didn't write those awful letters. I loved you and wanted to spend my life with you, but you don't believe me. Do you?"

"If that's true, why did you send me away?"

"I did what I had to do." Her lips quivered, but anger overcame her fear. "What about you? I needed you, but you ran."

"What? I don't understand?"

"There's nothing to understand. You didn't want me." The pain of his betrayal slashed into her heart.

He waved his hand. "Nothing you've said makes any sense."

"I don't want to discuss this. It hurts too much." She pressed a hand to her mouth.

"I need to know the truth." Jason slapped his hand on the table. "Tell me what happened!"

She jumped to her feet. "Leave me alone!"

Beth ran. Outside, rain drizzled over her face. She shivered. Jason's anger and bitterness battered her heart. But if he knew what she'd done, he would hate her. That she would never survive.

Rather than wait for the valet, Beth raced to her car and tumbled into the driver's seat. When she pulled out of the parking lot, the car swerved and the tires squealed. She swallowed a sob. Last night he'd been gentle and caring, but tonight there was no softness in him.

At work today, Beth had caught herself humming. It had been years since she'd felt so much hope for the future. She'd imagined Jason as her friend, lover, maybe more.

But his bitterness and relentless hunt for answers killed her hopes and did a death dance on her dreams. For eight long years, nightmares and memories haunted her. Every day she struggled under the weight of the anguish she endured for the sins she committed, but his contempt would kill her soul.

Beth blinked her eyes as she tried to see the road, but tears clouded her vision. Her chokehold on the steering wheel kept her hands from shaking—almost. It wasn't smart to drive while upset, but she couldn't take any more of his accusations. Should she leave town? Her shoulders drooped. Jason would still be here when she returned.

The day she'd sent Jason away, she'd cried, cursed, and bargained with the angels, but nothing changed what she'd had to do. She'd sent an explanation, but the letter came back, and so did every letter she sent after it. Shattered and with no hope, she'd folded under her parents' pressure.

As Beth drove into a sharp curve in the road, she glanced at the speedometer. In that moment of distraction, she lost control of the car. It fishtailed across the wet pavement. Her muscles stiffened, and she fought to stay on the road. She pulled on the steering wheel, but the car swung too far to the left. Her leg shook when she slammed on the brake.

The car skidded into the ditch. Her body strained against the seat belt as the car flipped once, twice before it crashed to a stop jerking her body. The airbag and seatbelt kept her from flying through the windshield, but her head bounced off the side window. Pain. The wail of a baby pierced the pain before her world went black.

CHAPTER SIX

Jason rubbed his forehead. "Damn." Why had he pushed so hard? They'd gotten along so well. They talked and laughed the way they had when they were teenagers. Last night, their loving had been much more than he'd hoped for. He'd begun to think they could have a life together.

Beth had looked devastated when she ran out, and she'd been crying. The roads were slippery and soaked with rain. Not a good combination for someone who was distraught to have to cope with. He paid the check and rushed after her. He might be frustrated, but he wanted her safe.

Jason tapped his foot while he waited for the valet to get his car. He pulled out of the driveway, and his tires slid across the pavement. The road was slick and treacherous from the oil mixing with the rain. The curves were dangerous for anyone driving too fast. His hands gripped the steering wheel.

He didn't know this road well and kept the car moving at a steady pace, although slower than the speed posted. His jaw clenched as he pressed on the gas and drove too fast through a sharp turn. The car skidded. He eased his foot off the gas pedal to get the car under control.

As he pulled out of the turn, his headlights reflected off something. He slowed the car and squinted as he tried to see what was in the ditch. Could it be—? His chest tightened until it hurt to breathe. "No!"

Beth's car lay, twisted and mangled, at the bottom of the gully.

He pulled his car to the side of the road but was careful to park it on the pavement. If he drove onto the shoulder, he'd get stuck in the mud. With his car's headlights pointed into the ditch, he looked for Beth but saw no movement.

Jason pulled his cell phone from his pocket and dialed the emergency number. The dispatcher answered, and he told her what he could. She asked him to stay on the line. "I can't. I have to get to her." He shoved the phone into his pocket.

He grabbed the flashlight from the glove compartment and stepped out into the cold rain. When he reached the edge of the steep incline, he flashed the light over the ditch. It was muddy and filling with water. It didn't matter, he needed to get to Beth.

He slid more than he walked down the side of the ravine and

trudged through slimy pools of rain. With each step, Jason whispered the prayers he learned from his mother before she left and hoped they worked better now than they had when he was a young boy. They hadn't stopped his biological father from pounding his anger out on his face until the day he'd gotten big enough to defend himself.

He slid the last few feet to the bottom of the ditch. His wet clothes stuck to his skin and his mud-covered shoes were cold on his feet. The flashlight dimmed. He shook it, and the light brightened. He slogged through the thick, cold mire as he made his way to Beth's car.

The driver's side was wedged into a Norway pine. It would be impossible to reach her from that side. He ran to the passenger door. The car was tipped off the ground. If he tried to get in, his weight might make it shift or drop to the ground.

Jason rubbed the back of his neck. Desperate to get her out, he prayed, *Please let her be alive*. He opened the door. "Beth? Can you hear me?" No reply. No sound.

He had to get her out, so he carefully sat on the seat. The car wobbled but didn't fall. One slow inch at a time he slid across to her. "Beth? Talk to me."

She didn't move. Then Jason heard a soft whimper and waves of relief rushed through him. Her breathing, raspy and erratic, was the sweetest sound he could hear. He found her pulse—weak. *Where is the ambulance?*

Jason focused his flashlight on Beth. Maybe he could drag her across the seat? A stream of blood dripped from her forehead, and her lip bled. He flashed the light on the inside of the car. A cracked door panel cut into her left side. Jason didn't know how deep the metal dug into her body. If he tried to pull her from the vehicle, the panel could go deeper. He couldn't risk hurting her more.

Damn. Jason closed his eyes for a moment. He'd never considered himself a selfish man, but his stubborn pride caused this tragedy. While Jason waited for help to arrive, he held Beth's limp hand and begged, "Angel, squeeze my hand. Please."

No response.

"I've called for help. They'll be here soon." He rubbed his forehead. "Don't leave me."

He didn't know how long he'd talked, but from a distance came the wail of sirens, and relief flowed through him. Headlights reflected across the ditch, and a rescue truck pulled to the side of the road. An ambulance parked behind it.

"The emergency team is here, and they'll get you out of the car and to the hospital."

The sheriff and paramedics gathered at the top of the gully. They talked, walked around, and pointed. Jason heaved a sigh of relief when the group split up and got busy. The sheriff spoke into a radio while another officer ran back to his vehicle. The paramedics sloshed through rain and mud, then slid into the ditch.

"Angel, can you hear me?" He caressed her cheek. "I never wanted—"

"Who's the driver?"

Jason turned his head. "Wh—what?"

A rain-soaked deputy, with 'Davis' sewn on his jacket, leaned into the car. "What's the driver's name?"

"Elizabeth Kingsley."

"Beth?" The man's eyebrows lifted, and his eyes widened. "What happened?"

"I think she lost control of the car. I saw skid marks on the road."

Davis nodded and walked around the car. When he returned, he talked with the other members of the team. The rain, falling harder now, drowned out their discussion, but Jason caught, "Impossible to get to her...." Were they giving up? He wanted to yell, but it wouldn't do Beth any good.

A woman with a blue Star of Life patch on her jacket leaned into the car. "Sir, you need to get out."

"I can't leave, she needs me."

"We need to check her injuries and vital signs."

He nodded then whispered to Beth, "I have to go, but I'll be close. Please, I couldn't bear to lose you again." He kissed her cheek and crawled out.

Jason slid from the car and stood with Davis while the EMT technician moved across the seat to get close enough to check on Beth. The rain fell in a heavy torrent and streams of water ran over Jason's face and down the back of his neck. His body trembled. He didn't know if it was due to the cold or fear.

More beams of light flashed over Beth's car. A tow truck parked at the edge of the ditch. The driver pulled a heavy chain and hook from the back.

Jason turned to the deputy. "What's he doing? He can't tow the car, she's still in there."

"The driver's door and front panel dug into the tree when the car slammed into it. Beth's legs are trapped. We can't get her out until the crushed metal is removed." The deputy sighed. "Once the tow truck pulls the car away from the tree, they'll use the hydraulic cutters to free her."

"The metal from the door is cutting into her side. If the car moves, it could do more damage."

"It's dangerous, but there is no better alternative."

It took precious time to hook the chain to the car. Jason paced. The metal creaked and groaned while the tow truck pulled the car. With each screech of metal, his nails cut deeper into his palms. From inside the car, he heard Beth's whimpers and moans. He tried to get to her, but the deputy grabbed his arm.

Jason struggled to get free. "I have to help her."

"No. You've got to let them do their work." The deputy pulled him back and held his arm. "They have to free her and take her to the hospital."

Jason rubbed his face and prayed.

The tow truck pulled the car far enough away from the tree to use the hydraulic cutters. As they cut and tore away the pieces of the car, Beth cried out.

Afraid of losing his dinner, Jason swallowed several times. Once Beth was in the ambulance, he climbed in with them. Then he took several deep breaths to slow his pounding pulse and listened as Beth struggle to breathe.

The ambulance pulled into the driveway of the Emergency entrance at the hospital. A doctor and nurse ran over while the technicians lifted Beth from the ambulance. They pushed the gurney into the Emergency Room while the EMTs reported her vital statistics and what they knew of her injuries.

Jason followed until a nurse grabbed his arm. She pointed to the lounge. He opened his mouth to argue, but she stopped him. In a calm voice, she said, "The doctors and nurses will take care of her." When the nurse led him to the lounge, he saw the clipboard she carried. "Tell me about the victim? What's her name and date of birth?"

After the nurse left, he sat with his head in his hands. Because of his selfish need for revenge, Beth was fighting for her life.

Jason checked the time. It had been twenty minutes since she went into the ER. He stalked to the door. Why hadn't anyone come to give him an update?

With a frustrated huff, he returned to his chair. Waiting wasn't something he did well.

There was one thing he could do. He could inform Beth's friends and family about the accident. He checked his watch. The shop was closed, but her parents should be home. He called, but a maid answered. They were out for the evening. He hated to leave a message, but they needed to know so they could come to the hospital.

After making the call, Jason returned to his chair. He slapped a fist into the palm of his hand when he remembered the haunted look on her face as she ran from him. The ER doors opened, and he jumped to his feet. The doctor rushed into the lounge.

"Mr. Richards?"

"Yes."

"I'm Edward Walters, Beth's doctor." He held his hand out.

Jason shook it. "How is she?"

"She's still unconscious." Dr. Walters rubbed a hand over his face. "At the moment, our concern is internal bleeding. If we don't operate soon, we may lose her. Is her family on their way? We need permission to do the surgery."

"I haven't been able to reach her parents, and she has no other relatives. Is there anyone else we can contact?"

"In situations like this, we can give treatment with the consent of a friend. Would that be you?"

"Yes. Do the surgery." Jason clasped his hands behind his back. "Will she live?"

"I won't lie to you, her condition is serious." The doctor folded his arms over his chest. "Until we do the surgery, we won't know the full extent of her injuries."

"What can you tell me?"

"She has a fractured left wrist and two broken ribs. We think one punctured her lung. She has a deep cut on her left side. It might be the source of the bleeding. After the surgery, we'll have more answers. We'll give you an update. I have to get back in there."

Jason stood, alone, in the middle of the empty waiting room with nothing to do but wait and wrestle with his guilt. He returned to his chair, but five minutes later he was back on his feet. It took ten steps to cross the room; he counted them—one, two, three—as he paced from one wall to the other.

He stopped to look out the window, but all he saw were Beth's tears as she ran from the restaurant. Later the click of shoes on the tile floor caught his attention. He turned. Beth's mother, Deidre, hurried to the room. She stopped at the entrance, and they stared at each other. Then she wiped a handkerchief over her wet cheeks and rushed to him.

She grabbed him and dug her fingers into his arm. "How is Beth?"

"Let's sit, and I'll tell you what I know." Jason helped Deidre to a chair then explained what he knew of Beth's injuries and the surgery.

Deidre's skin lost its color and tears ran in rivulets over her cheeks. Her sobs came from a place of such sorrow it hurt to listen to her.

Jason got her a cup of water, but there was nothing he could do or say to ease her pain. Instead, he wrapped an arm around her shoulder and held her while she cried. If only tears could wash away his guilt.

When she was calmer, he said, "The nurse asked for Beth's medical history. I am sure they would appreciate any information you can give them."

"I'll go talk to her." She got to her feet then looked down at him. "Thank you for being here for Beth."

When she left, he wondered if Deidre would thank him if she knew he'd caused the accident. He returned to the window and stared into the darkness. Beth's words played over and over in his mind, *Remembering only makes the pain and anger worse.*

"We should sit."

He looked over his shoulder, surprised he hadn't heard Deidre return.

"It will be a long night."

"Yeah." He rubbed his hand over his chin. "Would you like a cup of coffee?"

"Maybe later."

He nodded and sat across from her.

Deidre's eyebrows dipped. "The nurse said Beth's car crashed into a ditch. She's a good driver. Even with the rain, she should have been able to control her car. What happened?"

Jason's shoulders slumped. "We had dinner at the University Club. Brighton Beach Road has sharp curves. It's a challenge on a sunny day, but the rain made it treacherous."

He told Deidre what he knew of the accident, Beth being trapped, and how the rescue workers used the hydraulic cutters to free her.

"I suspect there's more to the story you haven't told me,"

Deidre looked into his eyes.

Jason turned away; his lips pressed together.

"It doesn't matter. My concern is for Beth and her recovery."

An hour later, they still had no updates. He couldn't sit any longer, so he paced again. Two hours later his patience snapped. "I need coffee. Do you want a cup?"

"Yes, with cream, please."

"You stay here in case the doctor comes." Jason cringed. He hadn't intended to issue an order. "I'm sorry—"

"No need to apologize." Deidre gave him a weary smile. "We're both tired."

Jason dealt with crises daily and never let emotion rule him. Then he'd seen Beth's car in the ditch, and his control cracked. But he was J.D. Richards, and he didn't break.

He went to the nurses' station. "Do you have any updates on Elizabeth Kingsley?"

"We know she's still in surgery."

He clenched his teeth.

The nurse gave him a sad smile. "Beth is strong. She'll make it through this."

"You know her?"

She nodded. "We work together at the women's shelter. She's a special lady."

"Yes, she is. Thank you." Jason stopped at the coffee station and poured two cups, one with cream. He returned to the lounge and held a cup out to Deidre, "I talked with a nurse. Beth is still in surgery."

Deidre took the coffee. "It's taking too long."

Based on what Beth had told him of her parents, he imagined self-centered, indifferent people who didn't bend for anyone, not even their daughter. The woman next to him, with worry and fear etched on her face, was a parent who cared deeply for her daughter.

He frowned. "Where's Archer?"

Deidre's shoulders sagged. She stared at the floor when she mumbled, "He couldn't be here."

"Is he out of town?"

She shook her head.

Jason pounded his hand on the arm of the chair. "He's home, isn't he?"

"I'm not sure."

"Unbelievable." He jumped to his feet and swore when coffee

splashed on his hand. "Archer's daughter is fighting for her life, and he can't be bothered to be here? Does he care about her at all?"

Deidre clutched Jason's hands. "Please, let's not talk about him. Our thoughts should be for Beth."

Jason took a deep breath. "Has Archer ever cared about her?"

Deidre's eyes closed for a moment. "I've always believed he loved her, but now—I don't know."

He ran a hand through his hair. Why was he surprised? No one was more important to Archer than Archer. Jason again stood at the window and stared into the darkness. Was he any better?

He had returned to Serenity Bay to show those who'd called him worthless that they'd been wrong and force them to acknowledge the success he'd achieved. But that hadn't been enough. He wanted to make Beth pay for using him, but he never considered the cost to appease his ego. Now, it was Beth who had to pay for his arrogance.

His right shoulder ached. He rubbed the muscles, but it didn't ease the tension. The next time he checked his watch, three hours had passed. Beth was still in surgery. He wanted to pound on something, but she needed him to be strong. He wouldn't fail her again.

Twenty minutes later the doors to surgery opened with a swoosh. Dr. Walters walked out.

Jason told Deidre, "It's Beth's doctor."

The doctor trudged towards them with fatigue and worry lines in his face. While they waited, the color drained from Deidre's cheeks and Jason hands hung in fists at his side.

"She made it through the surgery and is in Recovery. We'll move her to the Intensive Care Unit soon." The doctor rubbed his chin. "There was a great deal of internal damage where the door cut into her abdomen and ovary. That caused the internal bleeding. We had to remove the left ovary; the damage was too severe to save it. We repaired the other ovary and a tear in her uterus."

"Oh, my god." Deidre lifted her hand to her lips. "Will she be able to have children?"

Dr. Walters shook his head. "We won't know until after she's recovered, and we run tests."

Jason felt as though someone had punched him. Beth always wanted a large family. She'd be devastated if she couldn't have children.

The doctor continued. "There were two cracked ribs. One punctured her left lung. After we repaired the lung, we re-inflated it and inserted a tube to drain any fluids. Her left wrist is broken, but it's a clean break. We set the bone and put on a temporary splint."

Jason frowned. "Not a cast?"

"We want to wait until the swelling eases." Dr. Walters grimaced. "The next twenty-four hours are crucial. We are cautiously optimistic and will keep a close watch on her."

Deidre asked, "When can we see her?"

"When she's settled in a room. I am limiting her visits to two a day, for ten minutes, and only one person at a time. I'll let you decide who sees her."

Jason asked, "When will she regain consciousness?"

"We don't know. Now, we watch and wait."

Deidre asked, "You'll tell us if there's any change?"

"Of course." He put a hand over Deidre's. "Beth and I have worked on several projects together, I consider us good friends. I promise you, we'll do all we can to help her. In the meantime, you should rest. It will be a long, difficult recovery."

After the doctor had left, Jason grabbed her hand. "I have to see Beth first. Please?"

Deidre looked into his eyes. With a nod, she said, "All right, I'll go in for the second visit."

"Thank you." He exhaled, and his shoulders relaxed. "The doctor's right. You should go home and rest."

She raised an eyebrow. "Are you leaving?"

"I can't."

Deidre shook her head. "If something happened while I was gone...."

He pointed at the chairs. Shoulders slumped and feet dragging, they returned to their chairs.

They sat, neither of them saying a word, until Deidre said, "I read about you. You changed your name to J.D. Richards?"

Jason nodded. "After I moved to Chicago, I met Matt and Helen Richards. They took me in and made me part of their family."

A nurse walked into the lounge. "We've moved Beth into a room in the ICU. She's still unconscious, and we're keeping a close watch on her. One of you can go in for ten minutes."

"I'm going in," Jason rushed his words afraid Deidre might change her mind.

She nodded.

He followed the nurse.

"I'll take you to her room. You need to prepare yourself. It can be difficult to see someone we care about hooked up to so many tubes and wires." The nurse left him at the door.

Jason walked into the room and inhaled the burning scent of alcohol. He went to the bed and forced himself to breathe. Beth's skin matched the color of the white sheets covering her. The light above her bed cast a shadow over her face. Wires connected her to machines that clicked and hissed. Cuts and bruises covered her face and arms. She looked like she'd been in a fight—and lost.

He lifted her hand and cringed. It was limp, lifeless. His fingers shook as he pushed a strand of hair off her face. He was desperate to take her into his arms and warm her. With a soft brush of his lips, he kissed her forehead and whispered, "Angel, open your eyes for me. Please. I need to apologize."

No response, not even an eyelash twitched.

"I'm so sorry. I was wrong to push you." Tears pooled in his eyes. "You've got to get better even if you spend the rest of your life hating me."

Her face was a watery blur. He was J.D. Richards, with more power and money than one man needed, and he couldn't make this better.

There was a light pat on his arm. The nurse stood at his side.

"You must stay strong and believe she'll get better."

Jason nodded then he leaned over and whispered to Beth, "Please come back to us. We need you." He brushed his lips over hers. "I need you."

CHAPTER SEVEN

Ten steps to cross the room and six to the coffeemaker. Jason refilled his cup and counted eleven steps back to his chair. It took some persuading, but he'd convinced Deidre to go home.

So he sat here alone with only his thoughts for company. He leaned his head against the wall behind his chair. He thought of the first time he'd seen Beth. It had been at the city park.

Across the park, Amber's hands waved as she talked to a girl he'd never seen. The girl's hair spread across her shoulders and shimmered like an angel's halo in the sunlight.

He walked over. The angel looked too sweet and innocent for this side of town. He looked into her tear-filled eyes. Angels shouldn't cry. "Hey Amber, what's happening?"

"The pampered princess thought she'd cross the tracks." Amber sneered. "I told her to run back to her rich daddy. She doesn't belong here."

He looked at the girl, and his heart slammed against his ribs. He wanted to wipe away the sadness from her eyes. She spoke in a voice as luscious as creamy milk chocolate filled with caramel.

"I didn't think people here would care about my parents." Her shoulders slumped. "I guess it was a bad idea to come."

Shivers slid along his spine. "No, it wasn't."

She looked at him. A spark floated in the pool of tears. Was that hope? He understood the need to belong. "Stay."

Her sweet smile warmed him, and the angel claimed his heart.

"Jason."

A warm hand on his shoulder interrupted his thoughts of the past. He opened his eyes to find Deidre next to him. The sterile chill of the lounge vanquished the warmth of his memories. He checked the time. Eight hours since they'd had an update on Beth.

"You need to rest."

"I can't leave. She might wake, or..." He scrubbed his hands over his eyes.

"I checked at the nurse's station. They told me her vital signs haven't changed, but they are stable. I peeked into her room. She's resting and has more color." Deidre straightened her shoulders. "You promised, if I went home to sleep, you would take a break."

Surprised at the way she stood up to him, he grinned. "I lied."

She raised an eyebrow. He shook his head. If someone had asked him to describe Deidre, he would have compared her to a piece of fluff that would blow away in a light breeze. He never knew she possessed this determination or strength.

"All right. I could use a shower and a change of clothes." He stood and stretched. "But promise you'll phone me if you get any news. No matter what happens, I want to be with her."

"I've learned my lesson. If there's any change, I'll call."

"Lesson about what?"

"Nothing important." She pushed his arm. "Go."

Jason checked his watch. "I'll stop in at the shop and tell her friends what's happened. She called them her family."

Deidre nodded. "They've been more of a family to her than Archer and I ever were."

Before he left, Jason gave his number to Deidre and left it at the nurse's desk.

Ten minutes later, he stood outside Delectable Delights. It was full of customers and employees who chatted, laughed, and were unaware of how their lives were about to change. He rubbed his mouth and opened the door.

Abbey rushed to him. "Beth hasn't come in yet. I've called her, but she didn't answer her phone. She told me she was having dinner with you last night. Do you know where she is?"

"Let's sit." Jason put a hand on her back, but she didn't move.

She grabbed his arm. "Where is she?"

"There's been an accident."

"Beth!"

Everyone in the shop turned to stare. Before Jason could explain, Erik raced to her. He put an arm around Abbey's shoulders and led her to the chairs. Employees and customers gathered around.

He rubbed his hands together to ease the chill in his bones. "There was an accident last night. Beth's in the hospital." Gasps rippled through the crowd.

Jason told them what he knew about Beth's crash and explained how the firemen had to cut the car to get her out. He described her injuries and the surgery, but the hardest part was telling them she hadn't regained consciousness. Abbey cried, but she wasn't the only one shaken by the news. Shock and fear covered every face.

Erik looked at Abbey. "We have to go to the hospital."

Abbey nodded. "We'll close the shop."

Jason's stomach clenched. He didn't want to give them more bad news, but they needed to know. "She can't have visitors."

"I don't care." Abbey grabbed Erik's hand. "We have to be with her."

"We take care of each other." Erik wiped a hand over his eyes. "That's what family does."

Jason rubbed at the ache between his brows. "What you can do for Beth is to keep the shop open until she gets back. We don't want her to worry about the shop or you."

"You're right. We'll stay open, but we'll still be at the hospital." Abbey wiped her eyes. "We'll put together a schedule so everyone can visit. We'll take turns."

Jason released the breath he'd been holding. "That's a good idea."

The employees returned to work with tear-drenched eyes and choked sobs. While the customers sat at their tables with looks of stunned disbelief on their faces.

Abbey and Erik stood with Jason. She threw her arms around his waist. "Thank you for telling us what happened. Beth's not just our boss, she's the heart of our family. I can't lose her too." Abbey sobbed and ran to the kitchen.

Erik crossed his arms tight over his chest. "How did Beth crash into the ditch?"

"The rain mixed with the oil made the road slick. We think she drove too fast through a sharp curve and lost control of the car."

"What haven't you told us?" Erik moved a step closer to him. "Beth is a careful driver and never speeds. I tease her about driving below the speed limit."

Jason sighed. "She was upset."

Eyes narrowed, Erik glared at him. "About what?"

"That's between Beth and me."

"If I find out the accident was your fault..." After a last glare, Erik walked away.

By the time Jason got home, exhaustion had him shuffling his feet as he walked to his bedroom. Too tired to be neat, he dropped his clothes on the floor. He ran the water in the shower until steam filled the room, then stepped in to let the spray soothe his aches and relax his muscles.

After his shower, he returned to the bedroom and found a tray of food Lupita must have left. His stomach soured at the sight. Eager to get back to the hospital, he pulled on a fresh pair of slacks. He tried to button his pants, but his fingers were clumsy and his eyes blurred. Unable to fasten them, he gave in and lay on the bed to rest for a few minutes.

Jason rolled onto his back and stretched. His eyes flew open, and he looked at the clock. Two o'clock. He'd slept for five hours. He took another shower, this time a cold one to wipe away the sleep that dulled his senses.

After showering, he called the hospital. Beth remained in serious condition, but stable. It wasn't much, but the news kept his hope alive.

While he dressed, he noticed a fresh tray filled with his favorite foods, a Caesar salad, salmon with lemon-dill sauce, and new potatoes. His mouth watered, and he attacked his food as though he hadn't eaten in a week. After he had devoured his meal, he took the tray to the kitchen.

Marco and Lupita sat at the table, so he joined them. Lupita got him a cup of coffee while he told them about the accident. They asked if they could help. He thanked them, but there was nothing to do now but wait.

After he had answered their questions, Jason went to the study to call his father. He told him a friend had been in an accident, and he planned to stay at the hospital until she was out of danger. To his credit, Matt didn't ask questions. After he assured Jason he could handle the operations, Matt said, "Remember you have a family who loves you. If you need us, don't forget to call."

After talking to Matt, Jason sat with his fingers pressed together. Guilt and fear dug their claws into his soul. If she died, how would he live with himself? The answers he'd pushed for didn't seem so important now.

He returned to the hospital lounge, but Deidre didn't notice him until he stood in front of her. She looked up. Her eyes were red and swollen.

He sank into a chair. "What's happened?"

"A few minutes ago, Beth's doctor told me…"

"What?" He grabbed her hands.

"Beth's brain is bruised, and there's swelling." Deidre wiped her face. "They've started her on medication to ease the swelling, but there's no guarantee it will help. Beth might not regain consciousness."

"Damn." He jumped to his feet and dragged a hand through his hair. He turned to Deidre. "I want to bring in a neurosurgeon, someone who specializes in brain injuries."

"I—I'm certain Dr. Walters is doing all he can, but if you think it will help Beth, then do it. Just be sure you're doing it for Beth, not to soothe a guilty conscience."

Was Deidre right? Was he trying to atone for his guilt? He paced around the lounge. When it was time to visit Beth, he swallowed his fear and went to her room.

Beth's skin had a pink tone now, but her only movement was the rise and fall of her chest. Jason talked to her, pleaded, made promises, but got no response. When his ten minutes were up, he went out to the hall and leaned against the wall. He broke into a cold sweat and had to take several deep breaths before he dragged himself back to the waiting room.

Deidre stood and grabbed his arm. "How is she?"

Before he could answer, the sound of approaching footsteps had them turning to the door.

Dr. Walters walked in and said, "I checked on Beth. She hasn't regained consciousness, but there are signs that she's improving. She's breathing easier, and we've seen no evidence of other internal bleeding—"

"When will she wake up?" Deidre clutched the doctor's hand.

"Her body needs time to repair itself. Now that we have her on medication, we hope to see improvement soon." The doctor laid his hand over Deidre's. "It's important to stay positive. I've dealt with patients who said they heard people talking to them while they were in a coma. Beth needs to believe she will get better."

After the doctor left, they sat. Despair hung heavy in the room while the silence scraped Jason's nerves raw. His obsession with the past caused this accident. He'd done this to Beth. How would he live with himself knowing what he'd done?

He jerked when Deidre spoke.

"Several of Beth's employees and customers were here to check on her."

"I'm not surprised. I stopped in at the shop to tell her friends about the accident. Her customers were just as upset."

"Beth is a big part of this town."

"They wanted to close the shop. After I explained she couldn't see anyone, they agreed to take turns visiting."

People stopped in throughout the day. Deidre welcomed each person, introduced Jason, and chatted with the visitors. This side of her personality surprised him. When Deidre welcomed Abbey and Erik with a hug, his jaw dropped. Judging by shock on their faces, they hadn't expected her warm welcome.

"Thank you for coming." Deidre held their hands. "Beth is fortunate to have such good friends. Please sit with us."

In ten minutes, Deidre had Abbey and Erik telling stories of Beth's disasters while she learned to cook. They laughed and talked as though they'd been friends for years. He'd underestimated Beth's mother. Deidre Kingsley loved her daughter.

Once again, in the evening, Deidre went home to rest. When she returned in the morning, he again stopped in at Delectable Delights.

While he drank espresso, he shared the little information he had about Beth. Jason explained how he'd asked a neurosurgeon to review her case. He agreed with Dr. Walters' diagnosis and treatment plan. The specialist told Jason, in similar cases he'd handled, the outcomes had been positive.

By the time Jason got home, his head pounded. He took two aspirins, a hot shower, and crawled into bed.

When he woke, Jason rolled to his back and did an inventory—headache gone, body rested—time to get back to the hospital. After dressing, he went to find Lupita. He found her in the kitchen.

"I'm leaving and don't know when I'll be back."

She pulled a pan of his favorite chicken enchiladas out of the oven. "You need to eat."

"I'll get something at the hospital."

She said, "Your mother would worry if she knew you weren't eating."

Lupita knew which button to push. He sat, and she dished out the enchiladas. While he ate, Lupita lectured him about taking care of himself. He stuffed food in his mouth to stifle his chuckles.

When he returned to the hospital, Deidre told him about the visitors. Beth's employees and customers stopped in, so had council members, the mayor, several people from the women's shelter where Beth volunteered, and her neighbors.

Deidre smiled. "Beth always made friends, but I never knew she was so well-liked. I've missed so much of her life."

Beth's relationship with her parents had never been warm and caring. He was surprised by this side of Deidre and her regret about her relationship with Beth. "What was Beth like when she was young?"

A sparkle lit Deidre's eyes. "She was a happy child and so curious. For her fourth birthday, we gave her a doll with hair down to her waist. Beth loved Missy and spent hours combing her hair. A week later she ran in to show me how she'd cut Missy's hair. That poor doll looked like a porcupine her hair was so short. Beth was so proud of what she'd done. Then she handed me the doll and told me to make her hair long again."

He grinned. "Was Beth disappointed that the doll's hair didn't grow back?"

"Devastated. After that, Beth refused to let us cut her hair."

They laughed. During the hours they waited, worried, and talked, they became friends.

It wasn't until the following morning that Dr. Walters rushed in with a wide grin on his face. "Beth's awake. She's groggy but alert enough to ask for water. We'll keep her in ICU until we're sure she's out of danger. If she continues to improve, we should be able to move her into a private room tomorrow."

Jason could scarcely talk through his smile. "Can we see her?"

"I think she can have a visitor every four hours, but we'll keep the visits to ten minutes. She's better, but her condition is still serious. We want her to rest and remain calm." The doctor looked at Jason when he said, "Don't discuss anything that might upset her."

He shook the doctor's hand. "Thank you." Next to him, Deidre sniffled. He pulled her into his arms, and she soaked his shirt with her tears.

This time when he walked into Beth's room, he welcomed the clicks and beeps. They were proof she lived. But now, he faced another problem. Would she remember their argument and ban him from her room? Every muscle in his body tightened as he walked to her bed.

She looked so vulnerable with her battered face and the wires hooked to the machines. Jason shook his head. How had she survived the accident?

Her eyes flickered. "Jason?"

He held her hand. "Beth, I am so sorry. Can you forgive me?"

"Hurt..." She whimpered, and her hand went limp.

"Beth!" He panicked. As he reached for the button to call the nurse, he squeezed her hand, and she whimpered. He wiped a bead of sweat from his forehead.

"Oh, Angel, you've been through so much, but you're safe now. I won't let anyone hurt you." He brushed her cheek. "Not even me."

He returned to the lounge and told Deidre that Beth had been awake for a few seconds.

Deidre smiled and said, "She's coming back to us."

A few hours later, Dr. Walters walked into the lounge. "We have a problem."

"What's wrong?" Jason's hands clenched. Had he upset her?

"Beth said you were in her room earlier?"

Jason nodded. "She said my name and 'hurt.' I didn't think she heard what I said. She was sleeping when I left her."

The doctor rubbed his chin. "Beth said you look different. When I asked her to explain, she told me you looked older."

Deidre said, "I don't understand."

"I checked her eyes, but found nothing that would cause problems with her vision." He grimaced. "I asked what she remembered about the accident. Her response was, 'What accident?' She doesn't remember the crash."

Jason's stomach twisted. "Maybe it's too painful for her to recall."

"I considered that possibility, so I asked her to tell me what happened yesterday." Dr. Walters scratched his chin. "She told me about her eighteenth birthday party. When I questioned her, it became clear she doesn't recall anything that happened since that day."

Jason wondered if he looked as stunned as Deidre.

Deidre said, "Could you have missed something."

"We know her head slammed against the window." Jason took a deep breath. "Is it possible she has amnesia?"

"I need more information before I can make any diagnosis."

Jason pointed at the doctor. "You didn't answer my question. Could it be amnesia?"

"It's one possibility." Dr. Walters grimaced. "As you said, her head hit the window, and we know her brain swelled. These kinds of injuries can cause a memory loss. If that's the case, when the swelling eases, her memory will return."

He demanded, "When will you know?"

"I've ordered an MRI and other tests to make certain we didn't miss some other injury. I've also asked a colleague who has experience with these types of injuries to perform an evaluation."

The color drained from Deidre's face, and she dropped into a chair.

"Did anything happen around Beth's eighteen birthday?" The doctor asked. "Something she might not want to remember?"

"We celebrated the day after her party. She was excited and happy. I left Serenity Bay the next morning." Jason grimaced. "Two weeks later, I received a *Dear John* letter. Except for one quick visit, I stayed away until a few weeks ago." He looked at Deidre. "Did something happen after I left?"

She fidgeted in her seat and mumbled, "We traveled in Europe for several months."

Jason watched Deidre and waited for her to say something more. She pressed a hand to her trembling lips. *What is she hiding?*

Deidre twisted her handkerchief and asked the doctor, "What have you told Beth?"

"I told her I wanted to have some tests done to make certain we didn't miss anything. She wasn't upset, and it's important to keep her that way. There's always a chance we'll find another reason for the problem." Dr. Walters rubbed a hand over his face. "If we determine she has amnesia, I'd like you to be with me when I tell her, Deidre. We can't let her give up hope."

Jason frowned. "What do we say if she asks questions?"

"Even if you answer her questions, it won't bring her memory back. If you tell her about the past, she'll get frustrated that she can't remember it."

Deidre sobbed, "My poor Beth."

"After I review the test results and get the second opinion, we'll talk again. I'm sorry." The doctor walked away.

Jason sat and dropped his face into his hands. *What else can go wrong?*

Deidre murmured, "I'm going to see Beth."

He looked at her. "If she asks, will you tell her I'm here?"

With her shoulders slumped in defeat, she nodded and walked away.

Jason looked at his watch. Over twenty minutes since Deidre went to Beth's room. His nerves ragged, he jumped to his feet and paced. Another twenty minutes passed. He scrubbed his hand over his forehead. Something was wrong. He'd decided to check on Beth just as

Deidre shuffled into the lounge.

He rushed to her. "What's wrong?"

"Beth woke. She asked about the accident. I told her to rest and not to worry about it." Deidre dug into her pocket and pulled out her crumpled handkerchief. "She cried and wanted to know why I wouldn't answer her questions."

"I didn't know what to say." Deidre dropped into a chair. "I told Beth she might have a temporary memory loss. She asked what she'd forgotten and when I didn't tell her she became hysterical. I called the nurse. She gave Beth a sedative. I stayed until she fell asleep."

"You wanted to help. Don't blame yourself. You did what you thought was best."

"Nothing I did or said helped." Deidre trembled. "Beth sobbed as she fell asleep."

It was hours later before the doctor returned. He walked in without his usual smile. "The tests show no injuries other than those we've already identified. I talked to the neurologist. He assessed Beth and agrees with a diagnosis of Post-Traumatic Amnesia resulting in retrograde amnesia. We believe it's due to the swelling of her brain, and when that subsides, her memory will return."

They questioned the doctor. What could they do to help Beth? How long until her memory return? None of the answers reassured Jason and, from the look on her face, they didn't reassure Deidre either. Dr. Walters left, and they sat lost in their own thoughts.

When it was his turn to go to Beth's room, he struggled but managed a weak smile. "How are you feeling?"

"Like someone beat me with a baseball bat. Dr. Walters and Mother both talked about a crash. I don't remember an accident, and they won't tell me what happened. Will you tell me?"

"The doctor told us not to talk about the things you've forgotten. He's certain that, with rest and time, your memory will return." He brushed his thumb across Beth's lips. "I'm so sorry you were hurt."

"This wasn't your fault."

His shoulders drooped. "Beth—"

"I'm cold." She rubbed her arms.

He grabbed the blanket at the foot of her bed and spread it over her. "Is that better?"

"You take such good care of me." Beth yawned, and her eyes closed. "That's why I love you...."

Beth rubbed her forehead to ease the blinding pain that plagued her whenever she tried to recall the past. She should have memories of the time between her birthday and when she woke in the hospital, but she couldn't remember a single moment or event.

Her mother sat in a chair next to her bed. Beth wondered what she was reading. Since she'd learned she had amnesia, either Jason or her mother sat with her. It comforted her to have them near unless they scolded her as she tried to force her memory to return.

Earlier, the doctor had stopped in to check on her. She'd told him, "Why can't Mother and Jason talk about the things I've forgotten. I am certain, it would help me remember."

He'd said, "It doesn't work that way. You can't force your memory to return. When the swelling around your brain eases, it will come back on its own."

"But when will that be? I feel lost."

"I wish I could tell you when it will happen, but we don't know. You need to rest and avoid activities that could aggravate the problem. That includes trying to force your memories to return. It will only frustrate you and give you a headache."

After the doctor left, Beth became more determined to recover her past, but her reward for the effort was another headache. She pressed her temples.

Beth sobbed, "Tell me about the accident."

Deidre said, "Darling—"

"Why won't you answer my questions?" Beth demanded. "Did something awful happen that you don't want me to remember?"

Jason walked into the room. "Deidre, why don't you get a cup of coffee, and I'll sit with Beth."

Her mother's lips were pinched as she rushed from the room.

He stroked her cheek. "Beth, we want to answer your questions, but we have to do what's best for you and follow the doctor's instructions. I'd rather answer your questions than watch you struggle, but it wouldn't help."

"My life has a huge, gaping hole in it. I don't recall the accident, or how I ended up in the hospital. What if my memory never returns?" Her body shook from the force of her sobs. "I want to remember."

"Should I ask the nurse to give you a sedative?"

"No." She squeezed his hand. "I don't like how they make me

feel."

"I'll wait a few minutes. If you calm down, we won't call the nurse."

Beth took several deep breaths and laughed when she hiccupped. Jason took such good care of her, even if he didn't answer her questions. She gave him a shaky smile.

He sat next to her and pushed a strand of hair behind her ear. "Do you remember the first time we went to the lake together? I dived off the bridge, and you wanted to try. You were so excited about jumping until you hit the water and did that spectacular belly-flop."

Beth laughed so hard her stitches pulled and made her cringe. "Oh, don't make me laugh, it hurts."

"When you're better, we'll go to the lake, and you can jump off the bridge again."

She giggled. "I'll try not to do a belly-flop this time."

He drew circles over the back of her hand. A thought tickled at the edge of her mind, but a moment later it vanished. She yawned and closed her eyes.

When she woke, her mother sat in the chair. "That was a good nap. Do you feel better?"

"I'm not ready to run a race yet, but I'm getting there."

"The doctor said he'll release you in a few days. I want you to come home with me. You shouldn't be alone while you're recuperating."

"Where else would I go? If I didn't go home, Archer would be furious and tell me not to embarrass the family."

CHAPTER EIGHT

Jason drove to Delectable Delights. Until Beth could have visitors, he continued to visit the shop. But this morning, something was different. After he told them Beth was better, no one said a word. Most days they bombarded him with questions. He frowned and looked around.

Erik cleared his throat. "We talked to Dr. Walters. It took some convincing, but he agreed to let Abbey visit Beth."

Jason pursed his lips and looked at her. Nothing good would come from this. "You love Beth and want to be certain she's recovering, but if she doesn't remember you—well, I'm afraid you'll both be hurt."

Abbey smiled. "Beth will remember me. We're family. You told us to wait until she woke, and we did. Now you tell us she's better, but we still can't visit her. Well, I want to see Beth myself whether or not you agree."

Jason's shoulders fell. "If you insist on going to the hospital, I'll take you. When do you want to go?"

"I'm ready now."

During the drive, neither of them said a word. Abbey stared out the window and clutched her purse the way a drowning man clutches a life preserver. Jason wasn't in much better shape. His hands wrapped around the steering wheel until his knuckles were white.

This visit wouldn't be easy for Beth or Abbey. He said, "You have to know, even though Beth's memory hasn't returned, it doesn't mean she cares any less about you."

"She will remember me—remember us." Her lips trembled. "I don't have a family without her."

In the hospital, he led Abbey to the lounge. "Will you wait here? I want Beth to have a minute to prepare."

Abbey nodded. "Yes."

Jason forced a smile and walked into Beth's room. "Hello, Angel. Someone is here to see you."

"Who?"

Jason smiled, but his stomach made him sorry he'd eaten. "Abbey St. John."

"I don't remember anyone with that name." She looked suspicious. "Who is she?"

"She's your best friend." He squeezed her hand. "Your friends are worried about you. They want to be sure you're getting better. If the doctor allowed visits, they'd all be here. Since your visitors are restricted, they sent Abbey to check on you."

"What if I don't recognize her?"

"What if you do? Maybe seeing her will be what you need to trigger your memory."

She nodded, but her eyes were wide with fear.

Jason left and returned with Abbey. She ran over and pulled Beth into a tight hug.

Beth pulled away. "You—you're Abbey?"

Abbey smiled, but her lips trembled. "How are you? We've been so worried. They told us you didn't remember us, but I knew you would know me. We're more than best friends. We're family."

"I don't know you." Beth burst into tears, "Why don't I know my best friend?"

Abbey pleaded, "You have to remember me. We work together at the shop with Erik and Jamie and all the others."

Tears poured from Beth's eyes. "I don't remember you."

Abbey's face turned white. "Please, Beth, I'm Abbey."

"Jason...." Beth choked on her tears.

He squeezed her hand. "It's all right."

Beth's sobs shook her body. "Why can't I remember?"

He turned to Abbey. "Would you wait in the lounge? I'll be out in a few minutes."

She sobbed as she ran from the room. Jason wanted to comfort her, but his first priority was Beth.

"Beth, your memory will return. When it does, you'll remember your friends and family."

"My friends will hate me."

"Your friends love you, and they know you didn't want to forget them."

Her sobs broke his heart. He couldn't wait any longer and pressed the *Call* button. The nurse took one look at Beth and rushed out. When she returned, she carried a syringe. A few minutes after receiving the shot, Beth fell asleep. With a heavy sigh, Jason kissed her forehead and went to the lounge to find Abbey.

Abbey sat alone but looked up when he walked into the room. Tears ran from her eyes, but she didn't make a sound. "Beth didn't remember us. She didn't even know me."

"You haven't lost her. Beth's memory will return. When it does, she'll remember all of you and probably be embarrassed that she didn't recognize you."

Abbey got to her feet and shook a finger at Jason. "It's not her fault that she has amnesia. She shouldn't worry about us. We'll always be her family."

"What's most important now is to keep her from worrying about you or the shop. You keep Delectable Delights open for business. Beth would be devastated if someone lost their job or didn't get paid."

"You're right. I'll make sure the shop opens every day, and the employees keep their jobs. We'll make Beth proud." With the back of her hand, Abbey wiped away her tears. "But what will we do if her memory never returns?"

The next day the doctor released Beth from the hospital with instructions to get plenty of bed rest. Not that she had much choice. She couldn't get back to a life she didn't remember.

Her mother drove her home. When she saw the house, Beth shuddered. Her father liked to brag the house was the biggest in Serenity Bay and had it decorated by a designer brought in from New York. She called it the mausoleum.

Beth walked to her bedroom but had to stop often to catch her breath. Her mother helped her change into a nightgown and tucked her into bed. The snick of the door closing was the last sound Beth heard before she fell asleep.

She slept most of her first day at home. When she woke, she ate and used the bathroom. Exhausted, she climbed back into bed and fell asleep again.

The following morning Beth woke rested, but in desperate need of a shower. In the bathroom, she studied herself in the mirror. Her eyebrows dipped into a frown. She wasn't eighteen anymore. She'd asked why everyone looked older but hadn't realized she did too. *How old am I?*

"Beth?" Her mother called to her.

"In here. I am going to take a shower."

"Do you need help?"

"No, I can manage. I'll yell if I need you."

Beth stepped into the shower. The water, a gentle rainfall, slid over her body. It soothed the aches and washed away the fog that clouded her mind. When she returned to the bedroom, she found her mother reading from her favorite Daphne du Maurier book.

She and her mother watched movies, read, and talked. Beth discovered she and her mother had many more likes and dislikes in common than either of them knew. They both had a passion for classic movies, romance novels, and chocolate. But their most important discovery was how much they liked each other.

Later, Beth's eyes widened when her mother brought Jason to her room. They were chatting like old friends. Her mother never approved of Beth's friendship with him. What happened to change her mind? Did her father know Jason had come to visit? He disliked Jason with an intensity that she'd never understood and nothing she said had altered his opinion.

Jason carried two shopping bags. He walked over and kissed her forehead. "How are you?"

"I have some aches and pains, but I'm better. I just wish my memory would return."

"Your body is still healing. Soon you'll have your memory back too. Until then, I plan to distract you."

Beth tilted her head. "How will you do that?"

He lifted a bag onto the bed. "In this bag, we have the complete box set of the Monk series."

"I love Monk." Beth took the box. "I remember the early years, but not these later ones."

"We'll start with episode one and watch all of them. Before you decide, there's another choice." Jason pulled out a chess set. "Do you want to continue the lessons you were giving me?"

"If we had a deck of cards, you could try to teach me to play poker—again."

With a laugh, he reached into the bag and pulled out two decks of cards and poker chips.

Beth laughed and wrapped her arms around her waist. "Ouch! Don't make me laugh; it hurts."

Later that night, Beth opened a book to read before she went to sleep. Her door flew open and slammed against the wall. Beth looked up as her father stalked into the room.

"What do you want?"

"I want Richards to invest in my project, and I want you to arrange it."

"I don't know any Richards."

He smirked. "Your act might fool your mother and Richards,

but you don't fool me. I have to compliment you, though. Faking a memory loss is a good way to keep the man in town until you can get your hooks in him."

"You think my memory loss isn't real, that it's some plot?"

"I never thought you were smart enough to plan a scheme like this." He smirked. "Maybe you are my daughter after all."

"I don't want to trick anyone." Beth massaged her temples and reached for the medication the doctor had prescribed. "I don't recall anything after my birthday party until I woke in the hospital. I don't even recognize my friends. I hate this, and I would never *fake* losing my memory."

"I don't care if it's real or not." Archer paced back and forth. "I need capital to keep my Chicago project in business. I want you to convince Jason to put up the money."

"I don't understand what you're talking about, but I won't ask him for anything." She kneaded the back of her neck. "You've always thought he was worthless, but now you want him to do you some favor. If you want something from him, ask him yourself."

Archer's face darkened to a deep red. "Have you forgotten I make the rules in this family? When I tell you to do something, you don't say no or question me. You just do it. Get me that money, or I'll make you sorry you defied me." He stomped out.

Beth rolled her shoulders. She might have lost her memory, but she hadn't forgotten how Archer enjoyed issuing orders or the way he'd hound her until she obeyed. Thank goodness the pills she'd taken made her sleepy, otherwise Archer's rant would have kept her awake for hours.

The next day, Beth's mother stayed with her. They read, watched a movie, and ate together. It had been years since they'd spent time together that she enjoyed this much. Late that afternoon, her mother had an appointment, so Beth watched another movie.

Then her father stomped into the room. "Has Jason visited you today?"

She shook her head. Today was not a good day. Her body ached and the jackhammer pounding in her head made it difficult to think. She'd taken a pill for the pain, but it hadn't helped yet. Why did he have to bellow?

"You will talk to him today and convince him to invest in my project."

"No. I told you, if you want a favor from Jason, ask him

yourself." She pressed her fingers to her temples.

"He'd never do the deal if I asked. Not the mighty J.D. Richards." Archer mocked.

"Who's J.D. Richards?"

"Just talk to your precious Jason." Archer growled, "I want his money."

"What game are you playing?"

"Just do what I tell you." He grabbed her arm. "It will make my triumph so much more satisfying to have Richard's money in the deal."

"Leave me alone." She twisted to get free, but he tightened his hold on her. "Let go!"

Her mother rushed into the room. "Archer, what are you doing?"

"Stay back." He pointed at Deidre. "Elizabeth needs to be reminded, who's in charge. I gave her an order, and she'll do what I tell her."

"Beth was seriously injured. The doctor said she shouldn't get upset." Deidre knotted her hands. "Whatever you want, it can wait until she's better."

"No, it can't wait. I want Richards to back me. He'll do it if she asks him." He squeezed his fingers around her arm.

"You're hurting me!"

"You will talk to Richards." Archer flung her hand aside and marched out.

Beth rubbed her wrist.

Her mother rushed to her side. "I'm sorry. I never thought he'd disturb you."

"Don't apologize. You aren't responsible for his actions." Beth flexed her hand. "If I stay here, he'll harass me until I talk to Jason. Why does father think Jason has money? I have to leave."

Deidre pressed her lips together and nodded. "Where will you go? You shouldn't be alone until your memory returns."

Jason walked into the room. As he looked at Beth and her mother, his smile faded. "What's happened?"

Beth grimaced. "How would you like a roommate?"

Her mother helped her to pack a bag while Jason waited in the living room.

Beth studied the purple and blue bruise on her wrist. "Father will be furious when he finds out I've left. I'm worried about you."

"He'd never hurt me."

Beth laid a hand on her mother's arm. "Why do you stay with him? He doesn't even try to control his temper."

"I believe beneath the bitterness and anger, he's still the man I fell in love with." Deidre tried to smile, but it held no joy.

"He's not the man you married." Beth held her mother's hand. "Now he cares more about money and power than he does people—even his own family."

"It's true, he's changed, but Archer's had so many disappointments. After we married, my father groomed him to take over the business. Archer expected to inherit the company." Deidre sighed. "Your grandfather only left him twenty-two percent of the ownership, and Archer feels cheated."

"So father owns less stock than my twenty-five percent?"

Her mother nodded.

"Nana told me Grandfather didn't trust him."

"Father didn't trust anyone. He wanted to protect the company he worked so hard to build and make sure it remained in the family. When he died, I inherited the majority control for the company, and he set up the estate in a way that allows me to pass the ownership only to my children or grandchildren."

"I didn't know." Beth took her mother's hand in hers. "I'm worried father might take his anger out on you. Promise you'll call if his temper gets out of control."

Her mother nodded and patted her hand. "I'll be fine."

In the car, on the way to Jason's house, he asked, "Did Archer hurt you?"

"I have a bruise on my arm, but it isn't bad." They pulled into a driveway, and Beth stared at the elegant Victorian home. "This house belongs to the Simonsons."

"It's okay. I have permission to be here." He helped her from the car. "I know you're confused, but I need you to trust me."

"I've always trusted you."

"I will answer all your questions when you're better."

"Promise?"

"I promise. Now, let's get you to bed. Lupita prepared one of the guest rooms for you." Jason led her into the house and to the bedroom. "Do you want something to eat? Lupita can bring you a tray."

"No, I'm too tired to eat. I just want to crawl into bed."

"All right. Do you need help to change your clothes?"

Beth shook her head.

He kissed her forehead. "Rest well."

After she washed her face and put on a nightgown, she snuggled into the soft bed and closed her eyes.

A knock on the door woke her. "Yes?"

Jason walked in carrying a tray. "Good morning. I come bearing breakfast."

"Thank you." She smiled. "What time is it?"

"It's almost ten o'clock."

"I'm surprised I slept so long."

"You needed the rest, but now you need to eat." He set the tray on Beth's lap and pulled a small table next to his chair.

"Why are you living in the Simonsons' home?"

"We're friends. Now no more questions. Eat."

They were finishing breakfast when Lupita walked in with the doctor.

Beth's eyes widened. "Dr. Walters, why are you here?"

"I wanted to check on my favorite patient."

She turned to Jason, and her eyebrows lifted.

He said, "I asked him to come."

"I didn't think doctors made house calls?"

Dr. Walters grinned. "Don't let my other patients know I do this."

He made Jason leave the room while he examined Beth. Jason knocked twice before the doctor let him return. The doctor teased, "A little impatient?"

He shrugged. "Is Beth all right?"

"She has a couple of new bruises, but otherwise she's fine." The doctor put his things in the bag he carried. "Beth shouldn't have any problems as long as she takes the time to recover."

"Lupita and I will make sure she gets plenty of rest." He assured the doctor.

"Good." Dr. Walters pointed at Beth. "Avoid stressful situations even if it means you don't see your parents. Are you still having headaches?"

She nodded.

"Stop trying to force your memory to return."

Her voice trembled when she asked, "What if it never comes back?"

"It may come in spurts or all at once, but I am confident your memory will return." The doctor told Jason, "Don't miss her appointment next week."

Jason and Beth fell into a comfortable routine. He worked in his study during the day but ate his meals with her. Then in the evenings, they talked. They discussed the books she read and the movies she watched. Sometimes they watched movies together. She laughed when he told her how much he liked classic movies, and she asked him how he felt about chocolate.

Although Jason visited often, Beth spent a lot of time alone. She slept and read, but by the third day, she was bored and suffering a severe case of cabin fever.

Beth wanted to rebuild her strength so she could leave the bedroom. If she walked, it would restore her strength and stamina. When Beth stood, her legs buckled. Fortunately, she dropped onto the bed. Beth held onto the furniture for support and was able to walk to the dresser. Her legs shook as she shuffled back to bed. Although she was exhausted and struggled to breathe, Beth's mouth curved in a proud smile.

It took a few days, but soon Beth could circle the room without having to rest or hold onto the furniture. Ready to impress Jason, she made her way to his study. When she was close, Beth heard the deep rumble of his voice. She didn't want to interrupt his conversation and sat on a chair near the door to wait until he finished his call. Beth didn't pay attention to what was said until she heard her name.

"… Beth's trip to Europe with Deidre?"

Silence.

Why was he discussing her? Beth never traveled with her mother. She rubbed a hand over her forehead.

Jason asked, "How about the maid? Did you find her?"

Silence.

The jackhammer in her head pounded again.

"Beth has agreed to stay with me. It gives me time to question her." Silence. "Be careful. I don't want anyone to tell Beth a detective is asking questions."

Jason was having her investigated. Just like Archer, he'd do anything to get what he wanted.

As though a dam burst, memories rushed through her mind. She tried to make sense of the flood of thoughts, but she couldn't process the information fast enough.

At dinner, he'd pushed, prodded, and demanded until she'd run away. She'd driven too fast on the slick road. When she'd tried to slow the car, she'd lost control and skidded into the ditch. She'd barely been able to breathe through the pain.

"No!" Beth jumped to her feet, but the room spun in crazy circles. When she grabbed the chair, it scraped on the floor and screeched. She had to get back to her room.

Then she heard her name. There would be no escape. She looked into the face of the man who had cost her so much.

Jason took a step towards her.

Beth held her hand up. If he touched her, she'd fall apart.

Jason glowered. "What are you—?"

"How far would you have gone to get your answers? Would you have claimed to love me?" She took a step back but staggered when the room spun again. "You never cared..."

CHAPTER NINE

Beth moved her head and groaned. Someone pressed a damp cloth to her forehead. The soothing coolness eased the throbbing.

She frowned. Jason had been talking on the telephone. He'd warned someone to be careful not to let her find out he'd hired an investigator. She couldn't keep the tears from falling.

"Beth." Fingers brushed over her face. Jason.

Eyes closed, she turned away.

"Beth?"

"You spent time with me, had me stay here, so you could get answers. The night of the accident, you pushed and pushed. You wouldn't give up." She opened her eyes and looked at him. "You're no better than Archer. You never cared about me."

Lupita walked into her room followed by Dr. Walters. He wore his doctor smile. The one he used to show his concern, but would calm the patient. "Let's check you. Jason, would you leave us and close the door on your way out?"

Jason looked at her. "I'll be outside in case you need me."

"I don't need you." She turned her head away. "Not now. Not ever."

Years of Archer's emotional blackmail and verbal abuse had taught Beth how to protect her heart and soul. She was too smart to let anyone use her again, except she wasn't. While she dreamed of a second chance at a life with Jason, he'd manipulated her for his own purpose.

The doctor examined her and asked questions. Then he said, "Although parts of your memory have returned, you'll still find holes. Your brain needs to process the information, and it'll take time. So continue the bed rest and be patient. You have no new bruises, but I'd like you to come to my office tomorrow for a thorough examination."

After Dr. Walters had left, Jason returned. He stood next to her bed with his arms crossed and watched her. "For years I've felt cheated. Nine years ago I found out my dreams were lies. My world collapsed. You asked me to stay away, and I did. Then I got your letter about a secret and decided it was time for me to return to town."

"I never wrote to you."

"We're too old to play games."

"I'm not playing games." She glared at him. "You're accusing me of something I didn't do."

"I want to know what you're hiding." He rolled his shoulders then stalked out.

She stared at the ceiling. Her body and head ached, but her heart hurt more.

Jason returned with a red file. "Did you think I'd destroy the letters?" He opened the file and held out a sheet of paper.

She stared at it but didn't move.

He raised an eyebrow. "Afraid to read it?"

She lifted her chin. Careful not to touch him, she took the paper. The words were ugly.

You were never more than a fling I used you to amuse myself. I'd never marry the son of the town drunk. Don't come back. It would embarrass me to be seen with you. Elizabeth Marie Kingsley.

"How is this possible? It looks like my handwriting, but I swear I didn't write this." She shook her head. "You were never a fling. I loved you."

"When I came back to talk to you, you repeated the words in the letter. You even called me a fling."

"I said what I did to protect you."

Jason stared at her, his lips a tight, straight line. He pulled out another sheet of paper. "This is why I came back."

Beth's hand trembled when she took the paper. This letter hinted at secrets and told him to talk to her. This time there was no signature.

"I didn't send either of these letters. Who would have sent them?"

His brows knitted. "Even if you didn't send these letters, this one says you have a secret I should know. Is it true? Is there something I should know?"

"I don't—"

He jabbed a finger at her. "I want the truth."

"Why should I tell you anything?" Beth yelled, "You abandoned me."

Jason shouted, "You sent me away."

"I didn't have a choice."

"Right, because I embarrassed you."

"No. I was forced to say what I did." She'd fought for so long, but each year her hope withered a bit more. "I explained everything in a letter, but you never read it, did you? When I begged for your help, you ignored me. Why should I tell you anything?"

"Because I deserve to know the truth. I need to know."

Beth shuddered as her heart shattered into a million pieces and sobbed, "My baby...they took my baby!"

"Baby?" Jason stared at her. His mouth opened then closed with a snap. He stalked away then stomped back. "A baby?"

Beth's lips trembled. "Do you—remember our last night together?"

He nodded. An icy chill slid along his spine and froze every cell in his body.

"I was happy and looked forward to joining you in Minneapolis."

"But, your letter—"

"I didn't write those letters." Beth brushed the tears from her face, but more took their place. "Two weeks after you left, I started getting sick in the mornings. A home pregnancy test confirmed my suspicions. I was so happy until I realized you didn't want us."

"That's not true. I loved you and would have wanted our baby."

"You're lying!" She shouted, "If you cared, why didn't you come back? Why wouldn't you help us?"

"I didn't know." Jason rubbed the back of his neck.

"I wrote every day and begged for your help. The letters were returned, except two. You must have read them and decided you didn't want the burden of a family." Beth grabbed a tissue and wiped her eyes. "I tried to call you, but your phone number didn't work. What was I supposed to think?"

"My first two weeks in Minneapolis, I got a letter from you every day." Jason scowled. "Then they stopped until I got that last one. I didn't want to believe what I read, so I came back to town. You said you'd never marry someone like me."

Beth held a hand out. "After you left, I wrote and explained, but the letter came back unopened."

"I didn't get the letter. After seeing you, I couldn't stay in Minneapolis, so I went to Chicago." He scrubbed his hand over his face. "You asked me why I changed my name. I did it for the family, but also because I wanted to bury Jason Fischer. I wanted to bury a life filled with pain and disappointment."

Beth took a long, deep breath. "Archer made me say those things. He said if I told you about the baby or tried to leave with you, he would have you sent to prison."

"How would he have done that?"

She shrugged. "He never told me, but I couldn't let him hurt you."

He stared at her. "How did Archer learn about the pregnancy?"

"A maid found my test sticks and told him. He was furious and accused me of getting pregnant to humiliate him." She cried. "I was eighteen—desperate—alone."

"What about your grandmother? Wouldn't she help you?"

"She was eighty-seven and wasn't well." Beth wrung her hands. "I didn't want to upset her."

"But you don't have children."

"I told you, they took my baby. Archer sent me away to have my baby and give it up for adoption. That way no one would know about the pregnancy, and it would stay a dirty family secret. After I had the baby, I returned to Serenity Bay. While I was in gone, Archer arranged a marriage for me to a business associate—"

"Marriage?" Jason interrupted. "Why not keep the baby?"

"I tried. I promised to say the baby was my husband's. No one would know the truth. Archer told me, 'No man wants to raise a hoodlum's bastard.'"

"I argued and begged, but he wouldn't change his mind."

"So you went to Europe?" He clenched his fists.

"Mother and I told everyone we planned to travel in Europe, but we moved to Boston. Until the day I gave birth, I tried to find a way to keep my baby. Nothing worked." Beth pressed a hand to her mouth.

Jason handed her a glass of water and waited.

After taking a drink, she cleared her throat. "The day I gave birth was the worst of my life. They wouldn't let me see my son." She shivered, and tears ran from her eyes.

"It was a boy?" He jumped to his feet, and the papers scattered on the floor. "I have a son?"

"They took him from me." Beth's sobs tore at him. *Did she want my son or is that another lie?* "I wanted—my baby."

Jason turned on her. "He's my son, too."

"Nine years ago you didn't want him, but you want him now." She glared. "Why?"

"Your letters never reached me. I would have come back if I'd known." Jason paced. "Where is he? Who's taking care of him?"

"I don't know. I've searched for eight years, but haven't found him."

"Have you talked to your parents? They must know where he is."

"I've tried to talk to father about him, but he's always refused to discuss what he calls *my mess*."

"I'll find our son. When I do, you won't cut me out of his life." He stomped out.

Jason stalked to the liquor cabinet in his office and poured a drink. He held the glass and stared at the liquid gold. His birth father had used alcohol to numb the disappointments of life and used his fists on Jason to vent his anger. He left the drink on the cabinet and walked away.

Returning to Serenity Bay for vindication didn't seem so important anymore. But if he hadn't returned, he wouldn't know he had a child. Jason paced—back and forth. He had a son.

Beth placed their baby for adoption, was she forced or didn't she want him? She'd searched for him for eight years. At least that's what she claimed. It didn't matter. He'd find his son. Where was he? Was he happy? Safe? Loved?

Jason sat at his computer and opened a new file. People often asked him for his secret to success. They never believed him when he said there were no secrets or tricks. Success took good planning, learning every detail about your opponents, and a bulldog-with-a-fresh-piece-of-meat determination. He would use that same single-mindedness to search for his son.

His first call was to his closest advisor, Matt, the man who'd become a father to him. Three hours and several phone calls later, Jason returned to Beth's room. She stood near the bed, dressed, and packing her suitcase.

"You're leaving?"

She looked over her shoulder. "I'm going home." She dropped clothes into her suitcase.

"You were in a terrible automobile accident, underwent hours of surgery, and lost your memory. Your recovery won't be easy. You shouldn't be alone."

"I'll hire a nurse."

"Beth, you're hurt and angry, but so am I. I have a son. Where is he? Is he happy and healthy? Does he look like me? To find him, we must work together. It'll be easier if you stay here." He had to convince her to stay—for the search.

She kept packing.

He tried again. "I called Matt. He told me about an investigator, Gabriel Michael, who specializes in cases that involve children. I called him, and he agreed to meet with us. Our story caught his interest, and he wants to hear more before he decides whether to help us."

She stopped packing but didn't turn to face him. "I've hired several investigators, and none of them found our son. Why will he succeed when the others failed?"

"He's considered one of the best and only handles investigations others have given up. Once he accepts a case, he doesn't stop searching until he finds the child. No matter how long it takes." Jason sighed. "To give him the best chance for success, we have to tell him everything we can about the birth. There might be details you've forgotten to mention to the others that will help Michael."

She turned and stared at him.

"Please stay. Together we'll find our son." J.D. Richards never begged, but nothing had ever been this important. He took a deep breath. "Beth—"

"I'll stay." She took her clothes from the suitcase and walked to the dresser. "For now."

The tension seeped from his shoulders. "Will you answer one question?"

Her eyes narrowed when she looked at him. "What?"

"If you had to give up the baby, why did you agree to your father's arranged marriage?"

"After they took my baby, I didn't care what happened. Jacob seemed like a decent man and marrying him got me away from Archer."

"Was he good to you?"

"Jacob was thirty years older than me and treated me more like a daughter than a wife."

Jason jammed his hands in his pockets. "He didn't want the baby?"

"The way Archer talked, I thought he'd told Jacob about the pregnancy. But a week after we married, I found out Archer never said a word to him. Jacob was furious."

"Was he angry that you'd had a baby?"

"No, he was upset I was forced to give up my baby. When he was a child, Jacob got sick. It left him unable to have children. He would have welcomed my son. Jacob hired an investigator to search, but we never found him."

"Your husband sounds like a good man."

"He was and didn't deserve what happened to him. Someone spread rumors about Jacob's condition. I always believed it was my father."

Jason grimaced. "That sounds like something Archer would do."

"Jacob was humiliated."

"It would be difficult for any man to bear that kind of malicious gossip."

"Within a year, Archer forced Jacob out. Later I learned Archer never wanted a merger. He always intended to take over Jacob's company." She took a slow, deep breath. "Jacob lost his will to live. He had a stroke and died three months later."

"I'm sorry," Jason murmured.

"He was a good, kind man, and I cared for him. His mistake was trusting Archer. Father used him then tossed him aside like yesterday's garbage. I was a widow and hadn't even finished college."

"I'm surprised Archer didn't arrange another marriage for you."

Her face turned bright red. "He tried, but I refused to be part of his schemes."

Beth sat in her bedroom. She'd never forget the look on Jason's face when she told him about their baby. He'd looked stunned and angry. His reaction only made sense if he hadn't received her letters. Was he telling the truth?

A knock on the door pulled her from the guilt that had tormented her for years. Lupita walked in with dinner. Beth inhaled the sweet fragrance of oregano and tangy tomato sauce. She'd made eggplant lasagna that looked as good as it smelled. Beth wanted to eat but pushed the food around for a while before she set the tray aside.

She snuggled deeper into the mattress, but couldn't fall asleep. Could this investigator succeed? What if his new family refused to let her see him?

She wanted her son and walking away a second time wasn't an option. Beth clenched her teeth. The scared eighteen-year-old debutante had become a woman who would fight for her child.

In the early hours of the morning, she fell into a restless sleep. When she woke, her pillows and blanket were on the floor. At the foot of the bed the sheet laid in a tangled mess.

Beth took a hot shower, but the dullness from a sleepless night clouded her mind. She switched the water from hot to cold. When the icy water hit her body, she screeched and scrambled from the shower.

She finished dressing and went to the breakfast room. Jason was at the table drinking coffee. Lupita dashed in with the food that included scones from the shop.

After Lupita left, Beth asked, "What time do you expect Mr. Michael to arrive?"

"He telephoned an hour ago. His flight is late, but he's booked on the next one out of Atlanta. He'll get to town around seven this evening. We'll meet with him then."

"Good. In the meantime, could Marco take me to pick up my car? I need it to get to my appointment with the doctor at one. After I've seen him, I want to stop at the shop to see my friends."

"It seems you still have gaps in your memory. Santos towed your car to his shop. I talked to him. He said it's a total loss. You need to get a new one."

"Oh. Okay. I guess my memory is still faulty."

"When you're better, we'll drive to Minneapolis so you can shop for a new vehicle."

Beth's brow furrowed. "Well, can I borrow Marco for a few hours to visit Dr. Walters and my friends?"

"I'll drive you. After you see the doctor, if you're not too tired, we'll stop in at the shop."

"I don't want to bother you. Marco can take me."

"I'll take you. I hired my management team because they're the best. I'm sure they can manage the business for a few hours without me. Besides, your appointment isn't until this afternoon. That will give me plenty of time to handle urgent issues before we leave."

Beth nodded. She didn't want to be alone with him, but he hadn't given her a choice. They ate in silence. By the time they finished breakfast, Beth had a difficult time keeping her eyes open. After a last cup of tea, she went to her room and fell asleep.

A knock on the bedroom door woke her.

Jason opened the door. "I know you're tired, but we need to leave in half an hour for the doctor's office."

"I'll change and meet you downstairs."

Twenty minutes later Beth went to his study. The doors were closed. Was he talking about her again? She curled her hands into a tight fist as she remembered the conversation she'd heard. Beth didn't want a replay of that scene but didn't want him investigating her either.

She knocked once on the door and walked in.

Jason smiled and waved her to the sofa. She looked around the room. It was beautiful with its leather and mahogany furniture. Once seated, she listened to his conversation.

"No. I want the construction to be solid, no short cuts. It will have my family's name on it, and I want them to be proud of the complex."

Jason listened. "I don't care what the crew does to cut costs for other builders. That's not how I do business. If they can't do what I want, we'll bring in a new crew. Got it?" After a moment he said, "Great. Call me if you run into any other problems."

Beth stared at him. "You plan to go ahead and build the complex?"

"I may have had other reasons for returning to Serenity Bay, but I gave my word. I don't break promises."

"My father wouldn't have finished the complex once he'd gotten what he wanted."

"I'm not Archer." He smiled as he walked to the file cabinet. "We'll be on our way in a minute. First, I have to pick this lock."

"What?"

"I locked my file cabinet and can't open it."

"Was this an important skill for you to have?" She laughed. "Were you planning a career as a thief?"

"I forget where I hide my key, so a friend taught me to open the cabinet without one."

"This friend of yours, would that be the same man who is studying Swedish?"

He chuckled. "A man of many talents."

"What work did he do before you hired him?"

"If I told you, I'd have to kill you."

She shook her head and laughed.

After Jason told Lupita they were leaving, they walked out to the car. Marco knelt in the front flower bed, singing as he pulled weeds. Beth bit her lip. He might have a gift for languages, but his voice would send small animals, maybe even large ones, into hiding.

Beth called a cheery hello but didn't dare look at him. After they left the driveway and pulled onto the street, they both broke into laughter.

With tears in her eyes, she said, "I never knew a serenade could be so frightening. Do you think the flowers grow faster because Marco sings to them?"

"I think they're afraid he'll sing louder if they don't grow." He snickered, and their laughter filled the car.

After Dr. Walters had examined Beth, she and Jason met with him in his office. He said, "Beth, I'm happy with your progress."

"Is it good enough to return to work?"

He shook his head. "While you're better, your memory is faulty. I know you don't want to hear this, but you need rest if you want to make a full recovery."

"Abbey and the others will help me. I'll take breaks and naps."

The doctor crossed his arms.

Beth sighed. "I suppose that means I can't drive either?"

"It's not safe."

"Angel, give your body time to heal." Jason squeezed her shoulder. "You don't want full bed rest again, do you?"

Her shoulders dropped. "No."

The doctor said, "I'll check on you again next week. If you're better then, maybe we can relax some of the restrictions."

After they left the office, Jason drove to Delectable Delights. Beth clasped her hands so tightly her knuckles were white.

"What's wrong?" Jason asked.

"What if my friends are angry?"

"Why would they angry?"

"When Abbey came to see me, I didn't remember her."

"You didn't know anyone." He squeezed her knee. "Your friends love you. They'll be happy you're better and that you remember them."

He pulled into the shop's parking lot. More tired than she'd told Jason, she waited for him to help her out of the car. When she stood, her legs shook.

He held her arm as they walked into the shop then said, "You're getting tired. We'll make this a short visit."

She nodded.

From behind the counter came a squeal. Abbey raced over and pulled her into a tight hug. Tears poured from her eyes when she saw Abbey's smile. Then the other employees and customers stood to clap and cheer. She gave them a watery but happy smile.

There wasn't a dry eye in the shop. The employees from the kitchen came to join the happy reunion. Her friends passed Beth from one set of arms to another. Their faces reflected their joy and relief. But it was Beth's glowing eyes and joy-filled smile that took Jason's breath away.

He suggested they get her a cup of tea and find a place for her to sit. Abbey took Beth's arm and led her to one of the stuffed chairs.

Someone set a hot cup of tea in front of Beth. "It's your special blend."

Moments later, a plate with a warm scone appeared. She looked up at Erik.

"I call it Heavenly Delight."

She bit into the pastry, closed her eyes, and moaned. "Mmm. My favorites—raspberries and white chocolate." Her eyes fluttered open, and she smiled at Erik. "It's wonderful."

He turned bright red when everyone cheered. "We have a new scone on the menu."

Beth talked and laughed with her friends. These people were important to her. They were family and cared about her.

Someone asked, "When are you coming back to work?"

"Maybe next week. I wanted to start tomorrow, but the doctor won't clear me. I told him you would—"

"Listen to your doctor." Erik shook a finger. "Don't take any risks with your health. You rest and take as much time as you need to get well."

Beth smiled. "Thank you for understanding."

When she yawned, Jason said, "I need to get our patient home. She's had a long day."

Beth hugged her friends and promised to visit again. Her smile never wavered even when she yawned a second time. As Erik had said, they loved and watched over her as she did them because that's what family did.

Back in the car, Beth leaned back and fell asleep. She woke when his door slammed.

Jason walked around the car and helped her out. They walked into the house and on the table in the front hall was a note. Gabriel called. Beth yawned but followed Jason to the study. He pressed a button on the answering machine.

Gabriel said, *My flight to Minneapolis was delayed, and I missed my connecting flight to Serenity Bay. I won't get to town until late tonight. Let's meet at nine tomorrow morning.*

Jason said, "It's better this way. You need to rest before we meet with him. It won't be easy for you to talk about the past and our baby."

"You're right. I'm just disappointed."

"So am I." He led her to the stairs. "Do you want Lupita to bring you a tray for dinner?"

"Please." She clutched his hand. "Thank you for taking me to the shop. I miss my friends. It's good to know not everything has changed." Then she kissed his cheek.

In her bedroom, Beth changed clothes and crawled into bed. She flipped on the television and found one of her favorite movies. Her stomach rumbled. She hoped Lupita brought a dinner tray soon. In the meantime, she watched *To Catch a Thief* with the always debonair Cary Grant.

A few minutes into the movie, Lupita walked in with a full tray and set it on Beth's lap. The aroma made her mouth water. She'd made a French onion soup covered with melted cheese. There was a steak salad with seared steak, romaine, tomatoes, red onions, and blue cheese. For dessert, there was an apple tart Tatin.

Lupita said, "I thought you'd prefer a light dinner."

"This is light?" The salad was huge. "If I keep eating like this, I'll have to buy clothes in a larger size."

"It wouldn't hurt you to gain a few pounds, so eat everything. I'll return for the tray later."

After Beth ate, she snuggled under the blanket to watch the movie. She yawned as the tension seeped from her body.

Jason wore a cocky grin as he strolled across the park. He wore a black tee shirt that hugged the muscles of his chest and black jeans that emphasized his long, sinewy legs. Watching his hips roll and sway took her breath away.

He wrapped her in his arms and kissed her until she melted against his body. Her blood heated. Hot and needy, she shifted and rubbed against him.

Her eyes snapped opened. The morning sun shone through the window. Beth ran her tongue over her lips as she remembered the taste of Jason's kisses. An ache ignited between her thighs. She rubbed them together, but it didn't ease the hunger.

Beth vowed not to watch romantic movies before she went to sleep. Looking over at the clock, she saw a note next to it. *Gabriel will arrive at nine.* She showered and hoped it calmed her desire for Jason, because she'd already spent too much time drooling over him.

CHAPTER TEN

Jason waited for her at the bottom of the stairs. He wore a tight black tee shirt and black pants. Beth licked her lips. He looked sexier than he had in the dream that teased her last night. When she reached him, he handed her a cup of tea. She inhaled the aroma of cinnamon and orange. "Mmm. How did you know?"

"While we were at the shop, Abbey gave me instructions on the proper care of Elizabeth Kingsley."

"She didn't."

"Oh, yes." He laughed. "You drink strong tea with breakfast and the rest of the day you have strong, black coffee. Abbey sent me home with a tin of your favorite tea and a package of the coffee you prefer."

"I'm sorry. Abbey shouldn't have bothered you."

"Your friends are worried and want you to have whatever you need to recover. That's what family does." He took her arm and walked to the breakfast room. "There's more color in your cheeks today. How are you feeling?"

"Better. Refreshed."

"I checked on you earlier. You were restless and whimpering. I thought you might be having nightmares about the crash. I walked in to wake you, but the moans stopped, so I let you sleep. Were they nightmares?"

Although she tried to appear calm, her face grew hot. "I don't remember."

"If you have nightmares, you should tell the doctor, or we can find you a counselor."

"I'm fine. If the dreams become a problem, I'll let you know."

"Good." He chuckled. "I hope you're hungry. I walked into the kitchen for coffee and found Lupita singing with the radio while she fixed breakfast. You know what that means."

Beth nodded. "She made enough food for a platoon of soldiers and expects me to eat at least two helpings of everything. If I don't, she'll accuse me of worrying my mother."

They laughed and sat at the table. Lupita brought in her usual overloaded tray of food, and they filled their plates.

She asked, "How did you find Mr. Michael?"

"A few years ago, the son of one of Matt's friends was kidnapped. They hired Gabriel Michael to find the boy."

"Is he good?"

"Matt told me he takes cases other investigators consider lost causes, and his success rate is higher than the average."

"Did he find the boy?"

Jason nodded. "He did."

"Then we should hire him."

"It's not a matter of whether we hire him, but whether he'll take our case. He's particular about who he works with. If he agrees to work for us, we have to first agree to his terms."

"What are they?"

Jason counted off the reasons. "Someone he trusts must refer us. We must have a good reason for finding the child. We have to agree to act in the child's best interests."

"He sounds like the kind of investigator we need. Someone who won't give up."

"That's what I thought, so I had his background checked. Michael's firm has an excellent reputation and is one of the best in the country. There isn't much information about Michael and nothing over seven years old. It's as though he didn't exist before then."

"I don't care about his past, my concern is whether he can find my son." She tilted her head. "Tell me what to say to convince him to accept our case?"

"Just be honest and answer his questions, no matter how uncomfortable they make you."

"There are still gaps in my memory."

"Do your best. If we have to fill in the blanks later, we will."

"Why does he have two first names?"

"I don't know. You can ask Michael when he gets here."

After breakfast, they went to the study. Jason nagged Beth until she sat, her legs up, on the sofa. "This interview will drain you emotionally and physically."

He covered her with an afghan and put a pillow behind her back.

She objected. "This isn't the way to conduct a business meeting with someone we want to impress."

"Michael will understand. I told him about the accident." He crossed his arms. "We can't risk setting back your recovery."

The doorbell rang, and Beth grabbed his hand. "What will we do if he won't help us?"

Jason said, "Don't worry. He wouldn't be coming here if he

wasn't interested in our case. If he decides against us, we'll hire someone else. I promise we will find our son."

The heavy footsteps in the hall got closer until Gabriel Michael walked into the room. Beth shivered. He exuded confidence and strength. Never would he allow himself to fail.

His blond hair was tied back in a queue and hung to the middle of his back. Shadows in his translucent silver-gray eyes revealed the soul of the man who walked in the alleys of life's dark side. Gabriel Michael could handle himself and anyone who got in his way.

"Mr. Michael, I'm Jason Richards. Thank you for meeting with us." Jason shook his hand.

"Please call me Gabriel."

They walked to her, and Beth marveled at their similarities. Both men exuded power and authority. Anyone who saw them would know it was a mistake to cross either man.

"This is Elizabeth Kingsley—Beth."

Gabriel shook her hand. "Happy to meet you."

"Thank you for coming here. It's difficult for me to travel."

"Jason explained." Gabriel nodded.

"Before we start, would you like coffee, water, or something else?" Jason pointed to a cart. "If you're hungry, we have scones and other pastries."

Gabriel poured a large cup of the dark coffee.

She warned him. "It's very strong."

He took a long drink and smiled. "Perfect."

"Your story caught my interest. I wanted to hear more." Gabriel sat on a leather chair and took a notebook and pen from his briefcase. "So tell me about your son."

Jason said, "I'd like to tell you about the early years when we both lived in Serenity Bay."

While he told Gabriel about their time together and their plans to leave town, Beth's thoughts strayed. *How will I cope with his contempt when he finds out I abandoned our son?*

She listened as he described his life in Chicago and talked about the Richards family. When he talked about his marriage, she crossed her arms to hide her clenched hands.

Beth held her breath when he talked about that awful letter he'd received eight years ago. He explained that although her signature was on the letter, she hadn't sent it. She released the breath she'd been holding.

Then he told Gabriel about the letter he'd received a few months ago. With a smirk, he admitted returning to town to ask questions and discover the secrets hinted at in the letter. He handed Gabriel the folder with the letters. While he read them, Jason refilled his coffee cup.

Jason talked for more than two hours. Gabriel never interrupted. He waited to ask his questions after Jason finished his explanation.

After Jason had answered the last question, he suggested they break for lunch.

Beth's stomach was tight with tension. It would be her turn to talk about the past. Afraid she'd lose her lunch, Beth ate little of the food Lupita had prepared. When Jason left town, she hadn't known how alone he'd felt, or how it hurt him to leave without her. No wonder he'd been confused and angry when he got the letter telling him he'd been a fling.

When they returned to the study, it was Beth's turn. Even though it had been years since her life fell apart, the loss and fear still plagued her. Talking about it hurt, deeply, but to find her son she'd endure any pain.

"Until the day Jason went to Minneapolis, I didn't believe he would go without me. But he did." Beth stared at her hands. "We talked on the telephone and wrote every day, but I worried he wouldn't come back for me. Two weeks after he left, I started losing my breakfast. I bought a home pregnancy test. The results were positive."

She took a deep breath. "Later that day, a maid told Archer about the test stick she'd found. I think she hoped to get on his good side, but she didn't know, he doesn't have one. He wanted no one to know about the pregnancy, so he fired her."

Beth dug a tissue out of her pocket. "Father made arrangements for Mother and me to go to Boston. He ordered me to have the baby and place him for adoption. I wanted to keep my baby, but father said he had plans for me, and they didn't include my brat."

Lips trembling, she said, "I asked him for money and promised to go away. I even offered to give him my shares of company stock, but he refused. He said I was an embarrassment, and he didn't want his reputation ruined because of the mess I'd made."

Jason left his chair and sat next to her. Then he held her hand.

She looked into his eyes terrified of what she'd see. A tear slipped over her cheek when she saw pain and sorrow, but no anger or contempt. "I told Archer I wouldn't go to Boston. He said if I didn't give up the baby, he'd make trouble for Jason. I didn't know what he would do, but I had to protect you. I went along with his plan, although I hoped you'd come for me. But the day you came to see me, Archer was home and said he would have you sent to prison. I had to tell you his lies. After you left, I wrote to tell you why I said those things. The letter came back—unopened. A week later, Mother and I flew to Boston.

"I tried to run away, but the police found me. Then Archer hired a bodyguard. I wasn't allowed to go anywhere alone, but I managed to escape a second time. The guard tracked me to a motel and took me back." Tears poured from her eyes. "I wanted my baby."

Jason pulled her into his arms and held her while she cried. He stroked circles on her back. His gentle care soothed the part of her that still ached after all these years.

"Why don't we take a break?" Gabriel got to his feet. "We can finish tomorrow."

"I'd rather go on. If you'll give me a minute, I'll be fine." She stared at their joined hands. "Can I have a cup of coffee?"

Gabriel stood. "I'll get it."

By the time he handed Beth a cup, her tears had dried. "I'm better. I can do this." Her voice was steadier when she continued her story.

"At the hospital, a nurse felt sorry for me. I begged her to name the baby Marie if it was a girl." She looked at him. "If it was a boy, I wanted him called Daniel."

Jason Daniel Richards stared at her with eyes that glistened with unshed tears. "Daniel?"

Beth nodded. "Later, the nurse told me the baby was a boy. I wanted to hold him before they took him away, but Mother wouldn't let me. She said it would make the pain worse. After that, I didn't care what happened. A month after we returned to town, I married Jacob."

He brushed his thumb over her hand, and she appreciated the caress. It kept her anchored in the present instead of wandering in the despair of the past.

"After Jacob found out about Daniel, he hired an investigator to search, but the detective couldn't find any leads and quit the case. Jacob died, and I didn't have the money to hire another investigator. I became depressed and lost hope."

"Then I inherited grandmother's estate and hired another

investigator. The first of five. I want to know Daniel is healthy, happy, and loved. I'd like to be part of his life. But none of the men I hired could find him or uncover any information about where he might be living."

She put her hands over her face and cried. "I'm...sorry..."

"That's enough." Jason stood. "We can finish tomorrow. Gabriel, will you wait? I want to take Beth upstairs."

Jason carried her to the bedroom. He sat on the bed and held her while she cried. When she ran out of tears, he laid her down. She shivered, so he grabbed the quilt at the bottom of the bed and covered her.

"Do you want Lupita to bring you something to eat?"

She shook her head.

"Beth—"

"Please, not now. I want to rest." She shut her eyes and prayed for sleep.

Jason returned to his study, agitated and angry. He went to the liquor cabinet and poured two snifters of brandy. He handed one to Gabriel then rolled his glass between his hands before he took a drink.

The day he decided to make Beth pay for her sins, he hadn't known how she'd suffered. She'd lived through her parent's betrayal, the loss of their son, and his apparent abandonment. Instead of losing herself in the pain and betrayal, she remained a warm, loving woman.

"Will she be okay?" Gabriel scrubbed a hand over his chin. "Did we push too hard?"

"She's tired. A good night's sleep will help." Jason stared at the amber liquid.

"The depth of her strength amazes me."

Jason took a drink of his brandy. "Have you decided if you'll take our case?"

"I'll take it." Gabriel set his glass on a table. "She deserves to find out what's happened to her baby."

"Yeah, she does." Jason ran a hand through his hair. "So, what will you do first?"

"I want to hear the rest of her story. Also, I have two or three questions."

"Come for breakfast tomorrow. Beth should be able to answer your questions then."

"That'll work." Gabriel packed his notebook into his briefcase and stood. He scrubbed a hand over his face. "You know, her father's a bastard."

Jason smirked. "Yeah, I know."

Daniel cried. Poor darling needed her. Before she reached him, Jason picked him up. She reached out, but he stepped away.

"You gave our son away. You don't deserve to have him."

"I had to save you."

"You're lying."

She stretched her arms out and pleaded, "I'm not. I can't lose him again."

A heartbeat later a warm, soothing heat surrounded her. She sighed and snuggled into the warm cocoon where there were no nightmares.

Beth woke more rested and relaxed than she'd felt in years. While the talk about the past opened the old wounds, the burden felt lighter. She wanted to believe Gabriel could find their son, but so many others failed. Another disappointment would crush her.

Jason might fight for full custody, but it didn't matter if he did. She wasn't a helpless eighteen-year-old girl too weak to fight for her child. Now she was a strong, independent woman who would face any obstacle to keep her son.

Even if they shared custody, it would be a challenge to make it work with Jason in Illinois and her in Minnesota. She would worry about that later. First, they had to find Daniel. *Please let this time be different.*

Beth went down to breakfast. Jason and Gabriel sat at the table. They stood, and Jason pulled a chair out for her. She stared at him until he asked, "Do I have food on my face?"

"What? Uh, no. Sorry. I guess I'm not awake yet."

"Would you like coffee instead of tea?" He grinned.

"No." She took a scone from the basket of pastries. It was a raspberry-white chocolate scone. She thanked Jason.

"Thank Lupita. She's worried you're not eating enough and hoped the scones would tempt you."

"I'll thank her later." She turned to Gabriel. "Will you help us?"

"Yes. Before I can start, I have a few questions."

"There's still a lot I don't remember, but I'll tell you whatever I know."

Jason held Beth's hand and brushed his thumb over the back of her hand. "Are you sure?"

She nodded. "I will do whatever it takes to find Daniel."

After breakfast, they went to the study. She didn't argue about putting her legs up this time.

"There aren't that many questions. We'll try to get this done quickly so you can rest." Gabriel pulled out his notebook and pen. "Where in Boston did you live?"

"We had an apartment in the Back Bay area." She gave him the address.

Gabriel nodded as he wrote. "Where was Daniel born?"

"Boston City Hospital."

"Were there any problems with the birth? Did the doctor mention any concerns about the baby's health?"

"No. The doctor refused to talk about Daniel. Although he did tell me the baby was healthy." Beth frowned and rubbed her forehead. "You know—there was something odd that I'd forgotten. The doctor who delivered the baby wasn't the one I went to for prenatal care. Before I had the baby, I saw Dr. Jessop. But he wasn't the doctor who delivered Daniel. I didn't know him."

"Do you remember his name?"

"No. I'm sorry."

"I would have been surprised if you remembered." Gabriel tapped his pen on his tablet. "Is there any chance you know the name of the attorney who handled the adoption?"

She shook her head. "No. Archer arranged that and never told me his name. I've asked father for the man's name, but he refuses to answer my questions or discuss the pregnancy."

"I didn't think he'd give you that information, but I wanted to check. If you remember any other details, call me or send an email." Gabriel smiled. "In the meantime, I'll check the county records and hospital files for a birth certificate and medical information."

Jason asked, "Can you search without knowing who adopted him or the attorney who handled the adoption?"

Gabriel huffed. "It would be easier to search if we had that information, but there are places we can check."

Jason asked Beth, "How do you feel about talking to your parents?"

"For years I've asked Archer for the information, but he refuses to tell me anything. Although, he might tell J.D. Richards." She frowned. "But he won't give us the information for free. He'll want to be sure we know he's the one with the power."

"I swim with sharks bigger and meaner than Archer. I can handle him." Jason pulled her close then asked Gabriel. "Any more questions?"

Gabriel's eyes narrowed, and his pen tapped on his tablet.

"What's wrong?" Jason asked.

"You hired five investigators, and they all resigned. What reasons did they give for quitting?"

Beth shrugged. "I wondered about that, but their stories were the same. They found no trace of Daniel, and it would be a waste of money to continue to search."

Gabriel asked, "Who searched the longest?"

"The first investigator searched for almost eighteen months. He told me he'd found a good lead, but two weeks later he resigned."

Gabriel scratched his jaw. "Do you have the names, addresses, and phone numbers of your investigators? It would help if I could also get the dates they worked for you. Do you have that information?"

"It's at home. I'll get my file and email what I have later today. Do you think they might have information in their notes you can use?"

She watched Jason and Gabriel stare at each other, but neither said a word. What weren't they telling her? "If you need a written authorization to get the information, I can send letters to them."

"Don't worry about it. I'm sure they'll talk once I introduce myself." Gabriel crossed his legs. "I'll search for your son, because you deserve to know what happened to him. But you need to prepare yourselves. If he's with a good family who loves him, it would be wrong to tear them apart."

Beth twisted her hands. "I don't want to rip their family apart, but I would like to be part of his life. If his parents don't agree, I don't know how I'd cope with their decision. Whatever happens, I don't want him to be caught in the middle of a court battle."

Gabriel nodded then looked at Jason.

"I can't tell you what I'd do." He rolled his shoulders. "I've only known I had a son for a few days. I want to believe I'd do what's best for Daniel, but I don't know if I could walk away."

Gabriel stared at him. "I do this work for the children. They deserve to be happy and to know about their birth. But I'll do whatever it takes to protect him, even if I have to stop you from hurting him. Understood?"

Jason nodded.

Beth asked, "Where will you look first?"

Gabriel stood. "I think Boston. We might get lucky and find information in the hospital's records about the people who adopted him or the agency that placed Daniel."

After Gabriel left, Beth wanted to get the information she'd promised him. Marco drove her home. She talked to her housekeeper and reassured her. Then she packed her computer and the files on the investigators in her briefcase.

By the time they got back to Jason's house, Beth was exhausted. She decided to change into a bathing suit and laid by the pool. It wasn't often she took the time to enjoy a sunny day, but today was perfect for being outside. The sun's rays warmed her and soothed the tension in her body. She closed her eyes.

Beth hummed at the light caress on her shoulder. She arched her back and stretched. Her eyelids flickered open.

Jason stood over her. "Hello."

Her stomach fluttered. "Hi."

"I saw you from my study. Unless you want a painful sunburn, you should move into the shade. I'll even put suntan lotion on your back."

Beth gathered her towel and tote bag before she moved to a chair in the shade. Jason sat next to her and poured lotion into his hand. When he slid his hand over her skin, she shivered and bit back a moan while every bone in her body turned to mush.

"When do you want to talk to your parents?"

She shrugged. "I thought we'd wait to hear from Gabriel."

"We have to do this." He rubbed lotion on her arms. "The one person who knows the name of the attorney is your father. He might even have the name of the couple who adopted Daniel. We have to try."

"You're right." She exhaled. "I hate to ask my father for anything. He'll want us to pay for his help. I've thought about it, and I am certain he'll want you to invest in his latest project."

"Trust me. I can handle Archer." Jason stroked her arms. "I promised we'd find Daniel, and we will. He won't stop us."

She smiled. "I'll call Mother and ask if we can visit this evening."

"Let me know." He kissed her forehead and returned to his study.

An hour later, unable to put it off any longer, Beth called her mother.

Deidre was thrilled they wanted to visit. Beth hated not telling her the reason, but she didn't want to give Archer time to prepare.

At supper, she tried to eat, but the few bites she ate felt like soured milk in her stomach. By the time they parked the car at her parents' home, she'd shredded every tissue she had in her purse.

Jason pulled her close. "I negotiate with difficult people all the time, and I can handle Archer. If he wants money, that's what we'll give him. Whatever it takes, we'll get the information we need."

The butler opened the door. "Good evening, Miss Beth. You're looking well."

"Thank you, Thomas. How is your family?"

"They're well, Miss. My youngest son graduated from law school a week ago."

"That's wonderful. You must be very proud of him."

"We are, Miss."

"Where are my parents?"

"They're waiting for you in the front parlor."

"Thank you." She took Jason's hand, but at the closed doors to the parlor, she stopped.

He put an arm around her shoulder. "Your father can't hurt you anymore."

"No one has ever stopped him." She straightened her shoulders. "Let's do this."

Jason knocked and opened the door. Beth forced a smile and walked into the room.

Her mother sat in a chair next to the huge, marble fireplace. It was one of the few features she liked in this oversized mausoleum. Archer stood behind her leaning against the oak mantel.

Over the years, she'd learned to read Archer's moods. His smirk and raised eyebrow had her jaw clenching. He would be difficult.

Jason said, "Deidre, it's good to see you again."

She smiled. "I'm so glad you came to visit."

Beth said, "Jason, you remember my father."

They nodded, but neither of them put a hand out.

"Please sit." Deidre frowned and pointed to the sofa across from her. "Would you like something to drink? There is coffee and tea."

Jason shook his head.

Beth folded her hands together and said, "Not now, thank you."

Archer pulled away from the mantel. "You wanted to meet with us. Why?"

So, no polite chitchat. Beth said, "I told Jason about our son. We've hired an investigator to find him. It would help our search if you gave us the name of the attorney who handled the adoption and the doctor who delivered the baby."

Beth watched her parents' reactions. Her mother twisted her wedding ring and stared at Archer while her father narrowed his eyes and rubbed his chin. What was he plotting?

He said, "That unpleasantness is best left buried. I won't discuss it or the humiliation you caused me."

Beth inhaled. "The *it* you're referring to is our son. If you remember, you sent me to Boston and forced me to give up my son, so no one would learn about *your humiliation*."

Archer walked to the liquor cabinet and poured a drink. He returned to the fireplace without offering one to them. "I worked hard to clean up your mess. I'll not allow you to make that scandal public and sully my name."

Beth looked at Jason.

Although he looked relaxed, Jason's eyes were as cold and hard as icebergs when he said, "We will find our son, but the search would be easier if you gave us the information we need."

Archer sneered, "You can search for your brat, but I made sure you will never find him."

CHAPTER ELEVEN

Jason swallowed his anger. "What did you do?"

"I refused to let you ruin what I worked so hard to accomplish. It took years, but I made the name Kingsley respected and powerful."

"Answer my question," Jason demanded. "What did you do?"

"I needed Beth to stay in Serenity Bay. I'd made plans for her, and they didn't include leaving town with the son of the town drunk. Although if I'd known how much money you'd be worth, I would have sent her to you gift wrapped."

"How did you keep her here?"

Archer wore a cocky smirk. "You didn't know I pulled the strings while the two of you danced like mindless puppets. It's too bad you came back. But then if you hadn't, I wouldn't be able to gloat about besting the great J.D. Richards."

"You're boring me." Jason sat back. "You know what we want. What will it cost us?"

Beth stared at him. He squeezed her hand and hoped she'd let him handle Archer. She pressed into his side but didn't say a word.

Archer rubbed his hands together. "I have a project and need a partner to underwrite it. I want your financial backing. In exchange, I'll give you my files about Elizabeth and five percent ownership."

"What will this generous offer cost, two million or five?"

Archer smirked. "It's a bargain at twenty-five million dollars."

Jason bit his tongue. If he didn't, he'd tell Archer what he thought of him. Instead, he asked, "Would this be the project in Chicago?"

"That's the one."

Jason stared at Archer's smarmy smile. "Don't you care that you're breaking Beth's heart. This isn't the whim of a young girl. She deserves to know her son."

"I don't give a damn what Elizabeth wants. I won't let her humiliate this family."

"But, if I give you twenty-five million dollars, you'll tell us what we need to know?"

Archer shrugged.

"I've heard enough. Your reputation is well-deserved. You are a greedy bastard."

Beth gasped and turned to Jason.

Did she believe Archer would give them the information they

wanted? He'd take the money and never tell them what he knew. Archer didn't want them to find Daniel. He wanted the money.

"It's time to leave." Jason stood and held his hand out to Beth. He held his breath and hoped she didn't fight him. Archer would use their disagreement to drive a wedge between them. After a brief moment of hesitation, she took his hand.

They went to Deidre. She looked heartbroken.

Beth leaned over and kissed her cheek. "I'll call you."

He took Beth's arm and led her from the house. Her back was rigid. Jason expected anger and accusations, but he hadn't expected this icy detachment. He called to her, but she didn't respond. Then they pulled out of the driveway, and she attacked.

"You said you'd do anything to find Daniel. Father offered the information, and a share of his project, but you refused the offer. Why? You promised we'd find Daniel, but we'll never find him without his help."

"Archer's offer is a way to extort money. He has no intention of giving us the names we need even if we pay him the twenty-five million dollars."

"He would tell us."

"No, he wouldn't. He wants to get the money he needs to stay out of prison." Jason's hands tightened on the steering wheel. "Once he has the money, he'd use some excuse not to give us the information he promised."

"Prison? What do you mean?"

"His Chicago project, the one he wants me to invest in, is in financial trouble. There isn't enough money to complete the project. There's talk he's been siphoning funds out of the building accounts and putting it in his own pocket. The project is almost bankrupt. He's sold shares in the venture equal to over one hundred and twenty percent. That doesn't include the five percent he offered me."

"You're wrong. He isn't a crook." Her voice quivered.

"I hate to say this about your father, but you must know he doesn't have a good reputation. He's not known for honesty or fair play. My investigator, Jackson, checked, and what he learned was not flattering. Archer doesn't just bend the rules, he stomps on them." In his report, Jackson said, *Kingsley uses lies and blackmail to force others to comply with his plans. He will cheat or steal to get what he wants, usually power and money, and doesn't care who gets hurt.*

"You're wrong." She pressed her hands to her temples. "I know he operates close to the edge, but that's not illegal."

Jason couldn't have felt guiltier if he'd pulled the wings off a butterfly. To protect Beth from Archer's manipulations, she needed to know the truth about her father and his lack of ethics. Fifteen minutes later, he parked in his drive. Beth jumped out of the car and rushed into the house.

He raced after her. "Beth, let's have a drink."

"I'm going to bed."

Jason needed to explain why he refused to get involved in the Chicago project, and why Archer's demand was unreasonable. "We need to talk—"

Lupita walked out of the kitchen. "Mr. Michael phoned. He asked that you call no matter what time you got home."

Beth's face lit with hope, and she grabbed his arm. "Maybe he knows where Daniel is living."

"Thank you, Lupita." He led Beth to his office. "We'll call him, but first let's make you comfortable."

She sat on the sofa and kicked off her shoes. With a sigh, she put her legs up and pulled a throw over them.

Jason went to the liquor cabinet and poured two glasses of cognac. "Gabriel couldn't have found him so soon. But even if it's bad news, we'll keep searching. I promised we'd find Daniel and intend to keep that pledge."

She had a haunted look in her eyes. "I don't know what to believe anymore."

"Gabriel won't give up until he finds Daniel, and neither will we. If he runs into a roadblock, he'll go around it, roll over it, or destroy it. That's why he's the best."

"How do you know?"

"I recognize the same stubborn determination in him that I see in the mirror every morning."

Beth's lips curled at the corners. It wasn't her usual happy smile, the one that made her eyes sparkle, but at least it was a smile.

He went to the telephone and dialed.

After one ring, he heard, "Glad you got my message."

Gabriel's lack of greeting didn't surprise him. He wasn't a man who spent time on social pleasantries.

"Beth is with me, and I have the speaker on so we can both hear you. Do you have news about Daniel?"

"Not yet, but something happened, and I thought you should

know."

Jason's instincts shifted into overdrive. "What?"

"I stopped at the county offices to look for Daniel's records. On my way back to the hotel, I stopped for supper. While I ate, a man approached. He said his employer wants me to give up my search for Daniel."

Jason considered his options.

Gabriel said, "If I agree to walk away from the case, I'd be well-paid."

"Did he tell you who hired him?" Jason grimaced.

"I asked, but he didn't say. He told me to say I couldn't find your son, and it's a waste of money to continue my search."

Beth gasped.

Jason rubbed a hand over his chin. Those were the same words used by the investigators who dropped her case.

Gabriel said, "I asked about the money. He said the other investigators hadn't complained about the amounts of their payments."

Could they convince Michael to stick with their case by offering more money? "What did you tell him?"

Gabriel didn't hesitate. "The same thing I told you. I never give up an investigation once I agree to handle it."

If he wasn't calling to resign from the case, what was on his mind?

"How did he take your refusal?"

"He tried to change my mind. Soon he gave up and walked out." Gabriel chuckled. "When I left the restaurant, the nice man was waiting for me and tried some not-so-subtle persuasion. He now understands that I don't want his money. I don't expect to hear from him again, but you should take precautions in case he tries to persuade you or Beth to give up your search."

"Understood. Marco, my head of security, is already here. The rest of my security team is at my home in Illinois, but I'm sure they'll enjoy a visit to Serenity Bay."

Gabriel chuckled. "An excellent idea. I'll call in a few days." He ended the call.

The color drained from Beth's face. "Who would try to force Gabriel to give up our case? Why would anyone want to keep us from finding our baby?"

"Beth, we want to believe our fathers are honorable men who love us. But they aren't all candidates for Father of the Year."

"Archer would never do what you're suggesting. You assume the worse of everyone. I told you I didn't write those letters, but you thought I'd lied." She shivered. "Now you want me to believe my father wants to sabotage our search."

"You heard what he said. He 'pulled our strings like puppets' to keep you from leaving town. He cleaned up our mess and made sure we wouldn't be able to find Daniel. Those aren't the actions of a loving father."

"You're wrong. He's not heartless. He can't be." Beth waved her hands. "It doesn't matter. All I care about is finding my son."

"You mean *our* son, don't you?" A dark shadow fell over Jason's face.

"Yes, our son."

"I won't let you keep me away from Daniel."

"I'm not trying to exclude you. Can you say the same?" She jumped to her feet and ran from the room.

Daniel cried. She turned in a circle, but couldn't find him.

"You threw him away." The contempt in Jason's words sent shivers over her skin. "Now, he's mine, and you'll never see him again."

She ran toward his voice until she reached the edge of a murky void. The ground under her feet crumbled, and she fell... "No!"

Beth's eyes snapped open. Her lungs burned, and she inhaled a desperate breath. The nightgown she wore clung to her sweat-soaked skin. Hands shaking, it took several tries to get the twisted sheet off her legs and stumble to the bathroom.

Beth clung to the counter and stared into the mirror. The color had drained from her skin, and her eyes were filled with fear. She couldn't lose Daniel again.

With a dampened washcloth, she wiped the sweat from her body. After she put on a fresh gown and changed the sheets, she crawled into bed to spend another night reading. She huffed and rolled her eyes. Her books were at her parent's house.

Beth bit her lip. Why had she argued with Jason? Her whole life she wanted her father's love and approval, but she never got either. Archer admitted he'd manipulated them to keep her in town. Her shoulders slumped. It was time to acknowledge the truth. The only person Archer cared about was himself.

But was Jason any different? Did he still think she'd hid her pregnancy? Could he believe she would keep his son from him? She wanted his trust, but how could he give something he didn't have. All the lies and manipulation from the past continued to plague their lives.

Her eyes widened. She could prove she'd tried to tell him the truth. In her attic were boxes of mementos from her time with Jason. She'd kept the letters he sent her, and the letters that she'd sent but were returned.

She checked the time. Ten minutes to three. She never slept after a nightmare. Instead of counting the seconds until morning, she could go home to get the proof Jason needed.

Beth dressed and grabbed her purse. Wait, no car. Jason's car was in the garage, and he left his keys on the table in the front hall. If she got back before anyone woke, no one would know she'd borrowed his car.

Unable to sleep, Jason woke early and went to work in the study. Although Jason had coffee, he waited to eat breakfast with Beth. He owed her an apology. Archer might not be the best father, but he was the only one she had.

The grandfather clock chimed nine times. She never slept this late. They both liked to start their days early. At nine-forty-five, too impatient to wait any longer, he went to her bedroom. Was she so angry she'd skip breakfast? It didn't matter, she needed to eat.

He knocked on her bedroom door. No answer. He knocked again. "Beth?" No response. Was she still asleep, or didn't she want to talk to him? He opened the door. She wasn't in bed. He checked the bathroom. She wasn't there.

Had she left? Had she been that angry? He checked the closet and dresser drawers. Her clothes were there. Where did she go? He rushed downstairs to ask Lupita if she'd seen her. The doorbell rang as he reached the last stair. He didn't have the time or patience to welcome visitors. He pulled the door open.

Beth. Dust covered her clothes and hair. Along the side of her nose was a streak of dirt. She looked adorable.

Jason heaved a relieved sigh then bellowed, "Where have you been?"

"Home. I remembered these boxes in my attic and wanted to show them to you."

He looked at the boxes she held. "How did you get home?"

She held out his keys.

"The doctor hasn't cleared you to drive."

With a grin, she said, "I won't tell if you don't."

He took the boxes from her. "Why couldn't you wait for Marco to take you home?"

"I wanted to get these boxes. Before we go through them, I need to shower. Would you ask Lupita to bring us coffee?"

"What's in the boxes?"

"I won't be long."

He sighed. "I'll put these in my study."

She grabbed his arm. "Promise you won't open them without me."

"I promise."

Beth ran up the stairs, and he went to the study. What was so important that she needed to drive home? He set the boxes next to the sofa and returned to his desk. As Beth suggested, he called Lupita to ask her to bring coffee and pastries to the office.

He lifted an eyebrow when Beth returned fifteen minutes later. She must have taken the fastest shower of her life, which couldn't have been easy with her wrist in a cast.

When he saw the buttons on her blouse, he coughed. She looked at her clothes. With a roll of her eyes, she redid the mismatched buttons.

She shut and locked the door. Then she poured coffee and asked, "Do you want a cup?"

"Yes. Thank you." When she sat next to him, he said, "Tell me about the boxes."

"These are mementos. Reminders I kept from our time together and couldn't throw away." She stared into her coffee. "I kept the letters you sent me from Minneapolis and the ones I sent you that were returned unopened."

His eyes widened. "You kept them even though you thought I'd walked out on you?"

She shrugged and opened the first container. "These were memories of the best days of my life."

Inside was a wooden box covered with glass—a memory box. Jason reached to lift it out but stopped. He looked at Beth and asked, "Okay?"

She nodded.

With great care, he pulled out the keepsake. In it was a withered red rose and a dusty white lace handkerchief with Beth's initials embroidered on it. He ran his hand over the glass.

He'd given her the rose, and her grandmother gave her the handkerchief, for her sixteenth birthday. She'd put the birthday cards they'd given her in the box too. She took it from him and set it to the side.

Then he pulled out a stack of letters. They were the ones he sent after moving to Minneapolis. A pink lace ribbon held the bundle together. He remembered the ribbon. It was one of the handfuls he'd bought her at the Renaissance Fair.

She smiled. "Do you remember the weekend we drove to the cities to go to the festival?"

"I wanted to buy you a necklace, but you asked for the ribbons." He stopped and stared at her. "Why did you keep them?"

"I believed in our dreams and thought we could make them real. After you left, I didn't want them to die."

Beth returned the letters to the box. She put the cover on, and Jason set it on the floor. Then he set the other box on the table and waited while she opened it. On top was another stack of letters, but this time a black ribbon bound them. His name was on the top letter and next to it were the words, *Moved, Left No Address.*

Jason lifted out the bundle and ran his fingers over the letters.

She swallowed the lump in her throat. "I want you to read them."

He set them on the table. "These are private. I don't have the right—"

"I wrote those letters to you. If anyone has a right to read them, it's you." She stood. "I think I'll lay by the pool."

Jason's gut wrenched when she walked out. He'd returned to Serenity Bay to find out her secrets and make her pay for destroying his dreams. Again and again, she'd proclaimed her innocence, but he never believed her. To prove she hadn't lied, Beth brought him pieces of the past. His answers were here if he was strong enough to confront the truth.

He untied the faded, black ribbon and ruffled through the stack. The letters were stamped, *Moved, Left No Address.* It must have broken her heart to write to him only to have the letters returned. His heart ached, but he opened the first letter.

In it, Beth said she counted the days until he returned. She told him her grandmother was ill, but they planned to have a dinner to celebrate her graduation when she felt better. Excitement came through every word she wrote when she talked about their plans to marry and build a new life in Minneapolis. She told him she missed him and signed the letter—*Love, Beth*.

In every letter, she wrote of her love for him. When she told him about the pregnancy, her joy came through in each word she wrote. She begged him to return for her. He had to take a deep breath when she assured him they could raise their baby with the love and laughter they didn't have in their childhoods.

Then he read the letter she'd written the day he'd gone to confront her. Beth begged for his forgiveness. She wrote that Archer had threatened to have him arrested if she didn't send him away, and she'd been trying to protect him.

Please come for me. I love you and our baby. Archer has ordered me to place the baby for adoption. Don't let them take our baby.

Jason wiped a hand over his face. He'd been so wrong. Beth had needed him, and he'd failed her. When she sent him away, he'd felt betrayed. Her reward for protecting him had been his lack of faith and contempt. He'd been a fool.

He continued to read her words but frowned when the tone of her letters changed. She worried that something had happened to him. He didn't call or write, and her letters were being returned. She needed him to come back before Archer forced her to give up their baby.

He cringed when he read how she'd run away. She left with no money or clothes, only a desperate need to keep their baby. But the guard Archer had hired, found her and dragged her back to the Boston apartment.

Please help us. I won't ask you to take care of us, but I can't get away without help. I want to keep my baby. Please come to Boston before it's too late. Beth.

His heart bled for the girl who'd been so alone. He held the last letter. His chest was tight with fear. Did he have the courage to read the last letter?

After what he'd put Beth through, she deserved her pound of flesh. He pulled the letter from the envelope.

They took our baby. Now I've lost both of you. The pain makes it hard to breathe. Nothing matters anymore. I wish you loved me the way I love you. Goodbye. Beth.

J.D. Richards' heart bled, and the words on the letter became a watery blur.

A few months ago a letter invited him back to Serenity Bay to learn a secret. He'd returned to make Beth pay for destroying his dreams. Now he knew she'd been the one who had been betrayed. She'd withstood more pain and sorrow than any person should endure in a lifetime.

Not once during the time they'd been together had she belittled him or judged him unworthy. But at the first test of their love, he'd believed the worst. The day he went to see her, she'd been hesitant, wary. He'd decided she didn't want to see him. It had been so easy to believe she'd lied and made a fool of him.

Jason went to the patio doors and looked at Beth. She'd been so young and innocent when they met. He'd wondered how she could care for him, a damaged boy with no future. But her devotion never wavered and made him want to be worthy of her love.

Now her skin glistened in the midday sun, and her hair curled around her face like the halo of light she'd had the first time he'd seen her. She had always been lovely, but now she possessed a body he wanted to explore for the rest of his life.

Jason went to where she lay sleeping and watched her. At eighteen, Beth hadn't been strong enough to stand and fight her parents, but that hadn't stopped her from trying. She obeyed Archer only after he threatened to hurt Jason. Beth had done all she could to protect him.

He was careful not to wake her as he lifted her into his arms. She snuggled closer. When she murmured his name, he smiled and admitted what he'd always known. He fell in love with Beth the day he saw her in the park, and he'd love her until the day he died.

Could they put the lies and manipulation behind them? He laid her on the bed. Did she still love him, was that why she'd given him the letters? He needed to know because walking away was not an option.

Beth stretched and burrowed into the softness under her. Her eyes opened. She'd been on a lounge chair by the pool. How had she gotten to her bed? Jason.

She rolled onto her back. The silk sheet slid over her skin—her naked skin. Her cheeks heated. Jason must have removed her bathing suit. Her cheeks burned. He'd already seen her without clothes, but that had been in the heat of passion. Had he noticed the extra ten pounds she wanted to lose or the way her stomach rounded after their son's birth?

Her stomach growled. She looked at the clock. Past midnight. She'd missed supper, and her stomach demanded food. Lupita kept the refrigerator filled with snacks and had told her to help herself.

She put on her favorite nightgown, a figure-hugging, silk floor-length negligee with tight fitted sleeves. She loved the lush fabric brushing over her skin. Although it wasn't as luscious as Jason's mouth sliding over her body. Her stomach rumbled again. Food.

Beth went to the kitchen. Instead of disturbing the night with harsh lights, she used the glow of the moon to find her way. She opened the refrigerator and hunted for a snack. Cheesecake. Yummy. It was in a Delectable Delights box, so it must be one of Erik's creations.

She turned to get a knife and collided with a wall of hard muscle. Jason. Embarrassed to be caught raiding the refrigerator, she mumbled, "I was hungry."

She looked at him and felt the heat of a blush wash over her face. He wore slacks with no shirt or shoes. His hair was a sexy mess as though he'd just gotten out of bed. She swallowed. No man should look so delicious.

He nodded. "I'm not surprised."

"You're not?"

"You haven't eaten all day. I tried to wake you for dinner, but you made it clear you didn't want to be disturbed." He grinned. "You were snoring when I left your room."

She giggled. "I don't snore."

"Yes, you do. It's a cute little noise, but definitely a snore."

She tilted her head and smiled. "Do you want a piece of cheesecake?"

"Yes. I'll have coffee with mine." He asked, "Do you want a cup?"

"Is there enough for both of us?"

"Lupita makes a fresh pot if I work late." Jason walked to the opposite counter. "I'll pour the coffee while you cut the cheesecake."

They worked together to put the cheesecake and coffee on the table. He lit a candle and set it on the table next to a peach rose in a crystal bud vase.

With everything on the table, they sat next to each other. Beth took a bite of cheesecake, closed her eyes, and savored the flavor of the caramel macchiato cheesecake. "I love Erik's cheesecake. He tries new combinations and creates desserts that are decadent. I told him he has to stop or I'll weigh two hundred and fifty pounds."

"Lupita is still worried you aren't eating enough and called the shop. They put together a bag of goodies to tempt you. I guess it worked." Jason took a slow, deep breath. "Why didn't you show me the letters sooner?"

Beth shrugged. "It felt like you wanted to blame me. Besides, I wasn't sure they would change your mind."

"You were right."

She dropped her head and stared at the table to hide the pain those words inflicted. "You still think I'm lying?"

"No, that's not what I meant." He shifted in his seat. "I made you prove you were telling the truth, but I expected you to believe everything I said. I demanded your trust, but never gave mine in return. Can you forgive me?"

"Do you believe me now? Even the things I can't prove?"

"I do."

"Why?" She narrowed her eyes. "Because of the letters?"

"The letters proved what I already knew, but didn't want to admit. You're the same person I met twelve years ago. The one person who never cared who my parents were, or where I lived."

"Those things never mattered. Besides, my father may not have hit me, but he stomped all over my self-confidence."

He grimaced. "It's true that Archer manipulated us, but he wouldn't have succeeded if I'd had more faith in you."

"My loving father. All my life I wanted his love and approval but was never good enough to satisfy him. I thought the fault was mine. That, if I tried harder, I could make him care." She heaved a heavy sigh. "Now I wonder if he ever loved me."

"Don't waste your concern on him. He's not worth it." Jason pulled her onto his lap. "We'll find Daniel, and we won't let Archer stop us. Now that we know what he's done, we won't let him manipulate us any longer. Although there's one question I would like answered."

"What's that?"

"Who sent the anonymous letter and why?"

CHAPTER TWELVE

Jason watched her and brushed circles on her back. When she ran her tongue across her lips, he leaned in and stole her breath. When she opened to him, he slipped his tongue in and she lost herself in his heat. As he deepened the kiss, she slid her arms around his shoulders and pulled him closer.

He stroked her tongue and the inside of her mouth. Need flared at her core. Then he slipped a hand between them to cup her breast, and she made a soft mewling sound. When she shifted her hips, the globes of her butt pressed against the bulge of his cock.

"I want to make love to you." He cupped her cheek. "Tell me that's what you want."

She held out a hand. "So much I'm shaking."

He pulled her close and touched his forehead to hers. "Thank heaven."

Beth brushed her mouth over Jason's then kissed him with the hunger that flowed through her veins. His lips were hot on hers, and she couldn't get enough. She wanted to make love to him for the rest of her life, but she'd take whatever he offered. If they had only one night, she'd treasure it.

He pulled away.

Beth tried to pull him back. "What—"

"The table doesn't look very comfortable."

"The table?" Her eyes popped open, and her cheeks heated. "Oh."

"Yeah. Oh." He grinned and helped her to her feet. Then he took her hand and rushed to the study. She had to run to keep up and giggled at his impatience. He locked the door and pulled her to the sofa. Her body shook when his hands swept over her.

"This negligee is stunning, but now I want to feel your skin against mine."

He undid the button at the back and brushed the fabric off her shoulders. Her negligee drifted down her body until it pooled at her feet. He stepped back and his gaze brushed over her like a warm caress.

Beth reached for him. "Please."

Jason stepped close and kissed her with a fierceness that stole the breath from her body. Lust flooded her senses. Afraid she'd fall, Beth held onto his shoulders. He nipped at her lips before his tongue slipped into her mouth to caress and tease her.

When he cupped her breasts and rolled her nipples between his fingers, she moaned and arched her back. Then he leaned down and sucked on first one nipple then the other. Chills raced through her body from her head to her toes.

She pulled on him. "I need you in me."

He took a step back. Beth wobbled but stayed on her feet. She watched him as he pulled off his pants. When he stepped out of them, she wrapped her fingers around his erection.

His shaft jerked, and he muttered, "Tighter."

She tightened her hold, and he moaned.

When his head dropped forward, she fell to her knees. He lifted his head and looked at her. She gave him her most seductive smile. She ran her tongue along the blue vein from the base of his cock to the tip. When she reached the tip, a drop of cream oozed out of the tiny slit. Her tongue circled the purple head, and she licked it to catch the milky drop on her tongue. When he sucked in a breath, she took him into her mouth.

He growled, "Yes."

Beth sucked harder. When she swallowed, he moaned and fisted his hands. He rocked his hips working his shaft in and out of her mouth. She wanted to tease him and used her tongue to glide over the ridges of his shaft slow and easy.

"Enough!" He took a step back and pulled out of her mouth.

She frowned. "What's wrong?"

"I want to be inside you when I come."

"Oh."

"But first...it's my turn." He helped her to stand. Wrapping his arms around her, he lifted her off her feet. She leaned in to kiss him and wrapped her legs around his waist. With a sigh, she savored his taste and the satin softness of his lips. So lost in his kiss, she jerked when she felt the sofa under her. She laid back and shifted her hips.

Jason knelt between her legs then leaned over her. He teased her, brushing his mouth back and forth over her lips until she caught his bottom lip and nipped at it. Beth savored his kiss and felt the cream pool between her thighs. She ached to have his body fill her, and she lifted her hips to rub against him. "Please...."

"Soon." He placed light kisses on her eyes, cheeks, and ears. His mouth drifted over the skin of her throat until he got to that sensitive spot where her neck and shoulder met. He swirled circles with his tongue. Pleasure, fierce and wicked, streaked through her body.

Jason fondled Beth's breasts. When he rolled and pinched her nipples, she arched her back. He slipped from one breast to the other and used his teeth to tease her. Her muscles grew taut, and her back lifted off the sofa.

When his mouth left her breasts, she whimpered until he moved down her body scattering kisses on her ribs and stomach. His lips reached her slit and, before she could protest, he ran his tongue through her damp curls. She writhed at the erotic caress then gasped when his tongue stroked her clit. Nothing in her life prepared her for the intimacy of this act.

A heartbeat later, he pushed a finger into her sheath. Her hips bucked as she tried to force him deeper. Pleasure took command of her body and flung her into a whirlpool of intense sensation.

When he slipped a second finger in, her heart pounded a frantic beat. Jason leaned over her and swirled his tongue in her cream. Her breath came in short, desperate gasps, as she fought to survive the furor that gripped her body. She jerked her hips to meet his strokes desperate to release the tension building in every nerve and muscle of her body.

Then he pinched her sensitive nub, the air rushed from her lungs, and she shattered. She dug her nails into his shoulders while the walls of her pussy rippled around his fingers. He sucked on her slit to draw out each flutter of her orgasm.

She struggled to get air into her lungs, and as he crawled up her body, he nuzzled, licked, and tasted her skin until he reached her mouth. He took her lips in a kiss more passionate than any they'd shared. A kiss that left its imprint on her soul.

Jason slid his shaft over her slit coating it in her cream before he slid into her. He stroked in and out, in and out. His cock rasped over the sensitive walls of her heat. Beth wrapped her legs around his waist and lifted to meet his thrusts. Then she slid her hands around to his back.

In a few short strokes, he had her desperate for his possession. When she tightened her legs, his cock sunk deeper. Jason grunted, and his thrusts came faster. Desperate for orgasm, their demands turned savage.

They moved together in a hot, frenzied rhythm. Jason slipped his hands under Beth's hips. With his next thrust, he pushed so deep shivers raced through every part of her body. The muscles in her pussy clenched around his cock, and her world exploded. She rode the violent waves of her orgasm.

As though from a distance, Beth heard Jason roar her name. His hot seed pulsed into her and sent another wave of shudders through her body. Every part of her hummed with satisfaction. When he dropped to her side, she felt the heat radiate from his body.

Sweat covered Jason's brow, and his heart pounded a wild beat. After a deep breath, he draped an arm over her stomach. Eyes narrowed to slits, he looked at a sleeping Beth and smiled. Her beauty dazzled him, but her courage and spirit captivated him.

Their lovemaking had been so much more than he expected, but he already wanted her again. Only this time he didn't want to worry that they'd fall off the sofa. He stood and lifted her into his arms. She didn't wake, but a sweet smile curled her lips.

As he carried her to bed, he grinned at the cute not-quite-a-snore she made. Nine years ago, what they shared had been special because it had been young, innocent. But tonight had been much more. Their loving tonight held a promise of what they could have if they were willing to take a second chance to make a life together.

Careful not to wake her, Jason settled Beth in bed and climbed in next to her. Propped on one arm, he watched her. She'd survived the manipulation and betrayal of the past with her heart intact. Archer hadn't crushed the spirit of the young girl or the generous, loving woman she'd become.

Beth whimpered, and her body thrashed. Was this another nightmare of the accident? He pulled her close and brushed her hair back. "Shh. Sleep, Angel. I'll keep you safe."

She snuggled into his chest and sighed.

Jason wanted her to sleep next to him for the rest of his life. He needed a plan. What would it take to make her his?

In the morning, Jason woke to Beth with her arm and leg thrown over him. His stiff cock made its approval known, but he'd scheduled an early teleconference he couldn't miss. Jason slid out of bed to shower and dress. He kissed her forehead and forced himself to leave.

Two hours later, Jason's meeting ended, and he studied a proposal. Then a soft knock caught his attention, and he looked up to see Beth at the door. He rushed over and kissed her. With his arm around her, they went to breakfast.

After they had served themselves, Jason said, "I had an idea. Gabriel needs the information your father has, and Archer will never give it to us. There has to be a way we can get it." He paused. "Could we search his office?"

Beth gave him a sly smile. "I presume without him knowing?"

"That's my preference." Jason chuckled. "Archer manages every detail of his projects—even the minor ones. Someone that controlling wouldn't have trusted anyone else to handle the arrangements for the birth and adoption. Somewhere he must have the names and addresses of the people involved."

Beth's eyes lit with excitement, and she grabbed his hand. "You're right. When I was in high school, he lectured me if I didn't get the best grade in class. He had information about the classes I took, the names of my teachers, even the names of my classmates."

"Do you have any idea where he might keep the information about your pregnancy?"

"He has three file cabinets in his office that are locked. That must be where he keeps his important papers. He also has a safe, but I don't think even Mother knows the combination."

Jason rubbed his chin. "The pregnancy is old business. He has no reason to keep the file in the safe."

"There's a chance he keeps the information on his computer."

"Without his passwords, we couldn't get into the system to search."

Beth looked lost in thought. Then she said, "Tomorrow evening there's a birthday party for my mother. The house will be full of guests, most will be business associates, and Archer will play lord of the manor. He'll have someone at the door to be certain no one goes into his office, but I can get into the room."

Jason frowned. "No, I don't want to risk Archer catching you digging through his files. He's more volatile than you know. In the business world, his temper is legendary."

"What if you search?"

He nodded. "An excellent idea. How do I get in his office?"

"I'll drive to the party, and you'll hide in the back seat. I'll park in the rear of the house, near the office. After I've been at the party for a while, I'll go to Archer's office and unlock the doors to the patio. You'll be able to get in and search. You let me know when you're done, and I'll go back to lock the doors. If nothing is disturbed, Archer won't know you were there."

"This could work." He scratched the back of his neck. "How did you come up with this plan so fast?"

"I've been thinking about it for a while."

"Why would you do that?"

"I know Archer has the information I need to find Daniel." She straightened her back. "The investigators may have given up, but I won't stop until I find him."

Jason rubbed a hand over her shoulders. "We have thirty-six hours until the party. Enough time to work out the details. Can you make a diagram of Archer's office?"

"Yes. I'll make one of the house too. In case something goes wrong."

They walked out to the hall. "While you do that, I have to finish my review of two proposals. Then we can discuss the details of the plan, and you can help me memorize the diagram."

"All right. I want to change and sit by the pool while I draw. Let me know when you're ready to talk."

"This will work." Jason pulled her close and took her mouth in a heated kiss. He'd prefer to spend the day in bed with her legs wrapped around him, but he had to read through two contracts and get the changes back to his people today.

Jason's work took until lunch to finish. He looked out the patio doors expecting to see Beth by the pool, but she wasn't there. His heart hammered with a frantic beat. Had she taken his car again? He ran to the garage. As he raced past the living room, he glanced in and came to an abrupt stop. She sat on the floor with papers scattered around her.

She looked up and gave him a bright smile.

He rolled his shoulders and let out a shaky breath. Now certain he wanted to make a life with her, he worried she'd leave before he convinced her to give him another chance.

After lunch, they went to the study and sat on the sofa.

He chuckled. "That's a sweet shade of pink on your cheeks."

Her nose wrinkled, and his laughter filled the room. She pursed her lips while she handed him several sheets of paper. He looked at the drawing of her parents' house and Archer's office. With her help, he studied and memorized the layout of the rooms, especially the office.

"Will Archer get suspicious if I'm not at the party with you?"

"He'll strut all night proud that he intimidated you." She chuckled. "He'd never guess you were searching his office."

"I don't know if it's a good idea to let you go in there without me." Jason pulled her close and cupped her cheek. "Who'll discourage the men who try to sweep you off your feet?"

"They don't matter. Never have."

He kissed her long and hard. She grabbed his arms and hung on. When he leaned back to catch a breath, he said, "Don't want you to forget who's waiting for you."

"You're hard to forget." Beth tightened her arms around his neck and slid her lips over his chin. "There's been no other man since the day we met."

"Let's go upstairs." He ran his tongue in circles around her ear. "I want to feast on your luscious body."

She hummed with pleasure then followed him from the room. After several stops to kiss and tease each other, they made it to his bedroom.

Jason huffed. "Finally."

She laughed as he removed her shirt and the lace demi-bra.

"So beautiful." He cupped the soft-as-velvet mounds. "So perfect."

Jason blew a soft breath over her nipples and watched them tighten. Eager to press her skin against his, he wrestled with his shirt. At the sound of fabric ripping, he rolled his eyes while Beth laughed. He tossed the shirt aside and pulled her close.

He shifted her from side to side sliding her breasts over his chest. His eyes closed as he delighted in her silky softness. When she nipped at his lower lip, his eyes jerked open. He breathed in short, shaky gasps and fought to maintain his control. Beth deserved a slow, gentle loving, but if he didn't get them on the bed, he'd take her against the wall with a great deal of passion but little finesse.

Jason stepped back and grinned when she whimpered. He wanted nothing between them and unzipped her pants to push them to the floor along with her lace panties. His fingers were clumsy, but he pulled off the rest of his clothes.

As she stepped into his arms, her body rubbed against his, and he sucked in the air his lungs needed.

Her hands drifted over his shoulders, chest, and stomach until she reached his cock. With a coquettish tilt of her lips, she drew circles on the head of his shaft. A sexy smile on her face, she clasped his shaft then stroked up and down.

Beth released her hold on him and crawled onto the bed. When she leaned back on her elbows and spread her legs wide, he grinned. He did not intend to deny the invitation.

Jason knelt between her legs and let his hands skate over her thighs until he reached her mound. His thumb circled her slit, and her head dropped back. He spread her cream and dipped his fingers into her. She dropped back and lifted her hips.

"Oh, yes." She rolled her head.

"Don't move. Let me do the work." Jason pressed his palm against her mound, and her moans got louder. He pressed the palm of his hand against her clit, and she squirmed.

"Don't make me wait."

"I want to take my time and make slow, gentle love to you."

"But it feels so good." Beth squirmed. "Go slow next time."

He slid his cream-coated fingers out of her warmth and gripped his shaft. After he spread her juice over it, he stared into Beth's eyes as he stroked himself. Then she licked her lips, and his control snapped.

Jason shifted his hips and plunged his slick cock into her heat. She moaned each time her mound rubbed against his pelvis. On his next stroke, he slid so deep into her channel that his balls slapped against her skin.

Worried, he asked, "Am I hurting—?"

"Don't—stop."

He established a rhythm—thrust, retreat, do it again. When he fondled Beth's breasts, her moans got louder as she reached for orgasm. When he tweaked her nipples, she arched her back and climaxed. Her pussy clamped around his erection, and his hips bucked. He slammed into her, once, twice, three times and groaned as he came.

It was late the next morning when Jason woke. Beth still slept. They'd made love throughout the night. The sky had begun to lighten when, too tired to do more than wrap their arms around each other, they'd fallen asleep.

Jason propped his head on one arm and looked down at Beth. The time he'd spent with her breathed new life into his dreams for a wife and children. He'd be a fool to throw away this gift. Jason had been called many things, but fool was not one of them.

He brushed a strand of hair off her face. Could she love him again? She couldn't have lost herself in his arms if she didn't care for him, but did she want to spend her life with him? He could never settle for marrying for Daniel's sake. It would never be enough for him. He wanted everything. He wanted love.

Her eyes fluttered open.

"Good morning." He smiled.

She moved to roll into his arms but whimpered.

"What's wrong?"

Her cheeks glowed a bright red, and she stared at his chest. "I'm a little—sore."

"It's my fault. I couldn't get enough of you, and now you're paying for my exuberance."

"I wanted you too." She grinned. "You weren't in bed alone."

"For that, I thank you." He laughed and brushed his thumb over her lips. "You said I was your only lover, but what about your husband?"

"I told you he was sterile."

Jason nodded.

"He was also impotent."

"Did your father know about Jacob's issues when he arranged your marriage?"

"Yes, but he wanted his company and used me to get it. Jacob accepted Archer's offer because he wanted a wife. He'd been engaged, but his fiancée broke their engagement after he told her about his condition. He lived with his shame for years. I told him it didn't matter, but he never believed me."

"You cared about him?"

"I did. Even though we married for other reasons, he loved me in his own way and treated me with more respect than my father ever did." She shook her head. "He didn't deserve what Archer did to him."

"Neither did you." He kissed her. "While I'm taking a shower, I'll fill the whirlpool bath. A long soak will relieve the soreness."

"That would be wonderful."

"Before I phone the office, I'll ask Lupita to make breakfast. My call shouldn't last more than an hour. Will that be enough time?"

"If I soak any longer, I'll look like a prune."

"On your worst day, you couldn't be anything but beautiful."

Jason stole one last kiss. He showered and dressed, but the whole time he planned his strategy to win the most important prize of his life—Beth.

CHAPTER THIRTEEN

Beth and Jason discussed their plans. He memorized the layout of her parents' home. They shared ideas about where Archer kept his files other than in the cabinets. Beth worried that the information they wanted would be in the computer.

"If you want to get into his computer, I am sure you will need a password." Beth gave Jason a list of birthdays and anniversaries. "He might have used one of these, or a combination of them, as his password."

But they both knew the chance of Jason accessing Archer's electronic files was slim to none.

After lunch, Marco drove Beth to her home to get a gown for the party. The bedroom looked as though her closet exploded by the time she narrowed her choice to four. When she got back to Jason's house, she tried to nap but was too nervous to sleep.

By the time she dressed for the party, Beth's stomach ached. She wore the white silk, a Grecian-style gown that left her right shoulder bare. She arranged her hair in a loose upsweep of curls that draped over her bare shoulder. With a fond smile for her grandmother, she wore the pearl and diamond earrings Nana had given her for her eighteenth birthday. To complete the outfit, she wore a pair of strappy shoes with four-inch heels.

She looked in the mirror and smiled, but it disappeared a moment later. No matter how she looked, Archer found something to criticize. She took a deep breath, picked up her pearl beaded evening bag, the gift-wrapped box, and left her room.

When Beth reached the top of the stairs, she saw Jason pacing in the hall. As she walked down the stairs, her shoes clicked on the wood floor. Jason turned and watched her. She stopped on the last step to smooth her dress before she checked his reaction.

Jason's gaze slid over her, soft and warm, like a summer breeze. Beth took the hand he held out as she stepped off the bottom stair. With a twirl of his hand, he turned her in a circle.

She laughed in delight. "Don't you think the cast adds a certain flair to the outfit?"

"Think? Who can think? You're breathtaking." He frowned. "You'll turn heads at the party, and I won't be able to warn your admirers to keep their distance."

She kissed his cheek. "You're such a sweet-talker."

Beth stepped back and crossed her arms. He wore black jeans that hugged his long legs with a black tee shirt that showcased his chest and stomach. "You could play the handsome thief in that movie I watched the other day."

"Well, I try to dress appropriately for all occasions." He frowned. "Are you sure you don't want to eat before we leave?"

"No, I'm too nervous. If I get hungry, I'll have hors d'oeuvres at the party."

"Our plan will work." He squeezed her hand. "Archer will play the loving husband and gracious host, and nothing will pull him from the spotlight. It's the perfect time to search."

She squeezed his hand. "Promise you'll be careful. I couldn't bear it if something happened to you."

"I'll be fine." He tucked her hand into the crook of his arm. "Let's go to a birthday party."

Beth drove Jason's car while he sat on the floor behind her seat. Her hands grasped the steering wheel. "Remember, I'll turn the lights on when I go into the office and unlock the patio doors after the butler leaves. I'll forget my purse in Archer's office so I can go back and lock them. Don't forget to send me a text message when you get back to the car. You've got to find the information we need. What will we do if Archer catches—?"

"Angel, breathe."

"But—"

"If I don't find Archer's files on the adoption, it might take longer to locate Daniel, but we won't give up our search until we have him home with us."

"I'm almost at the house. Slide down and hide under the blanket."

She pulled up to the gate. The guard recognized her and waved. Beth returned his wave and drove to the house.

"The valets are parking guests' cars at the side of the house. I'll go around behind the house." She parked the car. "No one else is back here. The car is outside the office doors. Be sure you're alone before you get out of the car and don't forget to send me a text."

A hand snaked over the seat and rubbed her shoulder. "Everything will be fine."

She exhaled, loudly, and got out of the car. On her walk to the front of the house, the butterflies in her stomach became dive bombers. At the door, she lifted her chin and rang the bell. The door swung open.

"Miss Elizabeth, it's good to see you." The butler welcomed her.

"Thank you. How's that adorable grandson of yours?"

"He's well, miss, thank you for asking."

Beth walked to the ballroom. She stopped at the entrance and looked around for her parents. They were across the room. Her father stood with a man who waved his hands and stabbed at Archer with his finger. He looked angry and desperate. Her mother watched the two men and looked uncomfortable. *Is father trying to steal another company?*

Beth crossed the room to her mother. Along the way, she stopped to chat with friends and acquaintances. She received several invitations to dance but refused with a polite no. Beth grinned when she heard whispered mumbles of *Frost Queen,* the nickname her disappointed suitors had given her. Their jaws would drop if they knew how she'd melted in Jason's arms last night.

Deidre hugged her. "I am so glad you could join us. How are you?"

"Fine, but I'm eager to get this cast removed."

Archer turned his back on the angry man and glared. "How good of you to grace us with your presence."

"Father, it's lovely to see you, too." She turned and handed her mother a gift. "Happy birthday. I know it's a tradition to open your gifts after dinner, but will you open mine now?"

Archer sneered. "It would be inappropriate to open it now. Deidre will open it later along with her other gifts."

Her mother waved her hand. "Nonsense." She untied the ribbon around the small jewelry box and gasped when she lifted out the gold and diamond pendant of a mother holding a child. A tear slid down her cheek, but a broad smile lit her face.

Archer scolded, "Deidre, you're making a spectacle of yourself."

Her mother pulled her into a tight hug. "I love it. Help me put it on, will you?" Deidre held the pendant while Beth hooked the clasp and straightened the pendant.

Deidre clasped Beth's hands. "It is beautiful. Thank you."

Since her accident, Beth felt closer to her mother than she had in years. When she was a young girl, her mother had tucked her into bed at night and told her stories. She'd become distant as Beth got older. But since the accident, they talked and enjoyed spending time together again.

"I'll talk to you later." She kissed her mother's cheek. "I want a glass of wine."

Beth waited for her drink aware that Archer watched her. He couldn't know of their plan. The bartender handed her a glass of wine, and she took a sip.

After taking a deep breath to settle her nerves, she went to mingle and chat with the guests. Most of the people at the party were Archer's business associates, but a few guests were friends, like the mayor and other council members.

Ten minutes later she looked over to see her father once again in a heated discussion with the man he'd talked to earlier. She slipped away and went to his office. As she expected, a butler stood guard in front of the door. Beth forced a smile.

"Hello, Philip."

"Good evening, Miss Elizabeth."

"I've developed a dreadful headache. I need a few minutes of quiet and thought I'd go into the office."

"Would you like me to get you something for your pain?"

"No, thank you. I already took two aspirins."

He opened the door and turned on the lights. "I'll be sure you're not bothered."

"Thank you, Philip."

As soon as he closed the door, she set her purse behind a lamp and hurried to unlock the terrace doors. Then she went to the sofa and sat with her hands clenched tight. Her heart pounded an erratic beat.

The patio door opened with a soft swish, and Jason slipped into the room. After he closed the door, he straightened the curtains and crossed to her.

He knelt in front of her. "How are you?"

She shrugged.

"Don't do that." He lifted her chin. "I know you don't want to be here, and Archer will be difficult, but you can do this."

"I've had years to learn to deal with father." Beth put a hand over her heart. "It was Mother who surprised me. I gave her a birthday gift, and she cried. I haven't felt this close to her since I was a little girl."

"Your accident scared her. I think she regrets the strain in your relationship." Jason ran his thumb over her cheek. "You should get back out there. We don't want Archer to wonder where you've gone."

"Hide in case Philip checks the room after I leave." She got to her feet. "Don't forget to send me a text."

"I won't forget." He kissed her forehead then hid behind the file cabinets.

Beth pasted a smile on and walked out.

Jason studied the room. It had the warmth of a warehouse showroom filled with ostentatious oak furniture. The furniture looked new, and the leather-bound books in the floor-to-ceiling bookcases showed no wear as though they'd never been opened. An overly large executive desk with a leather chair behind it dominated the room.

He waited five minutes before beginning his search. Jason powered-on Archer's computer, but hoped he wouldn't have to guess the password.

Jason combed through the papers and folders in the desk drawers. He searched every drawer but didn't find even a slip of paper that mentioned Beth or Daniel. When Jason reached the last drawer, he raised an eyebrow in surprise. He'd found a file for Archer's Chicago project. He skimmed through it.

What he read confirmed the information Jackson had provided on Archer's finances. If he didn't shore up the Chicago project, he'd have to file bankruptcy in six months. With the twenty-five million Archer wanted from him, he could keep the project afloat for another year. Long enough to bring in a few more investors whose money he could embezzle to line his pockets. Jason returned the file to the drawer.

He moved to the locked file cabinets and used his picks to open them. He searched through the folders and papers. His shoulders slumped. The only papers in the drawers were bills, receipts, and bank statements. He locked the cabinets.

Discouraged, Jason checked his watch. He'd searched for forty minutes and was almost out of time. Either Archer hid the files somewhere else, or they were in the computer. He checked the computer and saw the flashing cursor, with a request for a password. He tried family names, dates of birth, and various combinations with no luck.

Jason rubbed the back of his neck. Even if Archer kept the information on the computer, he'd have backup copies somewhere. There was no external hard drive, and he didn't think Archer would store his information on the internet.

He crossed the room to the bookcases. Maybe he has copies of the files hidden behind the books. He pulled out two books, and a disk fell from The Merchant of Venice. He picked up the disk. It had *Venice Mall* written on it. That was the name of the Chicago project, the one Archer wanted him to finance. Did he keep all his backup disks in books? He pulled out a copy of King Lear. In it was a disk with *A.K. Industries–2015* written on it.

He read the names of the books on the shelf. Elizabeth I. When he opened it, there was a disk with *Elizabeth–Disk Two* written on it. There had to be a disk one. He looked for similar books and found Elizabeth Tudor, but there was no disk. Then he pulled The Young Elizabeth. Sure enough, inside was another disk with *Elizabeth–Disk One* written on it.

Jason put the disks in his jacket and re-shelved the books. Grateful he didn't have to figure out Archer's password, he turned off the computer. He looked around the room. Nothing appeared to be out of place. When he peeked outside, he didn't see anyone and ran to the car.

Beth walked around to chat with the guests and sipped her wine. When her phone vibrated, she excused herself and moved to a quiet corner. "Dinner tonight? J." A relieved breath rushed from her lungs.

Archer was at the back of the room looking out the window. She used his distraction to return to his office. Philip still guarded the door.

She gave him a bright smile. "I forgot my purse when I was here earlier."

He opened the door for her. Beth waited until he closed it then rushed to lock the patio doors and straighten the drapes. She checked the room. Archer never left papers on his desk or cabinets, and Jason hadn't left any out. Beth took a deep breath to calm her nerves, grabbed her purse, and left the office.

Years of Archer's training served her well. She returned to the ballroom with her smile in place and certain she looked every inch the Frost Queen they called her. Fifteen minutes later, impatient to leave, she said goodbye to her friends.

She went to her mother. "I've enjoyed the party, but it's time for me to go."

"Of course, darling. You need your rest." Deidre clasped her hands. "I'm glad you came. Now that you're feeling better, perhaps we could have lunch?"

"I'd like that. I'll call you in a day or two."

"Wonderful." Deidre kissed her cheek.

Outside, the valet said, "I'll get your car."

Her muscles tensed. "Thank you, but I'd rather walk and get some fresh air."

"Then I'll walk with you to be sure you're not bothered."

Beth chewed on her bottom lip worried the valet might see Jason. Then the front door opened, and a couple walked out. The tension left her shoulders, and she said, "You should help them."

"I'll watch until you get to your car to be certain you're safe."

She thanked him and walked to her car. She got in and shut the door. "Stay on the floor. I'm being watched."

Beth waved as she drove past the valet. She pulled onto the road and, when they were clear, she asked, "Was there any information about Daniel's birth or adoption? Did you find the name of the attorney Archer hired? Were you able to get into his computer? Tell me you found something—anything."

"I found two disks, but didn't have time to check them." He laid a hand on her shoulder. "Can I sit up now? I feel like a pretzel. They didn't design this floor for comfort."

Beth laughed and released the tension that had gripped her. After she parked in front of the house, Jason opened her door. She jumped out, threw her arms around his neck, and squealed, "We did it!"

"Yes, we did. It was a good plan."

Laughing, she did a jig. "I was so afraid it wouldn't work."

Jason chuckled. "You are officially a master thief. Now let's check the disks."

Happy smiles on their faces, they walked to the study. Jason pulled a chair next to his and together they sat by the computer. He hit the power button then took the disks from his pocket.

Beth's mouth fell open. "How were you able to get into Archer's computer files? Did you guess his password?"

"I didn't have to get into his computer." He explained how Archer hid the disks in his books. "I doubt he'll notice they're not there."

He inserted Disk Two. When the computer loaded the disk, it asked for a password.

She moaned. "We'll never figure out his passwords."

"Don't give up now. Let's start with the obvious ones like birth dates."

Jason tried Archer's, Deidre's, and Beth's birthdays, backward and forward. No success. He tried names with birthdays. No luck.

She slumped in her chair. "We'll never unlock the files."

"Why don't you—"

Someone kicked on the study door. Beth grabbed his arm.

He patted her hand. "It's only Lupita. She kicks if her hands are full." He went to open the door. Sure enough, Lupita waited with a tray.

Beth went to help Lupita. She'd prepared tomato and mozzarella bruschetta, Florentine artichoke dip with pita chips, slices of cheesecake, and coffee. She put an arm around Lupita's shoulders. "You are a treasure. If you ever leave Jason, you can come to work for me."

Jason slid his arm around Lupita's waist. "I wouldn't survive without her and Marco to take care of me."

Lupita laughed then pointed a finger at Jason. "You make sure the Senora eats. She needs to build up her strength." Lupita turned to her. "If you don't eat, your mother will worry."

Beth smiled and took another spoonful of dip.

He poured coffee into their cups while she filled two plates with food. They returned to their chairs and discussed possible passwords while they ate.

She said, "We tried birthdays and names, let's try common passwords."

"What are those?"

With a grin, she did a quick internet search and found lists of common passwords.

Jason typed letter and number combinations, but *Please Enter a Valid Password* kept flashing on the screen. An hour later, they still hadn't figured out the password.

"Maybe Archer used the books for more than storing the disks," Beth said. "Try the title of the book or the name of the author."

The title didn't work. Neither of them knew the author of Elizabeth I, but a quick search on the internet produced the name. A few keystrokes later a list of files appeared on the screen.

"Yes!" They hugged each other.

When they read through the list of files, Beth gasped.

Startled, Jason turned to her. "What's wrong?"

"There's a folder for each investigator I hired."

"Did you tell Archer that you were hiring them?"

With a slow shake of her head, she said, "No. I was afraid he would try to stop me."

He clicked on a folder titled *Anderson.* "There are notes and spreadsheets. Look at this. It's a list of dates and amounts."

"The first date is two days before he quit. Archer paid him to give up his search. He must have bought off all the investigators who worked for me, even the man Jacob hired. He sabotaged my search for Daniel." Beth pressed her lips together. "Is having an illegitimate grandson so horrible?"

"When we talked to your parents, Archer made no secret that he wanted to keep Daniel's existence hidden."

"I never thought—" She pointed to the computer screen. "Look, there's a folder for Gabriel."

He clicked to open the folder. "There isn't much in it, except a copy of an email to an investigator."

Beth said, "He hired an investigator to check into Gabriel's background. If he finds something, he'll use it to force him to quit, and we'll never find Daniel."

"Gabriel Michael isn't a man who is easy to intimidate."

"I don't understand why father wants to stop me from finding Daniel?" Beth shivered and wrapped her arms around her waist.

"Drink this." Jason handed her a glass of cognac.

She sniffled and set the glass on the desk. "I don't want anything."

"You'll feel better if you have a drink."

She sipped the liquor. It warmed her and soothed her jangled nerves.

He wrapped his arm around her shoulder and kissed her forehead. "Gabriel told us he never gives up an investigation once he accepts a case. Those thugs didn't scare him, and Archer won't either."

She nodded.

"Let's look at the other disk." Jason closed Disk Two and inserted Disk One.

She prayed it contained the information they needed to find Daniel. This time when the program asked for the password, Jason entered the author's name. He pulled up a long list of folders. He printed it so they could study the list.

His brows dipped into a vee. "Didn't you say you had the baby at Boston Hospital?"

"Yes. Boston City Hospital."

"It says you gave birth at Massachusetts General Hospital." He asked, "Did you go there?"

"No. Maybe my parents considered it as an alternative. Open the file."

He clicked on the icon, and the document opened.

She said, "According to this information, Archer had Daniel transferred to Massachusetts General. The attorney for the people who adopted him received a birth certificate that shows Massachusetts General as the hospital where he was born."

Beth read through the notes again. "Why move him?"

"An added precaution," said Jason. "Our son's name was recorded as Daniel Doe. There's no reference to the couple who adopted him or their attorney."

"How did father arrange this?"

"I don't know. I'd guess he bribed somebody." Jason stretched then looked at his watch. "It's close to three o'clock. We're too tired to make sense of this now. We can dig through the files in the morning after we've slept."

She yawned. "That's a good idea."

"Will you sleep with me? I'll rest easier if you're with me."

"I'd like that." Beth leaned against Jason's shoulder.

"Tomorrow, after we've looked at the files, we'll call Gabriel. He needs to know about the payoffs to the investigators and the investigator Archer hired to check on him."

"I still can't believe father paid those men to give up their searches. He doesn't care about anyone but himself." She wiped her eyes. "I thought he couldn't hurt me anymore."

Jason pressed his lips to her forehead. "Let it go for tonight. We'll deal with it after we've rested."

When they reached the balcony, she tried to step away, but he held her close.

"I have to get a nightgown."

"You won't need one." He wiggled his eyebrows. "You have your own personal heater."

The next morning, she woke when Jason climbed out of bed. "What time is it?"

"I have a teleconference with my executive staff. It'll take at least two hours." He pressed his lips to hers in a soft kiss. "In the meantime, why don't you rest? If you're not downstairs by the time I've finished my meeting, I'll be happy to wake you."

Her eyes closed. "Good idea."

Later, Beth stretched and sighed. Although she'd fallen back to sleep after Jason left, she slept better when he was next to her. When he held her, she didn't have the nightmares that haunted her nights for the last eight years.

Beth checked the time. Two hours since Jason had gone to his meeting. It should have ended by now. Desperate for a shower, she wrapped herself in one of Jason's shirts. She peeked out the door and hoped Lupita was in the kitchen. Beth laughed as she ran to her room.

After Beth showered and dressed, she went to Jason's study.

He frowned. "I am very disappointed. I wanted to wake you."

"You can wake me tomorrow. Now, we should call Gabriel."

"First, I'll let Lupita know we're hungry." He dialed and a moment later said, "Sleeping Beauty is awake. We have to call Gabriel, but then we'd love breakfast."

Beth whispered, "Sleeping Beauty?"

A smile curled his lips. "Great. We'll have coffee in the breakfast room while we wait." He dialed again.

"Michael."

"You're on the speaker, and Beth is with me."

"I have nothing to report. When I tried to get into the hospital records, they were reluctant to cooperate."

Beth said, "Jason found some information, but I don't know if it will help or make your job more difficult."

"Information, good or bad, provides leads," Gabriel said. "What do you have?"

Jason answered. "Beth is sure the birth took place at Boston City Hospital, but Archer had the baby transferred to Massachusetts General. The couple who adopted him received a forged birth certificate. It showed Massachusetts General as his place of birth, and the baby's name as Daniel Doe."

Gabriel said, "So your talk with Beth's parents went well?"

"Not really." She cleared her throat. "We had to *borrow* Archer's files."

Gabriel chuckled. "Sometimes that's how we get our best leads."

"There's more. Something we thought you needed to know." Jason said.

"That sounds ominous."

"Archer hired an investigator to check into your background. I'd guess he wants to find information he can use to blackmail you to get you off this case."

"Good for him." Gabriel snorted. "Let me know what he finds. I've searched for years."

Jason and Beth stared at each other.

"Do you have any other information?" Gabriel asked.

"We haven't gone through all the files yet. We'll do that today. If we find anything useful, we'll email it to you or call if it's urgent."

"Good. Unless I hear from you sooner, I'll call you after I check the hospitals." Gabriel ended the call.

Beth tilted her head. "He didn't seem concerned about Archer's investigation."

"His reaction was intriguing." Jason grabbed her hand. "Let's eat. Last night's burglary made me hungry."

She laughed as they went into breakfast. In an unspoken agreement, they discussed the recreation complex, work, friends, everything except Archer.

Too soon, Jason said, "We need to sort through the files on the disks."

Beth nodded and went with him to the study. She sat on the sofa and started her laptop computer. While he went to his desk to make copies of Archer's disks.

Jason brought the disks to her. "I know this isn't easy for you, but we need to get this done quickly. We need to find the information about the adoption before Archer discovers we have the disks. When he does, he'll try to keep us from finding Daniel. He won't succeed, but he could put up obstacles that will slow our search."

"We have to find Daniel. That is more important than how I feel about my father."

He kissed her forehead and returned to his computer. They'd agreed to split the work. Beth looked through half the files on Disk Two, and Jason checked the rest.

Two hours later she threw her hands in the air. "I found the name of the attorney Archer hired to handle the adoption. There's nothing about who adopted Daniel, or their attorney, but wouldn't Archer's attorney have that information in his files?"

"He should. Send that information to Gabriel. I sent you an email with his address."

They'd worked for another hour before Jason asked, "Have you finished?"

She rubbed her eyes. "Two more files."

"Why don't you let me go through them? I've finished my files." He went to her. "You look tired."

"I would like a nap."

"That's a good idea. If you look tired, the doctor will give you another lecture." He walked her to the door. "I'll wake you in time to get to the appointment."

Beth slept for two hours. After brushing her hair and teeth, she changed clothes. She went to the kitchen and found Lupita.

Lupita smiled and said, "You look rested."

"I feel better, but now I'm thirsty. Do you have lemonade or ice tea?"

"I'll get it." Lupita got Beth a drink. "While you napped, your mother called. She'd like you to call her back."

"Thank you. I'll call now." Beth asked, "Where's Jason?"

"Where else—in his study. You need to remind him, love and family are more important than work." Lupita handed her a glass of lemonade then shooed her from the kitchen.

Beth frowned. *He wants a family, but will he be a father who's involved in the children's lives or will they be less important than his work?*

Beth stopped at the telephone in the foyer to return her mother's call.

Deidre answered. "Hi, darling. I'm glad you got my message."

"What's wrong? Are you all right?"

"I'm fine. Archer asked me to invite you and Jason to the house this evening. He wants to talk about your baby."

After their last visit, she found it difficult to believe he wanted to find Daniel. "Are you certain that's what he wants to discuss? Has he changed his mind?"

"Yes. I can't tell you how happy this makes me."

"I'll ask Jason, but I'm sure he'll agree to go with me. Is eight o'clock good?"

"That's perfect."

Beth set the telephone on the table and turned to find Jason waiting. "Did you hear?"

"Yes, but I must have misunderstood. It sounded like your parents invited us over to talk about Daniel."

"Archer asked Mother to invite us. Now that we've read through those files, there's no way I believe he's had a change of heart. Either he found out we took the disks, or he wants fifty million dollars."

"Don't let it worry you." He took her in his arms. "I'll be with you. Together we can handle whatever Archer throws at us."

She asked, "Then you'll go with me?"

"I'm looking forward to it. Now, let's get rid of that cast."

CHAPTER FOURTEEN

Jason and Beth arrived at her parents' home a few minutes after eight. Deidre sat in the same chair by the fireplace, and Archer stood behind her. She rushed to Beth with a huge smile on her face.

"Darling, we're so glad you came to visit. You got your cast removed."

She hugged her mother. "The doctor took it off today. Now I can shower without plastic wrapped around my arm."

A smile on her face, Deidre squeezed Jason's hand. "It's good to see you again."

"Thank you for inviting us."

She waved them to the sofa. "Would you like coffee or tea?"

Beth said, "I'll have coffee. Jason?"

"I'll have coffee, too." Jason watched Kingsley. He hadn't uttered a word. Beth had been right. Jason would need every shark-eating skill he possessed to get through this visit.

Archer snapped, "Deidre, stop fluttering."

She poured coffee and handed cups to Beth and Jason.

Archer straightened away from the mantle and pounced. "At the party, I stepped over to a window for fresh air and saw someone outside my office. I couldn't see his face, but I'm sure it was a man. The next day I checked my office and found two computer disks were missing. They are the ones that contain information about Elizabeth and her mess." Archer glared at Jason. "You took those disks, and I want them back."

Deidre gasped and stared up at Archer.

Jason set his coffee cup on the table. "No." He put an arm around Beth's shoulders.

Archer's face darkened. "You took my property. I can have you arrested for theft."

Jason smirked. "If you did that, everyone would learn about the pregnancy."

Eyes wide, Deidre asked, "I thought you wanted to help them find their child?"

"Why would I do that? If he's found, everyone will know about their bastard. People will laugh at me."

Deidre's eyes filled with tears. "Why did you lie?"

"I needed you to get them here." He looked at Jason, a sneer on his face. "After all the trouble I went through to clean up your mess, do you think I'll let you air our dirty laundry now?"

"Our son is not dirty laundry." Beth's words rang with anger.

Archer bellowed, "Why did you tell Richards about the boy?"

"I didn't. Someone sent Jason a letter."

"Who sent it?" Archer's face was red and swollen with outrage.

Jason shrugged. "We don't know. It wasn't signed."

Archer shouted at Beth, "Admit it. You sent that letter to embarrass me!"

"I didn't send it, but I'd like to know who did."

Jason smiled. "Yes, we'd like to thank him."

"Well, it doesn't matter. You'll never find your brat. I made sure of that."

"Father—"

"Don't call me that. You've been nothing but a disappointment since the day you were born. I wanted a son, an heir to carry on my legacy. Instead, I got you—"

Jason interrupted. "You don't have a son, but you have a grandson. Help us find him."

"I told you the price for my help—twenty-five million dollars."

Beth's eyes narrowed. "We won't pay your extortion."

"For years I worked to make this family respectable, powerful. I refuse to let the grandson of the town drunk take over what I built." Archer pointed at her. "You are such a fool. Do you think a man like him cares about you or your brat? Richards is a shark. All he cares about is his next deal."

"You're wrong. Jason wants our son, and so do I."

Archer sneered. "You were so easy to manipulate. A few misplaced letters and missed telephone calls did the trick. When that wasn't enough, I only had to threaten your beloved Jason, and you did whatever I wanted."

"I would have done anything to protect him."

Jason scowled as his patience snapped. "You won't stop us from finding Daniel. So you can either help us or stay out of our way."

"You're a fool. Did you think I'd tell you where to find your bastard spawn? Even if you paid, I wouldn't have told you."

"Enough!" Deidre shouted.

Eyes wide, everyone turned to stare at her.

"Archer, you have to let go of your obsession with social status." Deidre begged, "Please tell them where to find their son."

"No." Archer crossed his arms over his chest.

"We were wrong to force Beth to give up her child. They deserve to know what happened to him."

Archer's face was the color of cayenne pepper. "This is none of your business!"

"Yes, it is. This is my family, too." Deidre turned to Jason. "I sent that letter to you. I hoped you'd want to find your son. Then you could make sure he's happy and safe. Beth, I didn't know you were searching, or I would have told you what I know. I'm sorry."

Archer grabbed Deidre's arm. "Be quiet."

Beth's mother struggled to shake off his hand, but he held on.

"I've been quiet for too long. Beth begged to keep her baby, and we shouldn't have forced her to give him away. You may not want our grandson, but I do and will help any way I can to find him."

"We will not discuss this any further." Archer dropped Deidre's arm and turned to Beth. "I expect the immediate return of those disks."

Beth stood. "Jason gave you our answer, and we won't change our minds."

Archer smirked at them. "It doesn't matter. The information you need to find your brat isn't on those disks."

Deidre turned to Jason and Beth. "The name of the couple who adopted your baby is Mr. and Mrs. Robert Anderson, and their attorney was Jack Woodson. They lived and worked in Boston."

Archer shouted, "I told you to stay out of this."

"I'm tired of your schemes and manipulations." Deidre straightened her shoulders. "I don't like the way you run this family or the business. I won't let you bankrupt the company Father worked so hard to build or drive our daughter from our lives."

"Don't challenge me, Deidre." Archer glared at her and bellowed, "I run this family, and you will do as I say."

Beth rushed to her mother. "Mom, come home with us. He's so angry. I'm afraid for you."

Archer yelled, "She cannot leave. I won't let her humiliate me."

Deidre patted her hand. "Your father would never hurt me. Besides, I've ignored Archer's behavior for too long. A discussion is overdue."

She hugged her mother. "I'll call you tomorrow."

Jason held Deidre's hand. "Thank you for sending the letter."

Legs weak and shaking, Beth gripped Jason's arm as they

walked to the car. She wanted to hide. When they got home, she planned to crawl into bed and pull the covers over her head. Never could she have imagined the depth of her father's betrayal.

At home, there was a message to call Gabriel. When they returned his call, as usual, he answered on the first ring.

"Glad you got my message."

"Sorry it's so late, but Archer found out we'd borrowed his disks."

"I'd bet a hundred dollars he wants them back."

"Yes, he does, but he won't get them. We found information and hope it helps in your search."

"Good, we need it. The lawyer Archer hired can't help us. Massachusetts requires attorneys to keep records for closed cases for seven years. He keeps his for eight years and then shreds them. Last year he destroyed the files on Daniel and the adoption. He only remembered one detail about the case. It involved a teenage girl whose father hired him."

Beth clenched her hands. "That's disappointing."

Jason brushed circles on her back. "Then it's good we got the names of the people who adopted Daniel, and their attorney." He passed on the information Deidre had given them.

Gabriel laughed. "I'm sure a lot more happened than what you've told me."

"Yes, but nothing vital to the search."

"From what you told me, I got the impression that Beth's parents were the ones who pushed her to give up your son. What's changed?"

"Remember the unsigned letter? Deidre sent it. She wants me to find Daniel. She didn't know Beth had been searching for years." Jason cupped her cheek.

"Now that we have the attorney and parents' names, we have a good place to begin our search for your son. I'll do background checks before I approach them. Surprises can bring trouble." Gabriel paused. "I'll send one of my female investigators to the hospitals. She might get the information they wouldn't give me. Down the road, you might need the hospital records. Would you sign a power of attorney, Beth?"

"Yes. We'll fax it to you."

Jason frowned. "Do you think the attorney still has his file?"

"I hope so. If the records were destroyed, he might recall some of the details of the case."

Jason asked, "Would you tell us what you learn from the background checks? We're most interested in what you find out about Mr. and Mrs. Anderson."

"No problem. Finding someone is like putting the pieces of a puzzle together. It takes time. Email me any other useful information you find in the files." Gabriel disconnected the call.

Jason pulled Beth into his arms. "It's time for bed."

"I won't be able to fall sleep yet. Maybe if I read, I'll relax enough to sleep."

"You need a soak in the whirlpool and a back rub." He gave her his best wolfish grin and waggled his eyebrows. "Then I'll give you my special relaxation treatment."

After a peaceful sleep, Beth opened her eyes and stretched. Jason's prescription to help her relax worked better than reading ever had.

After she had dressed, she called her mother. "Are you okay? What happened after we left?"

Deidre sighed. "Your father and I had a long talk about the family and business. Archer apologized for his behavior and has agreed to meet with a professional about his anger. He promised not to interfere with your search."

"Do you think he'll keep his promise?"

"Yes, I do."

"I hope so, for your sake." She wished she could be as optimistic as her mother. Archer had broken too many promises, and Beth didn't believe he'd changed.

After talking to her mother, Beth went to the study. Jason wasn't there. She saw the open patio doors and looked outside. He lay by the pool, asleep. She smiled and ran to change into her swimsuit. Ten minutes later she sat on the lounge chair next to him and studied his face.

As a teenager, he'd been handsome in a boyish way, but it had been the kindness he'd shown a young girl that won her devotion. Now, he possessed rugged good looks and a sexy arrogance, but it was the way he treated her, with respect and dignity, that made him special. He might swim with the sharks, but he hadn't lost himself. Jason was still the man she loved.

She leaned over and kissed him. When he opened his mouth, she slid her tongue in and stroked him. She loved the taste of him. After several breath-stealing moments, they pulled apart.

"That's a wake-up call I don't mind." He pulled her to him, but she stopped him with a hand on his chest.

"Jason, I'm worried—"

"About your mother?"

"No, I talked to her. She said Archer apologized, and he's agreed to get help to control his temper."

One corner of Jason's mouth curled. "Do you think he'll keep his promise?"

"No, but that's not..." Beth wrapped her arms around her waist. "What if Daniel is with parents and a family he loves? It would be cruel to take him from a home where he's happy."

"I've thought about that possibility, too. You're right, it wouldn't be fair to tear his life apart. I think there is a way to show our commitment to Daniel's well-being and get the approval we need to be part of his life."

"It's important to me not to put Daniel through a court battle, but I would do almost anything to spend time with him."

"I believe we'd have a better chance to get visitation rights or custody if...." He pulled on his ear. "We should get married."

Her mouth opened, but no sound came out.

Jason wrapped his hands around her tight fists. "We need to convince his parents that we want whatever is best for Daniel. That we won't shuffle him back and forth between our homes. It's important to give him a safe, stable, and happy place to live."

He wanted to marry her, but he wanted to marry for Daniel. Not once had he talked about their relationship. Would they be friends-with-benefits?

"Would it be a hardship to marry me?" He grinned. "I don't leave my clothes lying on the floor, I always put the cap back on the toothpaste, and I can support a family."

"Money was never a concern. I knew we'd manage." She waved a hand. "Are you certain you want to tie yourself to a wife? Maybe we should wait until we find Daniel to decide if we should marry? In a month or a year, I don't want you to regret that you married me."

"We care about each other and enjoy spending time together. I admire you. You're a kind, intelligent, and strong woman. We both love classic movies and chocolate. You've always wanted a large family, and I am happy to assist you with that. I believe we can build a good life together."

Beth stared at Jason. She heard his words, but did he mean what he said? He hadn't said anything of love or friendship. Did it matter? Would it be wise for her to marry him if he didn't love her? Was her love enough of a foundation for building a life together?

"Yes, I'll marry you."

Jason released the breath he'd held. "You won't regret it."

He kissed Beth and jumped to his feet then paced back and forth. "We'll apply for a license this afternoon. There's a five-working-day waiting period. We can get married next Wednesday. I'll find a judge to marry us unless you want a church ceremony? Did you have your heart set on a big wedding?"

As far as he was concerned, he didn't care where they got married, what they wore, or if anyone attended the ceremony. He wanted to get a ring on her hand before she changed her mind.

"No, a judge is fine." She wrinkled her nose. "Are you certain you want to marry me?"

He squeezed her hands. "I've never been surer of anything."

Beth's lips formed the sweetest smile he'd ever seen.

After lunch, they drove to the county offices to apply for a marriage license. Jason grinned when she wrote in the name she would use when they married—Elizabeth Marie Richards. After they finished the paperwork, he drove to the jewelry store.

Beth's shoulders were rigid, and she stared out the window.

"We can't get married without rings."

Had she changed her mind? She sent him a nervous smile then she reached into her purse. After a moment's hesitation, she handed him a small box.

The box looked familiar but not until he lifted the lid, did he remember. His eyes widened. In it were the wedding bands he'd saved for a year to buy. "You kept them."

Jason handed the box back to her. He jumped from the car and went around to open her door. When she climbed out, he kissed her. He wasn't ready to say the words, but he poured his love into their kiss. A love that hadn't faded even when he'd believed she'd betrayed him.

"I..." She hesitated. "I'd like to wear these rings when we're married. We don't need new ones."

"I'd like that, but you still need an engagement ring. I couldn't afford one nine years ago, but—." He grinned. "I can now. We need to have these rings checked for size. I want everything to be perfect."

She gave him a bright smile. "It already is."

It took a while to agree on an engagement ring. Although she thought the diamond was larger than necessary, she loved the emerald cut solitaire. After the jeweler checked the size of the wedding bands, they drove back to the house with smiles on their faces.

As they entered the house, her smile dimmed. Did she have doubts? Jason led her to the study and locked the door behind him. He wanted privacy while he convinced her that marriage was a good idea.

"Are you having second thoughts about getting married?"

"What? No. I mean—you're right. We need to give Daniel a stable home, not shuttle him back and forth."

He didn't want to hear her say their marriage would be convenient, but she only repeated what he'd said to get her to agree to his proposal. "Then why the sad face?"

"Your home and business are in Chicago. I'll have to leave Serenity Bay." Her voice shook. "I'll have to leave my friends and my mother."

"We'll come back often." He ran his hand over her arms. "Besides, you don't have to give up everything. You could open another shop there. Could you take Abbey or Erik to Chicago and leave the other one in charge here?"

"You wouldn't mind?"

"Angel, this will be a marriage, not a prison sentence."

"I know, but you—"

"My home is on Chicago's North Shore. It's an ideal area for a coffee shop. You could open a neighborhood business or go with a more upscale concept."

"I could leave Erik in charge of this shop. He might even agree to live in my house. I don't want to sell it, but it shouldn't sit vacant either."

"Do you think Abbey would move to Chicago?"

"Abbey has been restless. A move to Chicago might settle her wanderlust, at least for a while." Beth kissed Jason's chin. "Thank you."

"Why? What did I do?"

"You don't expect me to give up the work I love or be an ornament on your arm. That means a lot."

"You are a beautiful woman, but you're also intelligent, creative, and enjoy a challenge. I can't imagine you sitting around all day eating bonbons."

"I am marrying a wise man." She wound her arms around his waist and nipped at his lips.

"Glad I locked the door." He claimed her lips in a fiery kiss.

Later, they lay on the sofa wrapped in an afghan, their clothes scattered on the floor, as they gasped for breath. The telephone rang, but neither of them moved.

"Aren't you going to pick that up?" Beth asked.

Jason shrugged. "Someone will take a message."

After the third ring, Beth said, "Maybe you should answer it."

"If I tried to walk now, I'd fall on my face."

She giggled.

Jason yawned. "If no one answers, the service will take a message."

Two minutes later, Marco pounded on the door. "Mr. Michael wants to talk to you. Can you drag yourself to the telephone?"

Jason groaned then said, "Thank you, Marco."

A roar of laughter came from the other side of the door.

Jason struggled to get to his feet. "I'm glad I entertain him."

He hit the *SPEAKER* button on the telephone. "What have you found out?"

"I located the attorney for the people who adopted your son. He's a baby broker."

Wrapped in the blanket, Beth sat up. "He's a what?"

"He places infants with couples who will pay big dollars to adopt."

She gasped. "He's selling babies? That's despicable."

"Definitely scum," Gabriel said. "We need to learn more about him before we take any action. I don't want him to find out someone has checked on him. He might pack up and run. I sent in two of my operatives as a married couple. Their cover story is they're desperate to adopt a baby and have hinted they will pay any price."

"What did he say?" Jason asked.

"He took the bait." Gabriel snorted. "They have another appointment on Friday. He's promised to tell them if he can match them with a baby."

Beth asked, "What will you do now?"

"I want more information about him. My people are checking into his background. Once we have that, I'll figure out the best way to get in to see his files." Gabriel hesitated. "If I have to, I'll pay a midnight visit to his office."

"Whatever you do, don't get into so much trouble I can't bail you out of jail."

"Based on what I've learned, Woodson won't contact the police. He won't want them to look into his business practices, but that makes him more likely to run."

"Sounds like you know him." Jason grinned. "Anything else?"

"Yeah. We can't confirm the information you gave me for the Andersons. Either the name is wrong, or they used fake identifications. I won't know for sure until I can check into Woodson's files."

"This is closer than anyone has gotten, and we trust you'll do whatever is best. In the meantime, I'll keep Beth distracted." Jason winked at her. "If you're available, next Wednesday we're getting married. We'd like you to come."

"Congratulations. I wondered how long it would take you to figure out what a prize you had."

Jason smiled. "It took nine years to get this done, but I have staying power."

Gabriel laughed then disconnected the call.

Wrapped in the afghan, Beth got to her feet. Jason led her to the door, but she pulled away and ran back to the sofa.

Jason asked, "What's wrong?"

She bent to pick up his shirt. "I don't want Lupita and Marco to know what we were doing."

Jason coughed. "It will be our secret."

CHAPTER FIFTEEN

Several hours later they walked into the dining room.

Beth threw her arms around Jason. "Thank you!" The room was lit with candles and filled with flowers.

"It may be nine years later than we planned, but I don't want you to regret our marriage."

"I never will." She kissed him until her stomach rumbled. "Sorry, but the food smells so good. The aroma of the spices is making my mouth water. I smell basil, thyme, garlic...." She grabbed his hand and pulled him to the table, "Let's eat."

"I would never come between a woman and her food."

The wonderful aromas came from Lupita's pesto-stuffed pork chops, asparagus with parmesan and almonds, and orzo salad with basil flavored feta cheese. She told them to save room for the Italian Cream Cake from the shop, and Beth moaned. The meal was a culinary delight worthy of a five-star restaurant.

They wore matching smiles as they ate, talked, and made plans. Jason agreed he'd prefer a small, intimate ceremony with their families and friends who lived in Serenity Bay. After they returned from the honeymoon and moved to Chicago, they could have a second reception.

After dinner, Beth went to the parlor, and Jason went to his study. They called their family and friends to share the news of their marriage.

She called her mother first and smiled at her response.

"I am so happy for you. The two of you belong together."

"We wouldn't be if you hadn't sent that letter."

"Your father and I were wrong to interfere in your life. I can't tell you how much I regret forcing you to give up your son."

"We've put the past to rest. You should do the same."

"Darling, I love you very much. Now, I want to help. What can I do?"

Beth cleared her throat. "We don't have time for invitations and need someone to call our friends."

"I can do that. Have you put a guest list together?"

"We're working on it. I'll get it to you tomorrow."

They talked a while longer, and Beth's heart overflowed with love for her mother.

Next, she called Abbey.

Abbey asked, "Did you tell him—?"

"He's hired an investigator to search for our son." Then Beth told her what they'd learned about Archer. "Father said he manipulated us to keep me in town and away from Jason and took steps to make certain we could never find Daniel. Jason found the information when he broke into father's office."

Abbey laughed. "The plan worked?"

"Better than I expected."

"I'm glad the wine we drank when we came up with that plan didn't go to waste."

"We couldn't have found the information we need without your help." Beth asked, "Will you be my maid of honor?"

"I'd be proud to stand with you. Someone has to keep you from climbing out the bathroom window."

After they'd laughed, Beth said, "Nothing—and no one—will stop me from marrying him."

"I'm so happy for you and a little envious."

"Someday you'll find your Prince Charming."

"Yes, because there are so many of them running around Serenity Bay." Abbey laughed. "What will happen with the shop?"

Beth explained her plan to keep the shop in Serenity Bay open and establish a new one in Chicago. She asked Abbey if she would move with her to manage the Chicago location.

"Yes!" Abbey squealed. "I've been a little restless and have wanted an adventure, but I didn't want to leave you."

They chatted awhile longer and agreed to talk the next day.

Her last call was to Erik.

He announced, "I will create the wedding cake of your dreams. It will be so beautiful, you won't want to cut it."

She laughed and thanked him. "Erik, you're the best. That's why I want you to take over management of the shop in Serenity Bay." Beth explained her plans.

He thought a new shop was an awesome idea, but asked, "You won't do the baking, will you?"

With a laugh, Beth assured him she planned to hire a baker.

Erik promised not to disappoint her. "I have a few ideas I'd like to discuss."

She smiled at his excitement and knew she'd made a good decision.

After they had finished their calls, Jason and Beth sat on the patio with glasses of wine.

"How did your family take the news?" she asked.

"Mom and Dad couldn't be happier. Callie can't wait to be the *best woman*, but she's disappointed there won't be time for a bachelor party."

"Do they know our history?"

He brushed the back of her neck. "I told them we spent time together and made peace with our past. Then we fell in love again, and I begged you to marry me. I thought it best to wait to tell them about Daniel."

"What if they hate me for giving him away?"

"You were eighteen and survived an experience that could have broken you. Instead, you built a good life for yourself while you searched for our son. It's time to forgive yourself." He ran his thumb in circles on her palm. "The reason I thought it best not to tell them about Daniel yet is that I don't want to disappoint them if we don't find him."

"I agree." She kissed his chin. "With such short notice, will they be able to attend the wedding?"

"They're flying in tomorrow—"

"Tomorrow?" She jumped to her feet. "They can't come tomorrow. I need time to prepare. What if they don't like me or think I'm not good enough for you?"

"They'll love you." He pulled her onto his lap. "There is only one person whose opinion should concern you."

"Who?"

"Mine." With a sexy grin, he took her lips in a sweet kiss that quickly turned hot and needy.

Morning came too soon. Beth couldn't decide which outfit to wear and changed clothes three times before she chose. It didn't matter what she wore. His family knew their past and had to be unhappy with Jason's decision to marry her. They were coming to stop the wedding. *What's the proper attire to wear to get a heart broken?*

Unable to delay any longer, she went to the breakfast room. She pushed her food around her plate and guzzled coffee. Jason tried to reassure her, but her fear made it impossible to relax.

Lupita came in to tell them his family had arrived. Beth held his hand as they walked out to greet them.

Jason whispered, "Could you let the blood flow to my fingers."

"Oh. Sorry." Beth apologized but couldn't loosen her grip.

Jason laughed. She swallowed to keep from losing the little

food she'd eaten.

Outside, she stood at Jason's side and dug her nails into the arm he had around her waist. His family got out of the car, and she wondered if it was too late to hide in the bathroom.

"Jason." A young woman jumped into his arms. "It's about time my big brother got his head—"

"Callie." The woman, an older version of Jason's sister, shook her head. "Beth, excuse my daughter. Words pour out of her mouth before her brain is engaged."

She laughed with the others.

"Hi, Tiger. I'm glad you're here." He set Callie on her feet. "Beth, this is Matt and Helen Richards, and my *little sister*, Callie."

Helen beamed as she pulled Beth into a tight hug and said, "Grandchildren."

There were chuckles around them while a new set of arms pulled her into a crushing embrace. She looked into Matt's face.

"Welcome to the family." With a happy grin, he kissed her cheek. "We haven't stopped smiling since Jason told us you agreed to marry him."

Matt rolled his eyes when Callie tugged on his arm.

"My turn." She pulled Beth into a bear hug. "I admire your courage."

Beth frowned. "Courage?"

"You've agreed to marry the man others call a cold-blooded shark."

He winked at Beth. "I told you I swim with the sharks."

She laughed with the family and then said, "How about coffee, or would you like something else?"

The response was unanimous. "Coffee."

After Lupita had set out coffee and pastries, they talked, laughed, and got to know each other.

Helen clapped her hands. "We don't have a lot of time to prepare for the wedding, but we can get it done if we have a plan."

Beth laughed. "Now I know where Jason got his obsession with making plans."

Everyone, even Jason, laughed until Helen said, "I've scheduled a visit to a wedding boutique tomorrow."

"There isn't one in Serenity Bay." Beth's eyebrows drew together. "Are we going to drive to Minneapolis?"

"We're flying to Chicago."

"Chicago?" Beth said, "But my mother and Abbey—"

Helen held up a hand. "Jason gave me their names and telephone numbers. I called them last night. Abbey will be here for dinner and stay overnight. Then we'll pick up Deidre on the way to the airport."

Beth sat wide-eyed and listened to Helen's plans. She took charge with the force of a tornado sucking in everything in its path.

Helen patted her hand. "Let me tell you about the day we have planned for you. We'll spend the day at the boutique. A friend of mine, Wendy Rand, is a well-known wedding planner and has agreed to organize your day. She'll help you decide on flowers, decorations, dinner, and whatever else you need. Once you've made your choices, she'll make sure everything gets done."

Beth's mouth dropped. Jason put a finger under her chin to close it. Then he kissed her.

They planned a late supper so Abbey could join them. While they waited, the family settled into their rooms. Beth and Jason used the time to put together their guest list.

A short time later, Helen returned with an armful of bride magazines. She told Beth, "Look through these for ideas for your dress, the meal, flowers, and whatever else you would like to have."

After she had looked at two magazines, the wedding dresses began to look alike. When Abbey arrived, Beth pulled her into the living room. She gave Abbey a magazine and told her to pick a dress.

The best part of the day came when they gathered for dinner. Beth felt as comfortable with Jason's family as she did with her friends from the shop. They talked and joked and enjoyed being together. She laughed most at the stories they shared about Jason.

When Helen winked at her, Beth smothered a chuckle. She'd already learned what a sense of humor Helen possessed. "Beth, do you know any nice, single men you could introduce to Callie? If we don't find her a husband soon, she may never give me grandchildren."

Everyone laughed, except Callie. Her response was a long, drawn out, "Mother."

The next day, while they waited to board the plane, Beth clamped her hands together.

"What's wrong?" Helen slid an arm around her.

She shrugged. "I appreciate your help, but it will be impossible to have dresses fitted or find a caterer in time for the wedding. Even though we talked Jason into waiting until Saturday, no one can meet that deadline."

"There isn't a florist, dress designer, or caterer who wouldn't kill to be part of the whirlwind wedding of billionaire J.D. Richards to Elizabeth Kingsley." Callie laughed.

"I keep forgetting he's J.D. Richards." The heat of a blush washed over Beth's face.

Helen said, "The planner has five caterers scheduled to come in to present their menu suggestions for dinner. She also has several florists who will suggest flowers and arrangements, and the shop we'll be at carries one-of-a-kind designer dresses including several you saw in those magazines."

"What if I embarrass him?"

Helen put an arm around her. "You could never upset him. Jason doesn't care about his image or what others think. He wants you to have the wedding of your dreams."

Beth blinked back her tears.

Her day in Chicago was both amazing and crazy. She dealt with caterers, florists, and dresses in one day. It was an overwhelming task that couldn't have been done without Helen and the wedding planner. They had ideas and suggestions to transform the house and garden into a wonderland.

While Beth tried on another dress, Callie and Abbey walked up with identical smiles too innocent to believe. "What trouble have you two caused?"

"No trouble." Abbey laughed.

Callie said, "We have a gift for you."

Together they held up the sexiest negligee she'd ever seen. A sheer chiffon and lace confection with embroidered silk and pearl flowers in places to tease the imagination.

Abbey smirked and said, "If Jason doesn't lose his ability to speak the minute he sees you in this, the man is not human."

Beth grinned. "Not only will he be speechless, but he'll be on his knees before the sun rises."

That sent the women into side-shaking laughter.

After much debate, Beth picked a strapless wedding gown made of chiffon over satin created by a designer whose clothes she'd always admired. She loved the pearls and embroidery that covered the bodice of the dress and cascaded in a waterfall down the left side of the skirt. Beth chose a white satin and lace corset and thong. Her face heated when she imagined Jason taking them off—one piece at a time.

For Abbey, they picked a sleek, satin strapless dress in a burgundy. With her darker skin, the effect was dramatic and stunning. Deidre and Helen decided they wanted to wear floor-length dresses and found gowns that complemented the colors Beth had chosen.

As Jason's best woman, Callie intended to wear a tuxedo. Helen shook her head and said, "She's responsible for every gray hair on my head."

Happy but tired, the ladies flew back to Serenity Bay. Beth didn't believe they could plan a wedding in one day, but they'd done it. What made it special, though, was spending time with the amazing women of her family.

The one bump in the plans happened after Beth decided not to have her father escort her to Jason. Archer called to object to her decision. "I am your father. People will talk if I don't deliver you to Richards."

"This is our wedding, and we'll do what makes us happy. I don't want a show to impress your friends or business associates."

"How can you humiliate your family like this?"

"Goodbye, Father."

For years she'd tried to win his love, but now she knew the truth. He didn't love her and considered her a mistake, a disappointment. She refused to settle for the crumbs he tossed or put up with his abusive temper. Jason may not love her, but he respected her and treated her better than her father ever had.

The day of the wedding, Beth woke with a smile. She looked out the window to a morning bathed in sunshine. The day couldn't be more perfect. The ceremony was scheduled for the late afternoon to give the caterer, decorator, and others time to prepare.

From her window, Beth saw the trellis covered with organza, roses, and stargazer lilies, her favorite flowers. A few days earlier, Marco had strung crystal star-shaped lights that created rainbows when the sun reflected off them in the trees and bushes. After the sun set, the lighted stars sparkled and created a fairytale atmosphere.

They prepared the ballroom for the reception and dancing. It was an elegant room with a large Victorian crystal chandelier and three walls of windows from the ceiling to floor. She was eager to see how the room looked with the white, gauzy organza draped over the walls and windows. The tables were to have floral arrangements made with the same white roses and stargazer lilies used in her bouquet.

Beth hugged Erik when she saw the cake. He had created a

three layer masterpiece of white chocolate cake with a raspberry cream between the layers. The design on the frosting matched the lace and pearls on her dress. On top of the cake, Erik placed a crystal cake topper of a bride and groom dancing under a heart-shaped trellis.

Abbey and Lupita had both insisted on overseeing the caterer's work. "They might be the best, but they need someone around to deal with crises," Abbey said. Beth felt sorry for the caterer. The dinner menu was a leg of lamb stuffed with goat cheese, truffle potatoes au gratin, and candied ginger carrots. They had champagne and wine flown in from Jason's personal wine cellar.

In the afternoon, after a soak in a lavender scented bath, Beth dressed with Abbey and Callie's help. While Callie fastened the tiny buttons at her back, they teased Beth.

"Do you think Jason will have the patience to undo the buttons?" asked Abbey.

Callie leered. "Not if he knows what she's wearing under the dress."

They laughed.

Beth stared at the woman in her mirror and brushed a finger over her face. Her eyes sparkled. No risk was too great to be with Jason, not even a broken heart.

Soon it was time to begin the next chapter of her life. Beth stood at the door to the garden. The butterflies in her stomach had returned and waged war. Then she saw Jason. He watched her and wore a bright smile on his lips. He hadn't said the words, but she felt his love in the way he cared for her, supported her, and encouraged her. She returned his smile and walked to the man who owned her heart.

When she reached Jason, he kissed her hand and pulled her close. They listened to the minister. He spoke of patience and understanding, friendship and trust, and he talked about love. Neither of their smiles wavered during the ceremony. Then it was time to exchange vows. They had agreed that they wanted to write their own.

Jason held the wedding band she had treasured for nine years. He kissed it then slipped it onto her finger. "Beth, you are my angel, my love, and my joy. You are everything good and true in my life. I fell in love with you the day we met and will love you until the day I die."

Her lips trembled. He loved her. She gave him a shaky smile and slid the gold band on his finger. "Jason, I promise to be your friend, your wife, and your lover. I will laugh with you, support you, and love you every day of my life. I will be by your side in good times and bad because my heart and soul are yours—forever."

The minister pronounced them husband and wife. With those words, the fear that Beth might change her mind vanished and Jason's smile widened.

"At last you're mine." With love and joy flooding his heart, he lifted Beth into his arms and kissed her until he needed air. Pleased with the dazed look in her eyes, he kissed her again until the laughter and applause reminded him of their audience. After one last kiss, he whispered, "Later."

They turned to the guests to be introduced as husband and wife. Jason lifted her hand to his lips and kissed her fingers. The guests stood and cheered with one exception—Archer.

After a last kiss, they raced up the aisle to the open lawn. Then Jason lifted Beth and spun in a circle. She threw her arms wide and laughed while her dress billowed around them.

They held hands as they went to the ballroom to receive good wishes and congratulations. So many cameras flashed, Jason had to blink to get rid of the spots in his eyes. The best part of having their picture taken was the excuse it gave him to kiss Beth.

By the time they sat for dinner, one thought consumed him. *How soon can I get Beth alone?*

After the waiters served their salads, Jason watched Beth push her food around her plate. Worried, he asked, "What's wrong?"

She looked at him with tears that glistened on her eyelashes. "I never thought this day would come. I am so happy and love you so much."

"Angel, I love you too, always have, and always will." He pulled her onto his lap and kissed her to the delight of the guests who cheered for more. So he kissed her again and laughed when she blushed. "Now, no more tears. Eat. You need to keep up your stamina for tonight."

After dinner, a band replaced the quartet. Jason led her to the open floor, and they danced wrapped in each other's arms. As Jason turned Beth, he saw Gabriel off to the side of the room. When they finished their dance, they went to welcome him.

Jason smiled. "We're glad you could be here."

"The wedding isn't the reason for this visit." Gabriel shook Jason's hand and kissed Beth's cheek. He rubbed his chin. "I thought of waiting until after your honeymoon...."

Beth tightened her fingers around Jason's hand. "... but this was too important."

"Yeah."

"Let's go to my study." Jason lifted Beth's chin and whispered, "Whatever happens, we'll deal with it together."

She gave him a shaky smile. In the study, they sat and waited.

Gabriel rubbed the back of his neck. "Let me tell you what I know before you ask questions."

They nodded, and Beth moved closer to Jason.

"We tried to track down the adoptive parents with the name and information you gave us, but we couldn't find them. I wanted to try the hospitals again. This time I sent in a female operative. She got them to let her read Beth's records. In a file, she found a notation—a name—Addison. It could be the name of the adopting parents."

Gabriel scrubbed a hand over his face. "I decided it was time to check the information in Woodson's records. I took two of my men with me and paid a midnight visit to his office. He has a walk-in vault for his files. There are hundreds of files. We looked through a handful. It was enough to confirm that Woodson works with couples desperate for children and who will pay anything to adopt."

Jason asked, "Are you certain they're sales and not expensive adoptions?"

"Woodson keeps very detailed records," Gabriel said. "His fees are outrageous. Then, after a couple has adopted a child, he blackmails them. If they refuse to pay, he threatens to inform the authorities about the illegal adoption."

She gasped. "How does he get away with it?"

"There are people so desperate for children they will pay any price. He's arranged adoptions for some influential people who protect him."

"Why would people take such a risk?" She asked.

Gabriel's eyes darkened. "How much would you pay to get your son back?"

Beth and Jason looked at each other.

Gabriel shrugged. "Anyway, we got into his files and confirmed the information my operative found in the hospital records. The couple who adopted Daniel was Julia and Jeff Addison. I photographed the information and left the file in the vault. I don't want Woodson to know we're on to him, at least, not yet."

"Have you located the Addisons?" Jason frowned. "Wait. What

do you mean *was*?"

Gabriel ran his hand over his face. "There was a car crash."

"Oh, my God!" Beth gasped. "Daniel…"

"Daniel is fine. He was with a babysitter."

Jason shuddered. "What happened?"

"The Addisons were out for the evening. It was winter, and the roads were slippery. A truck lost control, crossed into their lane. Their car was demolished. They died at the scene of the accident."

Jason asked, "Was it an accident?"

Gabriel rolled his shoulders. "Good question."

Beth asked, "What happened to Daniel?"

"He had no other family, so he went into foster care. That happened a year and a half ago. I talked to my contact at Department of Children and Families to find out where he's living now. She's his caseworker."

Jason asked, "Do you think he's safe?"

"She's vigilant about safe placements for foster children."

"I'm sorry about the Addisons." Jason ran a hand through his hair. "But if Daniel is in foster care, we can file for custody without concern about a court fight or taking him from an adoptive family."

Jason looked at Beth. "How would you feel if we postpone our honeymoon?"

"Thank you." She squeezed his hand. "Gabriel, what can we do about Woodson? We can't let him continue to swindle people who want a family."

Gabriel's eyes narrowed and every muscle in his body tensed. "Don't worry about him. I'll make sure he gets what he deserves."

Jason hoped he was never on the receiving end of that look.

The door flew open, and Archer stomped into the study. Deidre raced after him. "Archer, please stay out of this. You agreed not to interfere."

"Did you think I meant it?" He turned to Gabriel. "Mr. Michael. I guess you didn't take my second warning any better than you did the first."

Jason's eyebrows pulled together. "There was a second warning?"

Gabriel shrugged. "I'd just left my office when two men stopped me. They suggested I drop my investigation. I wasn't certain who sent them until now." He laughed. "Did you think two third-rate thugs could make me back off the search? It backfired, Mr. Kingsley.

Like I told your messenger boys, I don't give up a case once I've agreed to take it."

"Elizabeth, you will stop this investigation." Archer raged. "If you don't, you will ruin all I've worked for."

She glared at her father. "You'll do anything to protect your inflated opinion of yourself, won't you?"

"I will not allow your bastard to be part of this family."

Deidre put her hand on his arm. "Archer, you promised."

He jerked his arm so hard Deidre lost her balance and fell to the floor.

She looked up at him, her mouth open, and her eyes filled with tears.

"Mother!" Beth ran to her.

Jason and Gabriel grabbed Archer.

He struggled to get free. "Let go of me. What do you think you're doing?"

She held her mother's hand. "Are you hurt?"

Tears ran from Deidre's eyes. She sobbed, "No."

"Deidre, we'll take you home." Jason said, "You can pack whatever you need and come back here."

"It wouldn't be right. You were just married and don't need your mother-in-law living with you. I'll get a room somewhere."

Jason shook his head. "We'd worry about your safety. If you're here, Archer won't be able to get through my security."

"Please, Mother."

"If you promise not to change your plans, I'll stay."

Another knock at the door. Jason grimaced. *Now what?*

His parents walked in and saw Deidre on the floor. They rushed to her, and Helen asked, "What happened?"

Beth pointed to Archer. "His temper is out of control, again."

Helen and Matt helped Deidre to her feet. "Jason, you need to return to your guests. We'll take care of Deidre. Why don't we take her upstairs?"

"No!" Beth said, "I'm sorry I didn't mean to yell. We have to take mother home to pack, and then she'll come back to stay here."

"We'll go with her." Helen patted Beth's arm. "You return to your guests."

Matt nodded. "We can help Deidre collect whatever she needs. If Marco is with us, we won't be any danger."

Jason asked Gabriel, "Would you keep Kingsley away from his

house until Deidre leaves?"

Gabriel's scowl promised retaliation if Archer bothered Deidre. "My pleasure."

Jason shrugged a shoulder. "After that, you can take him home or dump him in a ditch, the choice is yours."

Helen handed her purse to Beth. "There's powder and lipstick in there. Deidre, do you need a minute?"

"I'm fine, just shaken. I'd like to go now."

Beth returned Helen's purse. "Thank you."

Deidre put an arm around Beth, "I'm sorry this happened. But don't let Archer ruin your day. Don't give him the power to hurt you. This day should be a happy memory." Deidre glared at Archer, lifted her chin, and walked out.

Jason squeezed Beth's hand. "We don't have to return to the reception."

"Yes, we do. Mother is right. I won't let Archer ruin the happiest day of my life. Besides, I want to dance with you again."

"I love you." He brushed his fingers over her cheek. "Maybe we can get the band to play a jitterbug."

CHAPTER SIXTEEN

When they returned to the ballroom, the guests, unaware of the drama, teased them about their long absence. Jason laughed, and Beth blushed. Then the band played his jitterbug. He twirled her until she was breathless. She laughed when Erik pulled her into the chicken dance, but it didn't keep her from watching for her mother.

When she returned to Jason, he said, "Marco is with Deidre, and Gabriel promised to keep Archer away. They won't let him hurt her."

Then Jason distracted her. He pressed his hand to her cheek and his lips to hers in a kiss meant to comfort, but soon sizzled with heat. He lifted his head when the wolf whistles and enthusiastic applause broke through the lust that flared whenever they kissed. Flushed, they turned and bowed to their friends.

While Beth danced with their guests, Jason went to the study and called Mason Reed, owner of the River Inn. He got lucky. The bridal suite was available. It had a king-size bed, a Jacuzzi, and a balcony with a view of the river and forest. Jason made a few requests that Mason promised to arrange.

Jason got back to the reception at the same time Deidre returned with his parents. Beth ran to her mother and hugged her. Deidre reassured her she was fine. He told Beth and their families about their reservations at the River Inn.

Beth's reply was immediate, "I don't want to leave Mother."

Deidre said, "You need to celebrate your marriage and not worry about me. I'll be fine."

Helen put an arm around Beth. "Your mother needs time to figure out how to deal with all that's happened. She won't be alone. We'll stay here until you return."

"I can't avoid the problems in my marriage or bury my head in the sand any longer." Deidre frowned. "Archer's behavior has hurt the family and the business. It has to stop."

Beth nodded. "All right, but promise you'll call if he causes trouble."

Deidre laughed. "Gabriel made it clear that Archer is not welcome here."

Jason said, "Gabriel isn't a man you want to cross."

With a cocky grin, he lifted Beth into his arms. The musicians stopped playing, and he turned to their guests. "Thank you for helping us celebrate this happy day. Please stay and enjoy yourselves, but I've waited nine years to go on this honeymoon and refuse to wait any longer."

Beth laughed while the guests cheered and clapped. Jason carried her to the limousine under a shower of confetti. Before they got into the car, Beth reminded him she wanted to throw the bouquet. Jason turned, and she threw it over her shoulder. Loud laughter rang out. They turned to find Erik, his face a deep crimson, holding the bouquet.

Although it wasn't the honeymoon he planned, Jason wanted Beth to have happy memories of this day. He refused to let Archer ruin their wedding or cast a dark shadow over their marriage.

At the Inn, Mason greeted them and told Jason, "Your room is ready."

Beth opened her mouth, but he pressed a finger over her lips and winked. "It's a surprise." At the door to their suite, he again lifted Beth into his arms and walked into the room. "At last."

He kicked the door shut and took her mouth in a kiss that demanded all she had to give. She returned his kiss with an intensity that drove his need to the edge. When she parted her lips, his tongue slid in to tangle with hers. In desperate need of satisfaction, he caressed the sensitive skin of her mouth. He lowered her legs to the floor and brushed his hand over her cheek then stepped back.

Beth grabbed his arms. "Don't stop."

"I want to be certain no one disturbs us." He locked the door.

"Oh, Jason. This is beautiful."

He turned to find a fantasyland. He'd asked Mason for candles, but he never expected this. Lighted candles and vases of flowers were everywhere. Next to the Victorian style loveseat was a bucket of ice with a magnum of champagne set to chill. If they got hungry, on the table was a silver platter with hors d'oeuvres and desserts.

Jason dropped his coats and shirt then went to stand behind Beth. He wrapped his arms around her waist before kissing a path down her neck and shoulders. "You're beautiful in this dress, but you'll look even better out of it."

He flicked a button on the back of her dress. "I noticed these earlier. Did you do this to torture me?"

Beth grinned when she shrugged. "Callie thought it would be fun."

"Little sisters cannot be trusted," Jason mumbled while he struggled with the first button. After it had been undone, he managed the rest of the buttons without a problem. He turned Beth, but she'd crossed her arms and held her dress in place. He frowned and asked, "What's wrong?"

"I bought you a gift, but I didn't want to unveil it until I had your full attention."

"You have my complete, undivided attention." He grinned.

A coy smile curved her lips when she released her bodice and wiggled her hips. Her dress drifted to the floor and formed a white, chiffon cloud at her feet.

Jason's mouth fell open. Beth still wore white, but now she wore her satin and lace corset, lace thong, a garter belt and white thigh-high stockings. She was an invitation to sin no sane man could deny.

She stepped out of her dress and bent to pick it off the floor. On the back of her thong was a lace bow that teased his already overwrought senses.

Jason muttered, "Have mercy."

Beth looked at him over her shoulder and smiled.

His cock went from stiff to hard as steel. If he didn't bury himself in her soon, he might pass out from a lack of blood to his brain.

He took her dress and laid it over a chair. "If I had known what you were wearing under that dress, we would have skipped the reception—maybe even the ceremony."

"That's what Callie predicted." She laughed. "I guess she knows you well."

"She shouldn't tell you all my secrets."

"Well, I think she was optimistic. She said you'd have me in bed five minutes after I took off my dress. But I'm here in the sexiest lingerie I own, and you haven't taken advantage of me."

"What is wrong with me?" With a quick move, he lifted her, and she wrapped her legs around his hips. "Never let it be said I disappointed my bride."

Jason sat on the sofa, and Beth straddled his lap. With a light, soft touch, he stroked her skin. Then Jason cupped her face between his hands and captured her lips in a hungry kiss. He'd wanted to take his time, but his control fractured.

With a tug, he pulled on the top of the corset and uncovered her breasts. Jason used his mouth to make love to her. He fondled each mound and drew circles over them and then swirled his tongue over her nipples. He tormented the sensitive buds and blew air over each damp nub until she moaned.

Beth shifted her hips and rubbed against the bulge of his cock. He groaned when she touched his skin as she pulled his shirt out of his pants. Her fingers raked over his chest and stomach and sent waves of fire through his body.

She pulled his shirt open. The air cooled his skin and was a welcome relief from the heat that ravaged his body. He struggled to get his shirt off while she stroked his chest and stomach. But when she sucked a nipple into her mouth, lust ripped through him.

As Beth tortured him, he undid the hooks that held her lacy corset in place. He shuddered when a wisp of her warm breath drifted over his chest as he loosened the last hook. He tossed the enticing garment over his shoulder and gazed at the creamy skin he'd revealed. A seductive smile curled her lips when her breasts crushed against his chest.

Jason slid his hand between her thighs. He pushed her lace panties aside to tease her. He smiled when she moaned. Then her back arched, and she lifted her hips to grind against his hand.

"I want you in me."

"Soon."

She grabbed his wrist. "Can't wait."

She slid back so she could stroke him where he lay hidden in his pants. Then her eyebrows dipped as she concentrated on the zipper. When she freed him, his shaft jerked to rise hard and stiff between her thighs. She ran her hand up his cock and laughed when it bobbed.

"I have fallen in love with this little bow." Jason ran the palm of his hand over her butt until he reached the bow on the back of her thong. Then he pulled. "I'll buy you a dozen of these, but now I want it gone."

With the thong out of his way, he ran his hand through her wet curls. He whirled his fingers in her cream and spread it until he was certain she was ready for him then he said, "Lift onto your knees."

When she knelt, Beth held his cock at her entrance. "Like this?"

"Yes…" Jason slipped into her and wallowed in the pleasure of her soft heat wrapped around him.

Beth moved on his cock with slow, deliberate strokes. As she rode him, she rotated her hips and ground against his pelvis. Her sexy movements and the moans she made fueled his lust.

She rode him fast and hard. Her movements became frantic as she reached for her orgasm. Tingles raced along his spine. He couldn't hold back much longer. He dropped his hand between their bodies and teased her clit.

Her back stiffened. "Jason!" The muscles in her sheath clenched around his cock.

The feathery ripples wiped away the last of his restraint. He jerked his hips and arched his back as he throbbed and filled her.

Beth collapsed against Jason's chest. They clung to each other with their arms and legs entangled, sweat coating their bodies, and pounding hearts. He nuzzled her neck and inhaled the musky aroma of sex mixed with the sweet, fruity scent of honeysuckle.

On the second day of their honeymoon, Beth sat on Jason's lap as they fed each other between kisses and caresses. It was late when they woke. She'd reached for him, but Jason insisted they first eat the breakfast Mason brought to their room.

Jason's cell phone rang, and he scowled. "This better be urgent." She laughed and moved to another chair while he checked his phone. "It's Gabriel." He hit the *TALK* button.

"Richards."

"We found Daniel."

The words they'd waited to hear. Jason told Beth, "Gabriel's found Daniel."

Beth rushed to his side. "Turn on the speaker."

He hit the button. "Tell us."

"For the last fourteen months, Daniel has been at a farm in Massachusetts with the Brewer family."

Jason asked, "How is he?"

"He's happy and healthy. Over the years, the Brewers have taken in several foster children. They're generous people and good to the children in their care."

Beth asked, "Can we see Daniel?"

"His caseworker gave me the information on Daniel's foster family so I could check on them. She had one condition, I had to promise not to make contact until she gave the go ahead."

"At least we know where he's living."

Gabriel said, "I didn't want to risk Daniel's being moved before you petition for custody, so I explained your situation to his caseworker, Brenda Abernathy."

Beth asked, "Did that help?"

"Brenda promised not to move Daniel to give you time to apply for custody."

Jason wrapped his arm around her, and asked, "What do we do now?"

"You're to meet with Brenda Thursday at social services in Boston. She's a tough lady, but fair. She does whatever is necessary to take care of her kids."

"Gabriel, will you go with us?" Beth asked.

"I hoped you'd ask."

She clenched her hands. "Do you think we will get custody of Daniel?"

Gabriel didn't hesitate. "When I talked to Brenda and explained your situation, she was cautious but encouraging. Once you file all the paperwork and prove you're Daniel's biological parents, they'll conduct their investigations. If she doesn't find any problems, she'll recommend you be granted custody of Daniel."

Jason said, "My attorneys already have the general information put together."

Beth stared at him. "They are already working on this?"

He shrugged. "It's important to plan."

She hugged him. "I love you."

Gabriel chuckled. "The more information you can give Brenda on Thursday, the sooner she'll be able to do her reviews and process your petition."

Jason said, "We will have the forms and documents required by Massachusetts prepared before we meet."

Gabriel said, "Can I assume your filing for temporary custody and permanent guardianship."

"Yes. The lawyers are preparing that petition as well." Jason grinned. "Gabriel, we're grateful for all you've done."

"This is why I do this work. Let's not forget, the information you got from Beth's mother. We wouldn't have found Woodson without her help."

"Mother will be so happy."

Jason kissed her forehead. "We'll return to the house this afternoon and fly back to Chicago tomorrow."

"There's one last thing." Gabriel cleared his throat. "Someone got into Woodson's vault, and every file has been taken. If I find them, I plan to check into the adoptions he arranged."

Jason's brow furrowed. "Would you consider a silent partner? I'd like to fund your work. Who knows how many people adopted children through Woodson and have paid blackmail?"

"I'd welcome your support as long as you understand this won't be a profit-generating business."

Jason said, "I'm not concerned about profits. Children shouldn't be bought and sold."

Beth asked, "Gabriel, what did Woodson do when he learned his files were gone?"

"I heard he ran for the Canadian border. Like that will save him."

Although Beth enjoyed her time with Jason, she was too excited to relax. Her mother would be thrilled they'd found Daniel, but how would Jason's family take the news? Would they hate her for placing him for adoption?

The families welcomed Beth and Jason home with hugs and kisses.

Deidre frowned. "I thought you'd be away for a week. You didn't cut your honeymoon short because of me, did you?"

"We'll take time for a longer honeymoon after I move to Chicago." Beth wrapped an arm around her mother's shoulder. "Did Archer cause any problems while we were away?"

Helen squeezed Deidre's arm. "You're dealing with a painful situation and have made a difficult decision. Now, you need to tell Beth what you've decided."

Deidre folded her hands together and nodded. "Let's go to the study."

Beth and Jason sat on the sofa while Deidre stood by the fireplace and twisted her wedding ring. "Even after Mr. Michael told him to stay away, Archer came here anyway. He raised such a ruckus I agreed to talk to him. He tried to bully me so I would return to the house. I hadn't realized how out of control his temper was until he threatened to cut off my income."

"We won't let that happen." Jason's eyebrows drew together. "I'll put my attorneys to work on it."

"Thank you, but it's an empty threat. I own fifty-two percent of the company, and Beth has twenty-four percent. Archer resents that he doesn't have full ownership of the company. His bitterness eats at him and is, at least in part, responsible for his erratic behavior."

Deidre rubbed her hands over her arms. "Anyway, I told him I won't tolerate his abuse any longer. I threatened to file for a divorce if he didn't get help. He agreed to seek the help of a professional, but I refused to return to the house until he learns to control his anger."

Beth went to her mother and held her hand. "You can live here. We'll live in Chicago, and the house will be empty."

"We can talk about it." Deidre patted Beth's hand. "But I'm excited about having a home I can decorate the way I want it, not one staged by an interior designer with delusions of grandeur."

"Deidre, it's important to do what's best for yourself. Whatever you decide, we'll support you," Jason assured her.

"Thank you." She walked to the desk. "I will need your help to undo the mess Archer has made of the company."

Jason said, "You can count on us."

Deidre sighed. "I let him run the business without oversight for too long. I'd heard rumors about his business practices but ignored them. Before my father died, I promised to take care of the company he worked so hard to build. I failed him. Instead, I tried to soothe Archer's ego and let him run the company his way. Now the company is on the brink of bankruptcy."

"Mother, you didn't know what he was doing."

"I didn't want to know." Deidre rubbed her eyes. "While you were in the hospital, I took a hard look at my life. I let Archer's wishes interfere in my relationship with my daughter." She clenched her hands. "When he broke his promise to leave you alone, I'd had enough of his lies and manipulation."

Jason said, "Deidre, you did what you thought was best for your family."

"Did I?" She shrugged. "I wanted to keep peace in our family, but the cost was too high. It's time for a change."

"Father wore you down." Beth put an arm around her mother's shoulders. "We'll help you save Grandfather's company, and you will never lose me. I love you, and I'm proud of you."

While they dressed for dinner, Beth paced. "Your family will hate me. I got pregnant and gave up our son."

"You weren't in that boathouse alone. Besides, my family loves you, and they won't blame you for what happened. Although they may not be so easy on me."

"I don't want to tell them that my parents forced me to put Daniel up for adoption. They might get angry with mother, and she has so much to cope with already."

"They're my family, and I love them, but that doesn't mean they need to know every detail of our lives. We don't have to tell them why you placed Daniel for adoption. Now try not to worry." This time, when she walked across the room, Jason grabbed her and pulled her close for a kiss. "We've found Daniel. Our parents will be happy to have a grandchild, well, except Archer."

"I hope you're right."

"Let's go share our news."

They walked into the dining room. The families, including Marco and Lupita, sat at the table. Jason sat at the head of the table with Beth to his right.

He cleared his throat and took a drink of water. "We have something to tell you."

All eyes focused on him, he shifted in his seat. "You remember that I left Serenity Bay nine years ago. Well…the night before I left town, Beth got pregnant."

There were gasps around the table. Shocked eyes focused on Beth then turned back to Jason.

Matt looked angry and pursed his lips.

Helen asked, "Why didn't you tell us?"

"I didn't know until I came back to town last month." He squeezed Beth's hand.

"I tried to tell Jason about the pregnancy, but the letters I sent never reached him." Beth grimaced. "After our son's birth, I placed him for adoption. For years, I've searched for him."

Matt's eyes narrowed. "That's why you wanted Michael's number."

Jason smiled. "Gabriel found Daniel."

Helen asked, "His name is Daniel? Was he named after you?"

Jason nodded.

"You found him." Deidre rushed to Beth. Tears fell from her eyes, but she wore a smile that lit the room. "Where is he? Will you get him back?"

She hugged her mother. "He's in foster care."

"I have a grandson?" Helen rushed to hug Jason. "I'm grandmother."

Beth said, "The couple who adopted Daniel died in a car crash. For the last fourteen months, he's lived on a farm outside of Boston. Thursday we meet with his caseworker, and we'll file a petition for custody."

Callie frowned. "I don't understand. How did it happen?"

Jason grinned and said, "Well, there are birds and bees..."

Laughter filled the room, and Callie turned a deep, flaming shade of red.

Jason and Beth told them what they'd learned so far. They answered the questions they could, but there was so much they didn't know.

Beth said, "When we talk to his caseworker, we hope she'll tell us more about Daniel. We want to know about his life while he lived with his adoptive parents and in foster care."

Soon everyone was making plans for Daniel. Matt and Helen planned trips to the aquarium and the Planetarium. Marco said they needed to get a horse and saddle so he could teach Daniel to ride.

But it was Callie's plan that had everyone laughing. She'd pulled out her phone and typed so fast her fingers were a blur. Beth asked her what she was doing.

"I want to find a set of drums that Daniel can use to drive Jason crazy."

"Little sisters should be seen and not heard." Jason raised his wine glass. "I'd like to make a toast. To Deidre, who sent the letter that brought me back to Serenity Bay and gave us the information we needed to find our son. Thank you for the chance you've given us to be a family."

Everyone lifted their glasses. "To Deidre."

CHAPTER SEVENTEEN

The next day they flew to Chicago. Jason was glad the families planned to stay with them until after the Thursday meeting.

Jason and Beth spent hours with his attorneys, but when they flew to Boston Wednesday evening, they had the paperwork needed to apply for temporary and permanent custody. They stayed in a hotel on the waterfront, but Beth never looked out the windows. Instead, she paced. Every few minutes she'd sit and stare at the blank television screen.

The next time she got up, Jason pulled her onto his lap and kissed her. "We should go to dinner. I want to take you to my favorite restaurant."

"I'm not hungry." She clutched his arms. "What if they don't approve our petition? What will we do?"

"We'll get custody of Daniel. They have no reason to deny us." He ran his thumb over her cheek. "In the meantime, I don't want you making yourself sick with worry. You want to be healthy when we bring Daniel home, don't you?"

She nodded and laughed when her stomach rumbled. "Maybe I could eat."

"You'll like the food at this restaurant. They make the best lobster bisque I've ever had. But don't tell Lupita what I said, or she'll serve liver every night for a week."

After Jason and Beth finished dinner, they enjoyed a final cup of espresso.

"You were right. The food was delicious." Beth sipped her coffee. "But I like Lupita's cooking better."

"That's because she makes your favorite foods."

She laughed. "Our lives have changed so much since that day we met in the park."

"True, but one thing hasn't changed."

"What's that?"

"My love for you." He kissed her. "Let's go. I want to have my wicked way with you."

She jumped to her feet. "I'm ready."

He threw his head back and laughed.

The next morning, as Gabriel joined them for breakfast, he handed Beth an envelope.

"What is it?"

"A surprise."

She tore the envelope open and shook the contents onto the table. There were several pictures.

Beth's voice trembled. "Is this…?"

Gabriel nodded.

Hands shaking, she picked up the photographs and leaned against Jason. They studied the pictures.

"He's beautiful and looks like a miniature version of you."

"He has your blue eyes…." Jason's voice cracked. The pictures were of Daniel riding a tractor, running through a pumpkin patch, and picking apples. There were other children in the photos, especially a young boy with blond hair and gray eyes.

After Beth and Jason studied the pictures, she put them into her purse. "Thank you, Gabriel. I'll treasure them."

He smiled. "You're welcome."

Jason asked him, "Do you think it's too early to go to social services?"

"Maybe, but Brenda will understand."

At the office, Gabriel made the introductions. Brenda wasn't an inch over five feet tall and looked tiny next to Gabriel.

Beth shook her hand and said, "Ms. Abernathy, thank you for working us into your schedule so soon."

"Please, call me Brenda." She led them to a small conference room. "I'm glad we are able to get started with the process. I know you're eager to gain custody of Daniel."

Brenda arranged her files and tablet. "Gabriel gave me some basic information about your situation. He told me you're Daniel Addison's biological parents and want custody returned to you. Is that right?"

"Yes." Jason nodded. "We want to petition for permanent guardianship. Until our request is approved, we would like temporary custody."

Brenda said, "I checked and learned that you, Jason, live in Illinois, and Beth lives in Minnesota. How do you plan to share custody?"

He took Beth's hand. "Beth and I married last week. We will make our home in Chicago and raise our family there."

Brenda tapped her pen on the table. "What will happen if you don't get custody of Daniel? Will you end the marriage?"

He tightened his hold on Beth's hand and sent her a soft smile. "While we want custody of Daniel, we married because we love each other." He told Brenda they planned to live in Chicago, and Beth had plans to open another shop.

"Thank you for the explanation." Brenda nodded. "Why was Daniel placed for adoption? You may be his biological parents, but why should you get permanent custody?"

Beth explained. "I was eighteen and unwed when I got pregnant. My parents weren't happy about the pregnancy and wanted me to give up the baby. I wanted my son, but I couldn't fight them." She told Brenda the story of Daniel's birth and adoption. "For years, I've hired investigators to look for him."

Jason explained, "I've only known about Daniel for a short time, but I agreed with Beth that we had to find him. Gabriel handled a kidnapping case for a friend of my father's. After we explained the situation, Gabriel agreed to take our case."

Brenda chuckled. "Well, you got the best."

Beth smiled at Gabriel. "If he hadn't taken our case, I'm not sure we would have found Daniel. The other investigators we hired gave up the search."

Brenda had questions for them. After they provided her with answers, she said, "There's several forms and other paperwork you will need to complete before we can process your applications."

Beth smiled at the surprise on Brenda's face when Jason handed her two folders. "An advantage of having attorneys on retainer. These files contain the forms, letters, and financial information you need to process our requests for temporary and permanent custody. Would you verify all the forms and documents you need are there?"

Brenda looked through the files and smiled. "Your attorneys were thorough. I'll be able to get started on your petitions at once."

Jason held Beth's hand. "What do you think of our chances to gain custody of Daniel?"

Brenda smiled. "There's no doubt you can give Daniel a good home, and you are his biological parents. If our investigations turn up no surprises, you should get custody of your son."

With huge smiles on their faces, Jason and Beth returned to Chicago. Their families' smiled with excitement when they told them what Brenda said. Now, came the hard part. Waiting.

Beth explored her new home and searched for a location for the new coffee shop. She tried to keep busy, but she still worried about the adoption and often broke into tears. She appreciated that her mother stayed with them and did her best to distract Beth.

Helen, Matt, and Callie visited often or stayed for the weekends. During one of their visits, Helen suggested they redecorate a room for Daniel.

Beth discussed the idea with Jason. "I want to redo a bedroom and the playroom for Daniel. The moms and Callie offered to help."

"Good idea, but why don't you redecorate all the bedrooms? We both always wanted a large family, and we'll need the rooms."

Beth turned to the window.

He went to her and slid his arms around her. "Angel, what's wrong?"

"You know I've always wanted children, but the accident made that impossible. Doctor Walters said—I might never have children." She pressed her face against Jason's chest as tears rolled over her cheeks.

"Then we'll adopt children."

"You wouldn't object?"

"Whether we get children through adoption or by birth, they'll be ours. We'll love our family no matter how they come to us."

"I love you so much." She gave him a wet kiss.

"I love you too, and you shouldn't assume you can't have children. The doctor said it would be difficult, not impossible."

"Do you think it's possible?"

"We had one night together, and you got pregnant. It might take two nights, but I'm up to the challenge." He wagged his eyebrows at her.

She laughed. How could she have thought Jason didn't want her and Daniel?

With the help of Deidre, Helen, and Callie, Beth had fun redecorating the rooms. She obsessed over the paint samples and looked through book after book of wallpaper. They painted and wallpapered the rooms themselves.

Jason came home from work early one day to help. He walked into the bedroom and laughed so hard he bent at the waist with his hands braced on his knees. "You have more paint on your faces than on the walls."

She had the most fun shopping for furniture and toys. Soon the rooms were filled with everything a boy needed and enough toys to stock a store. Callie bought a set of drums and laughed at the horror on

Jason's face when they arrived.

The day of the home evaluation, Beth was sick to her stomach and spent the morning in the bathroom. When her stomach settled, she sat in Daniel's room and twisted her handkerchief. The social worker arrived, and Beth panicked. Jason wasn't home yet, and he'd promised to be with her for the assessment. Ten minutes after the social worker arrived, Jason rushed in with Matt. She wondered how many speed limits they'd broken to get home. A few minutes later, Helen and Callie came.

The social worker smiled. "Daniel will be fortunate to have such a loving and supportive family."

A tense week later, Jason walked into the house carrying a saddle and looking as happy as he'd been on the day they married. Matt walked next to him with a huge smile on his face.

"You two look like you raided the cookie jar." When Beth saw the saddle, she asked, "Isn't that premature?"

Jason shook his head. "Nope. Marco is worried about Daniel getting a late start. He was five when he rode his first horse. Daniel is eight."

"What if Daniel doesn't want to ride a horse?"

"Blasphemy. Don't let Marco hear you spout that heresy."

She gave him a weak smile. "What if they deny our application?"

Matt squeezed her hand and left them.

Jason grinned. "You don't have to worry any longer. Brenda called. There will be a hearing for temporary custody next Thursday. She believes the judge will agree with her recommendation to give us custody. If the judge agrees, we can bring Daniel home."

Beth ran to Jason who dropped the saddle to catch her. He lifted her into his arms. After a long kiss, Jason led her into the living room. Jason settled her on his lap then said, "It's time you let go of the guilt. You were eighteen when you had Daniel and had to give him up for adoption. The past doesn't matter. What's important is that he is coming home."

They sat with their arms around each other when Matt returned with the family. Lupita and Marco followed. They pushed a cart with coffee and a cake that read, *It's A Boy!*

The following Wednesday, Jason and Beth flew back to Massachusetts. Worried Beth would make herself sick, he suggested they go shopping. "There must be something Daniel needs."

Several hours had passed before they returned to the hotel. Jason laughed over the number of shopping bags they carried. The bags were full of clothes and games Beth insisted Daniel needed for the flight home. They had more clothes than Daniel would wear in a week, but the smile had returned to Beth's face.

Jason dropped his bags inside the front door and pulled her into his arms. He kissed her hard and long. She moaned. Impatient, he picked her up and rushed to the bedroom.

Much later, they met Gabriel for a celebratory dinner.

After they'd ordered their food, Jason told Gabriel, "I was sincere about my offer to fund your work to check Woodson's adoptions. Can you put together an estimate of the startup costs and expenses?"

"I already prepared a business plan with projected expenses and income." Gabriel handed a file to Jason. "This won't be a moneymaking operation, but we can do a lot of good."

"I'm not in this for money. Woodson sold children, and we don't know what harm he did. Children shouldn't suffer for his greed. If we can save one child or parent from the suffering Beth endured, I will consider the money well-spent."

Jason reviewed the financial information Gabriel put together and showed it to Beth. They both asked questions and made suggestions. "The costs you've projected are less than I expected. Will you be able to hire enough staff to give this project the attention it requires?"

Gabriel nodded. "My people are donating their time. Also, other firms have heard about Woodson's scam and offered their help."

"That's great." Jason grinned. "How soon can you get started?"

"My crew is already reviewing the files. We've identified a few placements that are questionable and may be unsafe. Those cases are our priority."

"I'm glad you've already moved ahead with the investigations. If you'll give me your bank information, my controller will transfer the funds to your account." He shook Gabriel's hand. "What's your next step?"

Gabriel chuckled. "Tomorrow I fly to Canada."

"Canada?"

"There's an attorney whose retirement is about to come to a quick end."

Jason and Beth chuckled.

Thursday morning they got ready to meet Brenda for the hearing. Before they left for the courthouse, Beth's stomach sent her to the bathroom. Jason held her hair back and wiped her face with a cloth. She drank a ginger ale and felt much better.

The hearing for temporary custody of Daniel was easier than they expected. The judge agreed with Brenda's recommendation and granted their petition, pending a decision on the permanent placement.

Jason and Beth walked out of the conference room holding hands and smiling. In the hallway, they hugged each other and Jason kissed the tears from Beth's face. Jason shook hands with Gabriel and Brenda.

Jason said, "We can't thank you enough for your help."

"I'm happy for you," said Brenda. "I alerted the Brewers about your hearing. They thought Daniel would be more comfortable if he met you in familiar surroundings. Hank and Jane suggested we meet at the farm."

Beth and Jason followed Gabriel to the farm.

They pulled up to a yellow, three-story farmhouse with green shutters and a wrap-around porch. A couple stood at the top of the stairs with four children. Daniel wasn't with them. The adults looked worried, frightened. Brenda and Gabriel smiled as they joined them, but then their smiles disappeared.

Jason held Beth's hand as they rushed to the porch. Brenda introduced them to Hank and Jane. While they shook hands, Jason asked, "What's wrong?"

"We can't find the boys," Hank said.

Jason's stomach twisted. "Which boys?"

"John and Daniel."

"What?" Beth grabbed Jason's arm. "Where did they go?"

"We don't know." Jane's eyes were wide with worry.

Hank put an arm around her shoulder. "We told Daniel his birth parents were coming and wanted him to live with them."

Jane clamped her hands together. "Daniel wants John to go with him; they consider themselves brothers. When we told them John would stay here, they begged to stay here."

"After we explained that wasn't possible, the two of them went outside. We haven't seen them since then." Hank rubbed the back of his neck. "The boys must be hiding. We checked the places where they play, but haven't found them. A few minutes before you arrived, Jeremy returned from checking the back road. He saw a black Hummer parked in the woods. No one in this area owns a Hummer."

Beth grabbed Jason's arm. "Do you think Archer—?"

"No." He squeezed her hand. "He doesn't know we found Daniel, or where he lives. The boys are just hiding."

"Dad," the boy who was a miniature version of Hank asked, "what about the deer stand?"

Hank nodded. "They could be back there."

Gabriel asked, "Can we check?"

"It's off the back road. We'll take my Jeep. We can drive to where the road ends, and it's only a short hike to the stand from there."

"Let's go," Beth said.

Jason grabbed her arm. "Beth, you should wait here. You haven't been well."

"I'm going. Now we can stand here and argue, or we can go find our son. What will it be?"

"Let's find the boys," Brenda said. Gabriel sputtered until Brenda pointed at him. "Not a word."

Hank chuckled and led them to his SUV.

Even though everyone wore seatbelts, they bounced every time they hit a rut or bump. Beth's face was a sickly shade of green, and Jason wished she'd stayed at the house.

Hank yelled, "This road ends around the curve. We'll walk from there."

When the truck rounded a turn, Jason was sure the truck was riding on two wheels. A few minutes later, they found the black Hummer parked at the end of the road.

Beth cried out, "Hurry!"

Hank parked so the Hummer couldn't leave, and everyone climbed out.

Worried about Beth, Jason squeezed her shoulders. "Will you stay back until we know what's going on? We don't know who's with the boys."

Gabriel said, "Brenda you wait too. Okay?"

Beth and Brenda said, "All right."

Hank took off running. Jason and Gabriel ran after him. Hank stopped and raised his hand. Jason opened his mouth to ask why he was waiting but snapped it shut when a man shouted.

"Daniel, we won't hurt you. We want to take you to your

grandfather."

"I don't have a grandfather."

"Sure you do, kid. He wants us to take you to him for a visit."

A young boy yelled, "He doesn't want to go with you."

"Was that John?" Jason whispered to Hank. He nodded.

They edged closer. Two men stood at the bottom of the tree and stared up into the deer stand. One man had dirt on his face and leaves in his hair.

Gabriel signaled to spread out.

"Come on, Daniel. Don't make this hard. Climb down and we'll take you for a ride on an airplane. You'd like that, right?"

"Joe, that kid's not coming down. Climb up there."

"Are you crazy? Getting hit with that bat was no fun. If you want that kid, you get him."

Jason grinned. Smart kids. Hank placed a finger over his lips. The boys had seen them.

The first man said, "Fine. I'll go up there."

Gabriel signaled to Jason and Hank to move. They edged forward but someone stepped on a twig and it snapped. Joe and his friend turned. Jason swung and knocked Joe on his ass. His friend got in a lucky punch and knocked Hank to his knees. Gabriel grabbed the man's arm and twisted it behind his back.

"Hank, are you okay?" Daniel yelled.

"Hank, did he hurt you?"

"I'm fine guys."

Beth and Brenda walk into the clearing.

Gabriel pulled out plastic zip tie handcuffs and cuffed both men. From the woods came the sound of running feet. Jason turned and curled his fists. Had Joe and his friend brought backup thugs? Two men ran towards them.

Hank grabbed his arm. "They work for me." He nodded to the men. "Lock these men in the storm cellar and call the sheriff. We'll give him statements when we get back, but right now we need to talk to the boys."

Gabriel handed the kidnappers over to Hanks men.

Hank said, "Guys, it's safe to come down."

John shook his head. "No. You'll let them take Daniel."

Brenda tried to convince the boys. "Daniel, your parents have been searching for you and want you to live with them."

"My parents died."

"Remember, I explained the Addisons were your adoptive parents. These are your birth parents, and they want you to live with them."

"I can't leave John." Daniel put his arm around John's shoulders. "We're blood brothers. He takes care of me, and I won't go anywhere without him."

"I am sure your parents will let you visit John in the summer and at holidays." Brenda tried to reassure him.

Jason said, "If it's okay with the Brewers, he can come for a long visit whenever you're out of school."

"No. I can't leave John. He'd miss me."

John's voice trembled. "We have to stay together."

Jason looked at Beth with a raised eyebrow.

She smiled. "We've always wanted a large family."

Jason asked, "Brenda, could John come with Daniel?"

"If Hank and Jane approve, John could visit for a week or two."

Beth asked, "We shouldn't separate brothers. Would it be possible for both boys to live with us?"

Hank and Brenda looked stunned, but Gabriel smiled.

Brenda said, "Are you sure? Two children are a lot of work."

"Like Beth said, we've always wanted children, and two boys who are already brothers is a great start." Jason said, "We also have a strong, supportive family to help us."

Brenda smiled. "Yes, you do. You'll need to submit another application, but based on the investigation we did for Daniel, I believe the judge will approve your petition."

"You'll have the paperwork by the end of next week."

Beth grabbed Jason's arm. "I don't want to force them to come with us. If they stay on the farm, we could come for visits until they're comfortable enough to go home with us."

Jason asked, "Are you sure? It will be difficult, but it would give the boys time to get to know us."

She nodded.

Jason turned to Hank. "Let's tell the boys we won't make them come with us, but we would like to meet them."

"Let me talk to them." Hank moved to the foot of the tree. "Boys, we won't force you to go anywhere, but I'd like you to meet these people. Daniel, wouldn't you like to meet your real parents?"

John asked, "You promise not to take Daniel away?"

"I promise not to make you go anywhere unless it's what you

want."

The boys had a whispered discussion. They climbed down but rushed to stand behind Hank.

Brenda smiled. "Boys, I'd like you to meet Beth and Jason Richards. Daniel, these are your birth parents."

He looked at Beth and Jason then tilted his head. "Are you my real parents?"

"Yes, we are. We've searched for you for a long time." Beth grasped Jason's arm. "We're happy to meet you—both of you."

"Aren't you going to say hello?" Hank asked.

John grumbled, "Hello."

Daniel muttered, "Hello."

The boys were the same height, but opposites in looks. Daniel had Jason's dark hair and Beth's blue eyes while John had light blonde hair and gray eyes.

Jason knelt to talk to them. "Boys, is it important that you stay together?"

Both of their heads bobbed.

"If you could be together, would you consider coming to Chicago with us?"

The boys looked at each other. Jason wished he knew what they were thinking.

"Guys, you should give this a try," Hank said. "These are nice people, and you'd have your own family."

Daniel looked up at Beth. "Are you really my parents?"

Beth knelt. "Yes, we are."

"Why didn't you want me? Didn't you love me?"

"Daniel, I've always loved you, but I couldn't keep you. It broke my heart to let you go. As soon as I could, I searched for you. I'm so happy we finally found you." She squeezed John's shoulder. "I would be so happy to have you as my sons."

Daniel asked, "How long would we stay."

Brenda said, "Boys, they want you to live with them and be a family."

John shook his head. "Grown-ups don't want little kids for always. When they don't want us anymore, can we come back to the farm?"

Jason's heart ached. No child should think he was disposable.

"That won't happen." Beth took their hands. "We want you to live with us and be our sons forever."

John asked, "Would we be a real family? All four of us?"

Jason nodded. "We'd be a great family."

"Would John be my real brother?" Daniel asked.

"Yes, he would."

"Forever?" John's eye narrowed. "Are you sure?"

A smile on her face, Beth dragged her fingers in a cross over her heart. "We promise."

John and Daniel looked at each other.

With a shrug, John said, "I guess we could try it."

"Okay." Daniel put his hands on his hips. "But we're not making any promises."

Beth hugged Daniel and tears fell from her eyes.

"We're so happy you'll live with us." Jason took John into his arms and hugged him. John looked skeptical. Jason knew John needed time to believe they loved him and wanted him in the family.

Beth said, "I want to meet my other son."

Jason said, "John, this is your new mother."

John and Daniel had another silent conversation. Then John asked, "Can—can we call you Mom and Dad?"

Beth burst into tears.

Daniel looked devastated, "We don't have to call her mom."

Jason smiled. "Mom is crying because she's happy, isn't that right Beth?"

She nodded. Then she wrapped her arms around both boys and smiled through her tears.

Jason stepped away to shake hands with Brenda. "Thank you for your help."

Her eyes were bright. "It's days like today that make me glad I do this work."

"I can't thank you enough for finding Daniel." Jason shook Gabriel's hand. "Keep me updated on what you find in your investigation into Woodson's placements. If I can help, let me know."

He helped Beth to her feet and wrapped his arm around her waist. She smiled while she cried. He told the boys, "Mom has waited a long time for her sons to come home. She needs time to adjust. In the meantime, your grandparents and aunt are waiting in Chicago to welcome you. I think Lupita might have a chocolate cake to celebrate."

Two young voices yelled, "Awesome."

Daniel looked at John. "Chocolate cake, my favorite."

John looked at him and grinned. "A new Mom and Dad."

They yelled, "High five!" Followed by a jump and slapping of hands.

After a few weeks together, Jason knew they'd made the right decision to bring John home with Daniel. The boys were best friends and helped each other adjust to their new lives.

Although they had a few bumps along the way.

Beth told the boys they could each pick a bedroom of his own. They had objected and insisted on being together. With the boys in the same room, bedtime became a delightful experience. After they were tucked in at night, Beth and Jason stood outside the room and listened to their sons' whispers and giggles until they fell asleep.

Then one night during dinner, Jason said, "Mom and I have something we want to discuss with you."

Daniel and John frowned and their eyes filled with fear.

To ease their concern, Jason rushed to say, "We'd like to adopt you and change your last names to Richards, but only if it's what you want too?"

Daniel tipped his head. "When a family makes important decisions, they should vote."

John nodded in agreement. "Yeah. We should vote."

Jason covered his mouth and coughed to smother his laughter. "You're right. We each get one vote. We are voting on whether John and Daniel will change their last names to Richards and be our sons forever. All in favor raise your hand."

His hand went up, and Beth raised hers. They watched and waited. With a nod of their heads, John and Daniel lifted their hands. There were smiles around the table, and Jason whispered a prayer of thanks. At last, he had the family he'd always wanted.

The next day, Beth had an appointment. Not wanting the family to worry, she didn't tell them about it. Later, as she drove home, she wore a huge grin. Her dreams had come true. She and Jason were married, and they had two wonderful sons. But this—this was a miracle.

She walked through the house until she heard Jason's and the boys' laughter. They'd planned to spend the day by the pool, and eager to join them, she ran to change into her swimsuit.

On her way to the pool, Beth stopped in the kitchen. When Lupita saw her smile, she hugged Beth and gave her a glass of ginger ale. Lupita told her lunch would be ready in a few minutes and sent her to join her men.

Jason welcomed her with a kiss. "You look very happy. What put that smile on your face?"

"Lunch is almost ready." Beth wanted to wait until they were alone to tell him her news. Then they could tell the boys together.

"You're happy about lunch?" Jason looked at her as though she'd lost her mind. To distract him, she leaned in for a kiss. The boys watched and giggled.

Daniel said, "I'm never kissing girls."

John shoved him. "She's not a girl; she's a mom."

Jason laughed.

Beth laughed, but soon tears ran down her cheeks.

Daniel frowned and said, "Being a mom must mean you cry a lot."

John nodded.

Lupita came out and set sandwiches on the table. There were peanut butter and jelly for the boys and tuna with pickles for Beth. When she smelled the tuna, Beth slapped a hand over her mouth and ran to the bathroom. Her stomach tightened then clenched as she gave up the breakfast she'd eaten.

A few minutes later she returned to the patio and dropped into a chair. Her skin was clammy, and her stomach ached. Jason pressed a cool cloth to her forehead and handed her the ginger ale. Her hand shook as she took a drink.

The boys looked worried. Daniel asked, "Mom, are you dying?"

"No. I just have an upset stomach." Beth clamped her teeth together and forced a smile.

Her eyes barely open, she watched Jason pull the boys close. "Guys, you don't need to worry about Mom. She's fine. When a woman is having a baby, she sometimes gets sick."

"A baby?" Daniel asked. Jason nodded, the boys gave each other a high five. "Yea."

John said, "We want a sister."

Daniel nodded. "We can teach her all kinds of important stuff. The best trees for climbing, how to dig worms for fishing, and how to throw a football."

"You'll be wonderful big brothers, whether it's a girl or boy." Beth turned to Jason. "How did you know? I just found out this morning."

He wrapped his arms around her. "I'm aware of everything that happens in my family." Then with a waggle of his eyebrows, he said, "I told you I was up to the challenge."

If you enjoyed KISS YESTERDAY GOODBYE, please let others know by leaving a review on the website where you purchased your copy or a reader's site such as Goodreads. I'd love to hear from you, so drop me a line at: dannirose@comcast.net

You can visit me on:

Facebook: https://www.facebook.com/dannirosewriter or

Twitter: https://twitter.com/dannirosewriter

Would you like to be notified about new releases and updates? Sign up for my newsletter at: http://dannirose.com/

Danni Rose is an award-winning author of sizzling historical and contemporary romance. When she's not reading, writing, or doing research for a new book, Danni is working with tiny glass beads to weave a new beadwork creation. Well, she is if her cat will get off her lap. It's true, Joan Wilder has nothing on this cat-lady.

Visit Danni or sign up for my newsletter at: http://dannirose.com/

Thank you for your support!